"It's a mess in there," Trew shook his head. "Every view has been full of pain, fear, and misery. Most players are hiding in small groups, struggling just to find warmth, food, and shelter to get them through the next day. Maybe it's better if people can't watch what's going on in there right now. I don't know if the fans would tune in."

"You know they'd tune in," Cooper said. "This is exactly the kind of thing they want to see."

"It shouldn't be," Trew said.

"Yet it is."

Books By TERRY SCHOTT

The Game is Life Series
The Game
Digital Heretic
Interlude - Brandon
Virtual Prophet

Also available at Amazon.com
The Gold Apples
Harvest *
Flight *
Timeless *

*short stories at the moment... well worth the 0.99

Virtual Prophet

Terry Schott

This is a work of fiction. Names, characters, businesses, places, events and incidents are either the products of the author's imagination or used in a fictitious manner.
Any resemblance to actual persons, living or dead, or actual events is purely coincidental.

Virtual Prophet
Copyright ©2013 by Terry Schott

Editing by Alan Seeger

All rights reserved.

This book or any portion thereof may not be reproduced or used in any manner whatsoever without the express written permission of the publisher except for the use of brief quotations in a book review

I dedicate this book to my two amazing children; Terry Christopher Schott, and Sydney Schott.

Sydney has always been the namer for these stories. Many of the wonderful characters we've all come to love and look forward to spending time with were named by my sweet daughter. Thanks so much Sydney for your creative input. Without you there would be no Danielle, Trew, Tygon, or many other great characters in the books!

Terry Christopher was sitting with me one day and he told me about a recent dream. Brandon's encounters with sloth, Owl, and the old man . Thanks for sharing that dream and allowing me to put it into the story, i think readers enjoyed it!

Huge thank you to my first reader Karen for reading the chapters each day and offering support and great advice and encouragement. You're a great help, Thanks again =)

Thank you Carl for loving this series. Since day one your excitement for the story has been awesome. Thank you also for your comments and feedback, along the way. This ending wouldn't have been written if not for a great discussion with you!

Thank you to everyone who follows me on the website, blog, Facebook, and Twitter. Thanks to everyone who buys the books on Amazon, and shares them with your friends and family. Thank you to those who blog about my books and suggest them to your circles of influence.

I love my fans, and I hope you all enjoy the ending of this story.

Already a new tale is creeping out of my skull. I look forward to sharing it with you.

Terry

1

49 hours before 'The Day of Darkness'

Thirteen.

I remember my name, but I'm not ready to use it yet. Perhaps I'll never use it. The poor wretch who answered to that name is no longer here, or maybe it's more accurate to say that he's no longer here alone.

I lean back and smile, enjoying the feel of sunshine on my face. I listen to the birds call out as they ride on the air currents above and the breeze blows softly off the water.

It's all so perfect.

People often take the simplest pleasures in life for granted. A person who has their health, freedom, and the ability to do whatever they want usually doesn't understand how wealthy they really are.

I started fading out when I was twelve. At first it was brief blackouts while playing with friends; falling down for no reason, stuff like that. Then the episodes became more frequent and lasted longer. I would go blank for a few minutes while sitting in the food court at the mall, or appear lost in thought during class with my pen frozen in place over my notebook.

A year passed before my parents realized I was having problems and took me to the doctors. After months of testing, experts sat across from my parents and collectively shrugged their shoulders. None of them had a single clue what my problem was, but they wished us good luck.

My parents should have put me into some kind of home or facility — someplace that could take care of me as my grip on reality slowly disappeared — but they didn't. They denied what was happening and moved away.

I remember briefly surfacing one day in an alley, wearing filthy clothes and surrounded by garbage. I'm not sure why, but that day I was self-aware for more than twelve hours. I had time to get cleaned up a bit, to eat, and attempt to call them. Their number had been disconnected, and directory assistance confirmed that there was no longer a listing for them at our home address.

I wasn't angry.

Over three years had passed since my last lucid day. It must have been horrible for them to deal with.

I don't remember much after that. It's easiest to pretend there is nothing worth remembering.

Then I woke up in a cage, standing in front of a man who could bring me out of what he called 'the Haze.' I'm not sure how long I was there; it doesn't really matter.

Eleven days ago. That's what matters most to me.

The man brought me out of my haze and told me it was permanent. He told me I could stay out here in the real world, along with my other half. My other half is apparently a genius level consciousness; an expert in quantum mechanics. During the past few days I've been able to piece together the understanding that the two halves were never able to be present as a single, integrated consciousness, although I'm not exactly certain why.

Eleven days ago, the man fixed that. He made me whole again for the first time in my adult life.

I've seen my reflection. I know living on the streets ages a person, but my best guess is that I'm in my late twenties, maybe early thirties.

I lost a lot of time, but my world looks very promising now.

When the man gave us our freedom, I knew immediately where to go. I made my way to the biggest city in Ontario, Canada; a large city surrounded by rich countryside, not too far out in the country. There are decent seasons for growing food and crops, and the population is large, but not huge compared to some other parts of the world.

Tomorrow I have an interview with one of the best physics labs in the country. I'm brilliant in the field of quantum mechanics; I'm certain they will hire me.

I don't sit and worry about anything that will happen tomorrow, though.

Today I sit on the shore of a lake, dip my feet in the water, and enjoy being a part of this amazing world.

Things are finally going my way.

2

24 hours before 'the Day of Darkness'

"We are very pleased to offer you a position at UniCaltrec Theoretical Physics Laboratory."

I smile and shake hands with my interviewer. "I'm so pleased," I say. "When can I start?"

"How does Monday sound?"

"It sounds great," I say. "I have some exciting theories that I think you'll be interested in, and the mathematical proofs I've compiled are very convincing."

She returns my portfolio and nods her head. "If they are half as elegant as what's contained in these papers, then I have no doubt you're going to show us some incredible new ways to look at the world from a quantum perspective."

I nod confidently. The papers I submitted as part of the job application are nothing compared to what I can truly do. This morning I researched current knowledge in the world on theoretical quantum physics. The information in my head makes the entire community of respected scientists look like five-year-olds playing with blocks.

I leave the laboratory and drive my rental car back into town. Unicaltrec's office is in a small city about half an hour outside of the metropolis. The population of this suburb is 56,000; large enough to contain all of life's creature comforts, but not so large that a person gets lost in the crowds. I pull into the hotel parking garage and head to my room.

Today is Friday, which means that I have a couple of days before I start my new job. I still have a considerable sum of money remaining from the duffle bag I was given by the man, and now that I have a job, money won't be a problem. I decide to go out for dinner and a movie; I haven't been to the movies since I was twelve years old.

I ask the concierge for recommendations and decide to try a nearby Italian restaurant. After an excellent meal, I get directions to the local theatre — they referred to it as a 'multiplex.' I decide on an action movie, and buy a large popcorn and a soft drink. Oh, my God, I forgot how delicious hot buttered popcorn was! I sit down in the theatre, happily eating and reading a movie magazine while I wait for the movie to start.

I notice people holding handheld devices and tapping away on them nonstop. "Excuse me," I say to a girl sitting a couple of seats away.

She looks up and stares at me.

I decide to be clever about my questions, asking just enough to get answers while trying not to sound totally out of the loop. "What model is that? It looks way better than my old beater."

The girl's eyes light up and she nods as she holds the phone up towards me. "Oh, yes, this is the SE33. It's the latest model smartphone! It can surf the internet much faster than the last generation phone and do so many other things. You know, it's still got a great camera, plus all my music is stored on it, and thousands of photos. But this one can do almost anything I need it to do."

She talks too fast and explains more than I can grasp. I just nod my head and try to absorb as much as I can. By the end of the conversation, which lasts only a minute or so, I understand that these phones can talk instantly to others, get any information a person could ever need, take movies and pictures, and play all the music a person could ever want to hear. I thank her for the demonstration and sit quietly, eating my popcorn and assimilating the information. During the years since I faded away, people have become much more dependent on technology. We had computers, but not much else. I decide I'll have to get myself one of these phones very soon.

The movie theatre darkens and the picture comes up on the screen. I notice small lights coming from seats throughout the theatre; many people are still focused intently on their phones, tapping away while the movie begins. It doesn't seem healthy to me, for some reason. Maybe I won't get a new phone after all.

I sit totally enthralled during the movie. Picture quality, sound, and acting have come a long way since I was a kid! It isn't until the movie is done and the lights come back up that I realize I've forgotten about my popcorn.

It's about 11 p.m. when I return to my hotel room. I get ready for bed and lie down, smiling as I recap the day in my head. I'm sure that to the average person, my day wouldn't be anything special, but to me it was magical. I think about where I was just a short time ago, and how long I've spent lost from this reality.

Today was one of the greatest days of my life, and it's only going to get better.

3

"Welcome back."

He opened his eyes and blinked them slowly. His neck was stiff, his mouth dry, and eyes blurry.

It'd been years since he'd woken up like this... almost thirty-eight.

A blurry shape entered his line of sight. He felt a hand touch his face and the cool splash of liquid bathing his eyes. He continued to blink, eyes moistening as the blurriness began to fade. "Thanks," he said. Then he chuckled. His voice had changed so much, but now it was back to normal.

"Can you sit up?" the voice asked him.

"In a minute or two," he said.

"Whenever you're ready."

"How 'bout a sip of water?"

"When you sit up."

A few moments later he raised his body to a seated position, groaning as he felt the burning of muscles that, for the past three months, had only moved with the help of physical attendants. "Oh, that really hurts," he said.

He looked around slowly before letting his eyes rest on the man sitting beside him.

"Father."

"Brandon."

"Where's everyone else?" Brandon asked.

"I'll fill you in later. Here — drink this." Thorn held a glass out to Brandon and the boy took it.

He sipped from the straw, careful to take small sips. "Any problems?"

Thorn pursed his lips. "A small one," he said.

Brandon continued to sip from the straw, waiting for Thorn to fill him in.

"Your avatar is still alive inside."

Brandon arched an eyebrow and moved the straw away from his mouth. "Trew tried to save me." It wasn't a question.

"Yes."

"How sweet of him." Brandon held the empty glass out and Thorn took it. Brandon started to rotate his limbs slowly, allowing the blood to flow and relax his muscles. "Did you show him the video?"

Thorn chuckled. "Your life story — as much of it as you wanted him to see? Yes, we showed him."

"And he's still functioning?"

"Of course he is," Thorn said. "You knew he would be."

"I was almost positive he would be..." Brandon said.

"Are you kidding me?"

"No," Brandon shook his head.

"You're gambling," Thorn said.

"You need luck to win," Brandon laughed. "A true player knows this, and helps guide situations to require the barest amount of luck at the most important moments. It's no more gambling than crossing a busy street after watching carefully to make certain conditions are most favourable to make it across alive."

Thorn looked at Brandon and sighed. They had argued about this for years, and neither agreed. "What do you think he will do now?"

"He'll follow his destiny."

"What does that mean?"

"It means everything is still on track, Father."

"But —"

"Yes," Brandon interrupted him. "Time is running out."

"Things have gone from bad to worse, son." Thorn leaned forward.

Brandon held up his hand. "I don't want to hear it."

Thorn frowned and began to speak, but Brandon cut him off. "Don't say a word. It won't help for me to know what's happening here."

"So you want to sit and pretend that the world isn't ending?" Thorn asked.

"No." Brandon laid back down on the table. "I want to know how soon you can put me back into the simulation."

Thorn frowned. "Your body needs to recharge and get physically strong again."

"That would take at least a couple of weeks. Years would pass inside the Sim. Things aren't as bad as you make them out to be if I have that much time, Father."

"We don't have that much time."

"Then answer my question." Brandon crossed one leg over the other and looked at the ceiling.

"If I put you back in right away, problems could occur," Thorn said.

Brandon's eyes sparkled like they did when he was close to the winning a game in the Centre. "So what I'm hearing is that it's possible to throw me back in immediately."

Thorn closed his eyes and nodded.

4

Non Player Characters. NPCs.

Trew's head moved slowly from side to side, looking at the people around him scurrying from one task to the next. He couldn't hear them over the buzz in his brain. They seemed to move slower than normal.

None of us are real, he thought to himself. Billions of us, bits of computer code with minds programmed by some mainframe master to complete tasks.

He didn't have time for this. Why had Thorn showed him the truth? Was it even the truth? If it was, and they were all NPCs, then did that change anything?

Trew shook his head quickly, trying to clear thoughts that he didn't want to consider. I don't know why Thorn wanted me to know this, but it doesn't matter. This life feels real to me, to all of us. The lives I've experienced in the Game may have been virtual, but they made me who I am today. If I don't snap out of this, we will all die, and that's not something I'm going to let happen.

"It doesn't matter," he said forcefully.

"What doesn't matter, Trew?" Michelle asked.

Trew looked around the table. It was full of team members waiting for him to begin the meeting. Brandon had dropped a little over a day ago. They'd lost contact with the Game at the same time.

No one on Tygon had any idea what was going on inside the Game.

Hopefully that was about to change.

"Give me the news, Michelle." Trew said. He was sitting at the head of the table — Brandon's seat.

Michelle stood beside the main viewer which displayed various graphs and charts. She looked weary and haggard; the last twenty-nine hours had felt like weeks to all of them.

"It's a mess," she said. "Brandon is in stable condition, but there's no sign that he'll wake up. As far as the Game is concerned... we still can't get a signal." She paused to look at Trew, hoping he would announce that she was wrong and he'd somehow found a way. Trew nodded in agreement and Michelle continued to speak. "Ejected players are being separated and sequestered according to the geographical regions that they were playing in. From hours of intense interviewing as they wake up, we're slowly beginning to piece together some of the major developments happening in there."

"How's Danielle doing?" one of the team mates asked.

"She's doing well," Michelle said. "She's surrounded herself with Timeless and carved out a base of operations in what used to be Cambridge, Canada. It's been almost two years since 'the Day' occurred inside the Game, and they've built themselves an impressive colony."

"How impressive?" Lilith asked.

"Ejected players all refer to the groups that are forming as 'tribes.' Most tribes consist of less than twenty individuals," Michelle pointed to a graph. "There are reports of some extraordinary leaders who've managed to build groups somewhere in the neighbourhood of 200 to 400 people."

"That's a serious accomplishment, considering the conditions," Lilith said. "The simple task of growing enough food to feed that many mouths would require a lot of hard work and cooperation.

Preventing dissension, squabbling, and challenges to authority would be a constant threat to the stability of groups."

"Yes," Michelle agreed. "Most tribes seem to reach a certain level, and then they implode for the reasons you just mentioned."

"How many people are in Danielle's tribe?" Trew asked.

"Well, that's the thing," Michelle said. "If we can believe the reports from players exiting the Game, and they all seem to agree with each other, then Danielle's tribe is large."

"I didn't hear a number in that sentence, Michelle." Trew said.

"Forty-five thousand," Michelle said.

Everyone sat in stunned silence.

"How are they able to maintain a group that size?" someone finally asked.

"The Gamers," Trew guessed.

"That's right," Michelle agreed. "Gamers are flocking to her. New groups of Gamers appear almost daily to join her. When they arrive, Gamers are welcomed as brothers and sisters and given portions of the city to settle. There is order, law, and a sense of togetherness that the entire group embraces."

"What do they do with non-Gamers?" Trew asked.

"They interview all newcomers," Michelle said. "If the admissions committee doesn't like what they hear, they send them on their way."

"That must cause trouble," Lilith said.

"Not very often," Michelle said. "Most accept a safe escort to the border and cross the bridge into Buffalo. A group of Gamers maintains a post at the border to keep the area secure and to make certain no one tries to come back once they cross over into Buffalo. Those who are denied entrance into Danni's colony are in no position to argue, and there are good opportunities in Buffalo. There are safe communities over there, just not many large ones."

"Any other large colonies like Danni's?" Trew asked.

"Nothing even comes close," Michelle shook her head.

"We need to be able to see what's going on in there," Trew said. He looked around the table expectantly, but everyone avoided his gaze.

"No one has any ideas on how to re-establish a video link?" he asked. The room remained silent.

Trew stood up. "Okay, this isn't really our area of expertise, anyway. Cooper, come with me. The rest of you do what you can to sort the information coming in. I want to know what caused this and what we can do to end it. At the very least we need to bring the video feeds up so fans can keep watching and spending money. An event like this has never happened before, and from a business end of things we're missing out on making massive profits."

Michelle frowned at Trew. He noticed her look and nodded his head. "That's right, I'm not just Trew the player anymore. I'm Brandon Strayne's successor, and I intend to surpass his accomplishments, impressive as they were."

Trew looked around the room to make certain everyone understood, then nodded and walked out the door with Cooper and Michelle following closely on his heels.

5

Danielle

I stand on top of the main gate and watch the Greeters below. The sun feels warm on my skin, and I grip the wooden ramparts lightly as I look down at the tired little tribe that has arrived to join us. Guards sit comfortably on the ground as well as on either side of me up here.

Angelica smiles comfortably as she moves amongst the newcomers, stopping to speak with each person, and then nodding pleasantly before moving on to the next. After a time, she looks up to meet my gaze and raises her hand to make a simple signal.

I nod and return the signal. She's telling me that they are Gamers.

I turn away and look towards the large courtyard off in the distance. We built the main settlement to resemble an old fort from the past. It adds credibility and a sense of safety to residents, although the Colony hasn't faced any major threats since it was created over a year ago. The courtyard is full of activity today; they're making preparations for a big celebration tonight.

Today is my 62nd birthday.

Everyone says I look more like I'm in my late thirties. I laugh and tell them I don't think I look a day over twenty-eight... but I must admit that I do look good for my age.

When I made the decision to live for 140 years, I wanted to reach that age with Trew, but he's been gone from the Game for over twenty years; I haven't seen him in more than two.

I smile. I wouldn't get much sympathy if I complained about such a thing out loud. 'Poor me, it's been two years since I've lain with my husband who died twenty years ago!' I did have it better than the rest, and I appreciated every second of it.

I don't think they can see us since the Day of Darkness occurred — the fans on Tygon, I mean. It's impossible to know for certain. Maybe only the meditation link stopped working. The old methods of hearing from Brandon and the others have stopped as well; newspapers and internet technology no longer exist. We're all running blind, which is both scary and comforting at the same time.

If no one can hear me, then why do I still talk to myself?

I shrug and climb down the rampart. I needed the break, but it's time to get back to work. This enormous group of souls can't function smoothly without a leader.

I walk towards my office building, nodding and smiling to people as I pass them.

"Happy Birthday, Danni!" a young girl calls out from across the street. "Are you excited about the big party tonight?"

I smile and wave, "Can't wait," I lie cheerfully. "See you there!"

There'll be thousands of people gathered to celebrate in the main courtyard, and thousands more all over the city. I shudder at the thought of the extra food and stores that will be consumed because everyone wants to celebrate my birthday, but Stephanie assures me we have the supplies to spare. Harvests have been bountiful, and the people need a reason to unwind. Life hasn't been kind to most of them since the Day.

The Day. That's what everyone calls it. Its official title, 'The Day of Darkness,' is too much of a mouthful to say every time, so it's been shortened to 'the Day.' Not the big mushroom clouds of radioactive destruction, or toxic clouds of chemical weapons, or even the outbreak of deadly disease that we all guessed would end civilization.

Just inconvenience. That's what brought the world to its knees and kicked us back into the dark ages. The power stopped working. We could no longer send messages to our friends across the world. The lights no longer came on when we flipped the switch.

Of course, it was much worse than that. Electricity, oil, gas — none of these things function anymore. Automobiles were pretty useful, when they worked. As dead husks of metal, they are one of the biggest pains in the arse we have in this new world of ours. Horsepower reverted back to horses; it's a shame so many people started eating them when they got hungry. I could use another thousand horses to help us work the land.

Old farmers are the most treasured resource in our Colony. They live like lords and ladies as they teach us how to use knowledge which almost died out with them. Overnight they went from being ignored fossils to revered teachers.

Life can be funny like that.

I open the door to my office and grab a cup of water from the pail before I head to my desk. This is my private office, my thinking place. Most people leave me alone when I come here.

"Happy birthday, old girl."

Most, but not all. I smirk as Carl steps from the corner of the room. There's barely any shadow there, but he doesn't seem to need much to wrap it around him like a cloak of invisibility. Out of habit, my eyes flit to his, verifying that he's still on our side. Yep, gold flecks instead of red. Checking Timeless eyes is a habit I developed after one changed unexpectedly last year. The first thing this one wanted to do when she changed was start killing innocent people. Carl says that doesn't happen often, and Raphael agreed with him. Still, that was a bad day. If more had been around to see it, things could have turned unpleasant for our Timeless.

"Old girl?" I ask. "Coming from an ancient, withered creature like yourself, that's funny."

He smiles, although his smile still looks somewhat like a starving tiger that has come across a baby deer all alone. Either the last few years of practice have made it look less intimidating, or I'm getting used to it. "I'm told by many that I don't look anywhere close to my true age."

"What number is that again?" I ask.

He shrugs, "A few thousand years."

I squint my eyes and look him up and down critically. "Okay, then, I would have to agree with them. I would have guessed only a little over a thousand. If you're more than that then, yeah, you look decent."

He sniffs dismissively and sits down in my chair. "So tonight is gonna be a big party."

I frown and grab him a glass of water. Then I place it on the seat across from mine. He slowly gets up, walks over to pick up his cup, and sits down. I move to my chair and sit, putting my feet up on the old, worn surface of the pale wooden desk, crossing my feet at the ankles and putting my arms behind my head. "Too big a party for too small of a reason," I say.

He nods, but I know he doesn't agree. Try as he might to show us all otherwise, being an Eternal agrees with Carl. The easiest way to tell is when the small children attack him and start playing with him. He grumbles and roars at first, but the kids see through that, and in moments he's throwing them into the air and safely catching them. He mutters and complains, but spends hours entertaining the little ones.

"How do you feel about skipping out of the party early?" he asks.

"If the reason is good enough, count me in. Come to think of it, even if the reason is lame, feel free to count me in," she smiles. "What did you have in mind?"

He drains his cup of water and puts it on the desk. Then he wipes his mouth with the back of his hand and gives me a serious look. "The other day I detected a stray Timeless, so I went to check it out."

I swing my legs off the desk and sit up straighter. "Who did you take with you?" I ask.

"No one," he shakes his head. "This was a powerful energy signal, and one that I was pretty sure I recognized, so I went to check it out by myself."

"That was stupid, Carl," I say.

Carl shrugs and stares at me blankly. He doesn't like being scolded, and I don't do it often. I take a deep breath and decide to let it slide.

"What colour eyes?" I ask.

"Crimson." He turns his head towards the front window and pretends to look out. "Someone you know, too."

"I don't know many Infernals," I say.

"I don't know much about that," he stands up and walks to the glass pane. "There's been a safe meeting offered. For tonight. I'll be your escort."

"And Raphael," I say.

Carl shakes his head.

"You know Raphael wouldn't agree to that," I say. "He insists on being with me when meeting new Timeless."

Carl looks back at me and shrugs his shoulders. "What can I tell you, Danni? Anyone else shows, the meeting doesn't happen."

I look at him for a few moments.

"You know you're safe with me," he says. "No matter what colour my eyes are."

I don't know that. But I would bet on it, under most circumstances. "Who is it?"

Carl comes back and sits down. He grins, and this time it seems less pleasant. "The Devil himself has travelled from far away to wish you a happy birthday, Danni."

"Daniel?" I ask. My gut jumps and I feel anxious.

"The one and only."

I look at him for a few seconds. Then I nod.

"Set it up."

6

Trew closed his eyes and rubbed the back of his neck. Taking a deep breath, he considered the information the top minds in the Game had just delivered.

All twelve Games Masters sat around a table. Many looked embarrassed and uncomfortable with the news their leader, Foundation, had just shared.

Foundation looked most uncomfortable of all. He was middle-aged, with thinning black hair and thick glasses resting on a tiny nose. His skin was splotchy and Trew guessed it'd been years since he'd eaten properly or exercised. Physical conditioning aside, he was extremely intelligent. Trew had studied the careers of all the Games Masters; Foundation was brilliant when it came to computers and the mechanics of the Game. After decades of working in the business, only the most skilled individuals could hope for a chance to become a Games Master, and the true stresses began after the title was attained. The average career of a Games Master was less than two years. The man who currently held the title of Foundation had been part of the Twelve for over fifteen years, and leader of that prestigious group for nine of those.

"I wish we could be of more help, sir," Foundation said to Trew.

Trew sat and stared at the desk, processing what he'd just learned. Most of the details were new, but he couldn't see any information that might help solve this crisis.

"I need results," Trew said.

"Sir, we are limited with what can be attempted," Foundation explained. "The Game tolerates minimal tampering or interference."

"I understand," Trew raised his hand, "but I'm not asking you to interfere with the Game directly. Instead, I want you to focus on the feeds."

"The feeds?" another Games Master asked.

"Yes," Trew said. "The Game is still functioning?"

"Everything indicates that it is," Foundation said. "Hundreds of thousands of players are waking up after being ejected and report that the Game continues to function."

"Exactly," Trew nodded. "So assume the Game is fine and it's simply a signal transmission issue."

"Worldwide?"

"Yes." Trew knew he was talking to the wrong experts. This was a simple problem when viewed from the correct perspective. He shook his head and decided to deliver the challenge anyway. "The Game works; Tygon works. The bridge between the two has been blocked."

"How?" one of the Games Masters asked.

"That is the question," Trew said. "Everyone involved must be asking two questions; how has the bridge been blocked, and how do we unblock it?"

The group looked at each other and nodded.

"Contact me if you come up with anything." Trew stood and walked toward the door.

Cooper was waiting outside. He joined Trew and the two men entered the elevator.

"Anything promising?" Cooper asked.

"No, but I think I've set them on the right path."

"Where to next?"

"The one Games Master who might have ideas that we can use." Trew pressed an elevator button.

===

"Hey, Trew, how's Brandon doing?"

Trew and Hack hugged briefly, then moved to the living area of his underground apartment. The thirteenth 'secret' Games Master turned a large monitor around to face them, grabbed a wireless keyboard and flopped down into a chair beside his visitors.

"He's still on life support, but the doctors are saying that it doesn't look good," Trew said. Cooper made a sour face beside him, but said nothing.

"Brain function?" Hack asked.

"They can't detect any."

Hack shook his head and ran his hand through his hair. "Might be time to cut him loose, Trew," he said.

"What if this blackout is tied to his body continuing to function?" Trew asked.

Both Cooper and Hack looked at Trew in surprise.

"Damn," Cooper said.

"You think that might be possible?" Hack asked.

"He dropped the same time the screens went blank," Trew said grimly.

"So what happens if he stops breathing?" Hack asked.

"Maybe the feeds come back up," Cooper said.

"Or maybe the Game stops functioning," Trew countered, "and over a billion kids die on their tables."

"Well, that could be a problem," Hack said.

The men sat thinking about the implications of both unplugging Brandon's body and leaving it connected.

"Tell me you have a way to see what's happening in there," Trew said.

Hack shook his head in frustration. "I got nothing, so far," he admitted.

"What factors are you looking at?"

"The Game functions, so there must be a block between us and it."

"Thank you," Trew exhaled. He was glad at least one Games Master was on the right track. "So what's the most effective way to bridge that gap?"

"I have to determine which side it comes from. So far everything points to the block being put up from inside the Game," Hack admitted.

"Who would be able to do something like that?" Trew asked.

"They would have to know they were in a Game," Cooper said. "Which narrows it down to a few thousand; maybe only hundreds."

"Infernals," Trew guessed.

"Or Eternals," Cooper shrugged. "They do things that they believe are good, but that doesn't always mean it's what's good for us here."

"I don't know much about Timeless," Trew admitted.

Cooper chuckled and nodded his head. "Feel free to ask me anything you like. Let's get out of here first, though," he glanced at Hack. "No offence, but there are things you can't know."

Hack shrugged with indifference and looked at his computer screen. "No problem. I'll keep working on this end to look for our culprit. If you think of anything else, you know how to contact me."

The two men stood up and left the apartment.

"You know a lot about the Timeless?" Trew asked as they waited for the elevator.

Cooper snorted. "Yeah, you could say that."

"You've researched them?"

"I've done more than research the Timeless," Cooper said as the elevator door opened. "I created them."

7

"**This looks like** my part of town," Cooper said as he scanned the crowd for signs of threat. "Not exactly the kind of place I'd expect to find one of the world's premier artists."

Trew pulled up his collar to protect himself from both the cold and the possibility of being recognized. "Not many people know about this artist," he said. A young man nearby squinted at Trew, but after a moment he looked elsewhere and moved on. Watching him depart, Trew continued to walk towards his destination. "This artist is renowned on a different world. Only a few people know that she was recently ejected from the Game."

The two men crossed the street and stopped in front of a rundown, abandoned building. It was once a storefront, but the windows were boarded up and covered with layers of thick dirt. Trew approached the door and tried the handle; it was locked. He was about to knock when a voice spoke up from a few feet away.

"This way, friends."

Trew looked to his left and saw the speaker. A young boy of about fifteen years old, he possessed the calm presence of a player. Cooper lazily looked him up and down, then nodded at Trew, and they followed him around the corner to a side door.

They entered a dimly lit hallway with low ceilings and damp stone walls. The hallway ended in a well-lit room where six kids of various ages were standing around. In the middle of the room was a chair with a boy sitting in it. The distinctive hum of a tattoo gun could be heard as the artist bent over the young boy's arm, occasionally stopping to wipe away excess ink and dip the needle into fresh colour.

Without looking up from her work, the girl spoke in the direction of the newcomers. "Hey, Trew, good to finally meet you."

"Hi, Janicka," Trew said. "Thanks for agreeing to see me."

"The pleasure is all mine," she said. "Come on over and take a look."

Trew walked over to inspect her handiwork. On the young man's shoulder was the image of two eyes, both greenish brown. One eye had gold flecks suspended in the cornea, while the other had crimson red ones. The artwork was incredible; he would have sworn it was a photograph of the eyes of an actual Timeless.

"Perfectly done," Trew said.

"Thanks," Janicka said, smiling slightly as she turned away to reload her needle.

"How did you get out of the Game Centre so quickly?" Trew asked. "They're detaining everyone who gets ejected from the Game for debriefing."

Janicka shrugged. "Perhaps they overlooked me in the confusion. There are quite a few players leaving the Game at the moment; maybe they simply can't detain them all."

Trew nodded. In the 37 hours since contact had been lost, an incredibly large number of players had exited the Game. Since the death of the player's avatar was the only way to exit, there was a massive event occurring in the Game that viewers were hungry to know about. For Game fans all over Tygon, this blackout was like being a drug addict with no fix in sight. Trew was one of the few who knew the true extent of what was occurring, as much as they could piece together so far, at least. It was grim in there.

"Okay, this is all finished," she said. "Tanner will dress it for you and give you instructions on how to take care of it."

Janicka walked to the nearby table and poured three glasses of tea from a pot. She sat in one of the chairs, indicating that Cooper and Trew should join her.

"You were with her?" Trew asked.

"Mmhmm," Janicka nodded.

"And?"

"And she's doing well, all things considered."

"I need details, Janicka." Trew said.

"I'll give you two hours' worth of details."

"Why two hours?" Trew asked.

Janicka smiled. "That's how long it will take me to ink your new tattoo." She reached behind her and grabbed a folder that contained loose sheets of artwork. Flipping through them quickly, she took one out and pushed it across the table.

Trew looked at it and nodded appreciatively. "It's beautiful," he said.

"That's the one she picked for you," Janicka said. "For all of us, actually." Janicka pulled up the sleeve of her shirt slightly to reveal the same artwork displayed on the front of her right shoulder. Trew looked around and saw that each of the kids in the room were revealing the identical tattoo on various parts of their bodies.

"What's the significance?" Trew asked.

"It designates that we're part of the movement," Janicka smiled. "You're not a Gamer if you don't have this somewhere on your body, in Danni's colony at least."

Trew liked the idea. "Okay, then," he said. "Time for me to get a tattoo."

Janicka drained her tea and stood. "Yeah, Danni said you might like the idea." She moved over to her workstation and patted the chair. "Hop on up here and I'll tell you how your wife has been doing these past few years. She also made me memorize a few messages to give to you."

Trew moved to sit in Janicka's chair. "Let's get to work then, shall we?" he asked.

Janicka smiled as the tattoo gun came alive with a sharp click followed by a dull humming sound.

8

"**Happy birthday, Danni!**"

"Thanks," Danielle said in a cool tone. "I hope you didn't bring me any presents."

The Devil stood and walked towards the large fire that burned brightly in the small clearing.

Carl had helped Danni sneak away from the festivities once darkness had fallen and the large crowds had begun to gather in smaller groups to play music and dance with each other. She'd had to give Raph and Stephanie the slip, which she didn't feel totally comfortable with, but Carl had assured her everything would be fine.

Now here they were, standing in the middle of a small clearing a few kilometres from the Colony. Daniel was alone, smiling with arms spread wide as he walked toward the flames, which appeared to dance and change colours as he got closer to them. Without stopping, Daniel walked directly into the blaze and strolled through the fire, emerging unharmed, close to his visitors. He raised his eyebrows in mock surprise and stopped a respectful distance from the pair.

"Fire," he said. "It's just not as hot as it used to be. You know, before the Day."

Danni shook her head and surveyed the area. There was a blanket on the ground with a picnic basket and two bottles of wine. Three chairs were placed close together; Danni walked to one and sat down. Carl followed her, bending down to grab one of the bottles and throwing it high into the air before sitting down beside her. Danni's eyes flicked upwards to follow the arc of the bottle. As it began to descend, she held out her hand and it sped straight towards her palm, making a sharp snapping sound as it made contact with her hand. She rolled her head slightly and the cork exploded out of the top of the bottle, then she held it behind her shoulder and began to pour...

Carl had a glass in position to catch the glowing blue liquid as it streamed out of the bottle. He made a faint tinging noise, and Danni stopped pouring for the count of three, resuming as Carl placed the second glass underneath the stream.

The entire time Danni kept her eyes locked on the Devil's.

Daniel chuckled and walked toward the empty seat, sitting down and extending his hand to take the glass of wine Carl was offering. With a nod of thanks he waited until Danni filled the third, then raised his glass in a toast.

"Here's to another sixty-two years," he said.

"I'll drink to that," Danni nodded and clinked glasses with the two men before taking a drink. She couldn't help but smile as she tasted the wine; it was the favourite drink of the Timeless. She'd sampled it once before when she first met Daniel; it was a pleasant treat, although she wouldn't admit it to him.

Daniel took a drink from his own glass. "The second bottle is for you to take with you."

"Thank you," she said.

"You're most welcome," he said. "I recommend that you save it for special occasions; there is no more being made at the moment."

"You came all this way just to share a drink with me on my birthday?" Danni asked sweetly. "I'm flattered."

"I came to pick up a friend. The birthday drink was just a pleasant coincidence."

"Your friend must not live near here... our settlement is the only populated group for kilometres all around."

Daniel nodded. "It turns out that my friend is living in your settlement," he said.

"That's not pleasant news for me to hear," Danni frowned with concern. "You've planted a mole in my home, and now you expect me to give them to you?"

"Oh, no, you misunderstand me," the Devil said. "He's not one of mine... yet. He just happens to be living safely inside your walls at the moment."

"I see." Danni took another sip of her wine. "I doubt very much that he will want to join you, especially after I have a chat with him."

Daniel drank from his glass as he looked into the fire. "I think we might be able to come to some sort of agreement on this, Danni," he said.

"I can't imagine the two of us ever reaching an agreement on anything."

"You still owe me Gamer lives." Daniel flashed a dangerous grin.

"You owe me for the ones you took," Dani replied. Daniel's eyes turned to ice. "If you want to settle up on old debts, that suits me," she added.

"Carl," Daniel looked at his old Captain. "How many Gamers were you short when you abandoned us?"

Carl's eyes were flat as he growled the answer. "A hundred thousand."

"That's more than you have in your rather large group at the moment, I think." Daniel put a leg over his chair and swung it comfortably. "Since it's your birthday, and I've come all this way with so little backup, I will forgive the hundred thousand Gamer lives still outstanding on my ledger books." He raised his glass towards Danni and arched an eyebrow. "You give me the one soul in your camp that I came for, and I won't bother you or yours ever again. What do you say to that, Danielle?"

Danielle glared at the Devil for a long time. Finally she gave him a smile of her own and asked, "What's this person's name?"

===

Thirteen

"You came in with the new group today, didn't you?" a voice asks from the darkness.

I look over and see an old man materialize as he gets closer to the fire. He's smiling, but it doesn't do much to improve his appearance. He's filthy, although I detect no odour as he sits down beside me.

His hair is standing all over the place, with bits of twig and dirt in it. There's a plastic crinkling sound coming from his outfit, and as he sits down with a light thud I see that he's covered entirely in black and green garbage bags. He sighs contentedly and stretches his feet towards the fire. Black army boots with no laces dangle loosely from his skinny, hairless legs. His hands clink musically as he extends them towards the fire for warmth.

"Are your gloves made out of red pop bottle caps?" I ask.

He pulls them quickly towards himself and holds them closely to his red bulbous nose. "Yes!" he exclaims, "Red bottle caps! I had forgotten what they were called. Thank you, my new friend, for helping me to remember!"

I shift away from him slightly and nod my head. "No problem," I say, as I look back towards the fire. There's music all around us with hundreds of people dancing happily. Many in my group have joined them, but I prefer to sit out of the way and watch. We have just enjoyed our first big meal in months, and I want to let it settle peacefully.

"Glad to be off the road and surrounded by protection for a change?" the old man asks.

I look at him to see if he's speaking to me directly, or in general terms. His gaze is on the fire, and it looks innocent enough. I nod and answer his question. "It's very stressful to be out there with only a small group for protection," I admit.

"Well, you're all safe here now," the man reaches forward and snags a discarded chicken leg from a plate nearby. He munches on it enthusiastically and looks at me again. Despite his filthy appearance, his eyes appear sharp and clever.

"So you didn't tell me your name," he says.

"You haven't told me yours, either," I counter.

"Fair enough," he nods, "but I did ask you first."

I open my mouth to give him my new name. Not the one I remember, but one that makes people comfortable. Before I can say anything he raises his hand and wags a finger. "Tut tut tut," he says. "Unless you're going to tell me your real name, I don't want you to even utter a sound."

The words catch in my throat. There's no way this old man knows what he's talking about. I smile and assume he's the local idiot. He likely plays this game with everyone he meets for the first time. I take a breath to answer him again, but the words he says next steal my voice away.

"You're Thirteen, right?" he asks.

My mouth snaps shut and I sit there looking at him. My mind is racing. How does he know that? I decide that I'm not going to admit anything to him. I smile and say, "That's not a name, that's a number, old man."

"Indeed it is," he nods gently. "But in this case, it appears to be your name, young fellow. Don't bother to deny it. I know a number when I see one. Three is in the camp as well, you know?"

There's another one of us in the camp? he thought. I don't remember any of them, but I wonder if they would remember me.

The old man chuckles and shakes his head as if he's reading my mind. "I doubt she would recognize you if she saw you. Don't worry my boy, your secret's safe with me."

"There's no secret, friend," I say. "My name isn't Thirteen."

The old man stands up and tosses the chicken leg into the fire, wiping his greasy hands on his garbage bag covering as he shakes his head. "That's too bad," he says. "Someone is coming to get Thirteen, and he will need my help to avoid it from happening. If I don't find him soon, he'll be in serious trouble." Then he begins to walk away.

"Wait!" I call out.

The man stops, his gloves clinking like singing birds as he turns back towards me.

"I am called Thirteen by some," I admit.

The old man nods. "Then come with me, boy. We need to get you someplace safe for a little while."

He begins to walk quickly into the darkness. I hurry to keep up with him.

9

Danielle

The Devil descends from the sky and stalks towards me with fire in his eyes. "I thought you agreed to this too easily," he snaps.

"What's the problem?" I ask.

"He's not there."

"Perhaps flying and trying to sense him at the same time is beyond your abilities," Carl suggests.

Daniel opens his mouth to speak and then snaps it shut as hatred smolders in his eyes. Carl smirks; I think he's enjoying himself.

"Don't forget who runs the show on the red side of things," Daniel says. "Odds are very good that I'll be your boss again, Carl. When that happens, I'll remember the difficulties those gold flecks in your eyes have caused me."

"Even if I turn back soon, I doubt you'll still be alive and in charge." Carl's tone is menacing. "If you want to start throwing threats around, though, we can certainly play that game right now."

I move between them before they start to claw at each other like animals. "Okay, boys, both of you have impressive muscles. Now calm down and focus on the task at hand."

They continue glower at each other, but Daniel looks at me and nods grimly.

"Do you know for certain he was in our camp?" I ask.

"Of course he was," he says. "His group was on the road and arrived at your front gates this morning. There's no way you turned away a group of Gamers, is there?"

"We accepted the group that turned up this morning," I confirm. "You told me he isn't a Gamer."

"He isn't, but the majority of his group are."

I walk over to the chairs and grab the remaining full bottle of Timeless wine. "Well, I don't know what to tell you, Daniel. I gave you permission to take him, and now you say he isn't in my camp. Why don't you take one more fly over and search very carefully for him. If you don't find him, then get lost." I smile sweetly. "I look forward to never seeing you or your crew near my colony again. Ever."

Daniel smiles and shakes his head. "That promise required that I leave with my prize. If I don't get him today, then I'll come back as often as I like until I find him."

I shake my head. "No, you won't. You have one hour to do your business and get out of here. The next time I see you, I'll view it as a declaration of war. If you push me, then we will fight you, and I promise things will get very messy."

I take a step forward so that my face is close to his and give him my best intimidating look, which has become impressive thanks to observing Carl for these past few years. "I have enough Eternals here to kick you from the Game, Daniel. Don't push me. I've got nothing left to lose and everything to gain from making you dead."

Daniel looks at me for a moment, and then one corner of his mouth turns upwards into an amused grin. "Calm down, girl," he chuckles. "I come looking for one individual and you start talking about going to war?"

"I'm serious." I continue to stare at him.

He looks into my eyes and nods. "I can see that you are," he says. "I was just playing with you, Danni. Some birthday fun." He raises his hand and makes a twirling motion with his index finger. Behind him, a glowing white doorway materializes.

Just before he steps through, he looks over his shoulder and grins. "Take care of yourself, Danni. It's a tough world out there now."

Then he's gone.

I look at Carl. He holds up his hand for a moment and turns his head from side to side, as if listening for something. Finally, he nods. "He's gone."

I move back to the fire and sit down in one of the chairs. "Well, that was fun," I say.

Carl chuckles and moves to sit beside me. "You had me going when you said that he could take someone from the camp."

I pour the remainder of the wine from the first bottle into our glasses. "I was serious about that," I say. "If he'd found who he was looking for, then he could have taken him."

"Really?" Carl asks.

"Absolutely," I say. "I was fairly certain that he wouldn't be there, though. We stalled him for long enough here."

"Who got him out of the camp?"

I look sideways over the top of my wine glass and arch my eyebrow.

"The old man," Carl says.

"The old man," I agree.

"How did you know he was in town?" he asks. "No Timeless can sense when he comes or goes."

"I don't know," I shrug. "I always seem to be aware of him."

"Who is he? I've met some strange creatures over the years, but this old man is... noteworthy."

I wonder who the old man is, too. I was surprised to find out the Timeless had never heard of him. "He's a friend, that much is certain," I say. "I find myself wondering more about the man Daniel came looking for."

"Me too," Carl admits.

"Hopefully when the old man brings him back we can get some answers."

10

"You've been on Tygon before, right?"

Cooper looked up from inspecting the new tattoo on his right bicep and let his sleeve fall back into place. "Yes," he replied. He leaned back and put his feet up on Trew's desk. Trew was still looking for answers, and the office where Sylvia resided was the next logical place to look.

"Why did it cost Brandon his life this time?"

Cooper shook his head. "The answer to that question is pointless at this moment."

Trew had heard this answer before, so he kept asking new questions. "Do you know why video feeds have been lost?"

"No, but I would guess that it was planned."

"By whom?"

Cooper smiled and ran his hands through his hair. "There's only one person on Tygon who could have set something like this up."

"Brandon?" Trew asked.

"That's where I'd put my money. You've seen what he was like as a kid. I mean, he still is a kid... you know what I'm getting at. The best players are ten, maybe twelve steps in front of the rest. With Brandon it was always like he'd finished the current game and was one or two entire contests ahead of everyone else."

"So what do you think we should do next?"

Cooper shook his head with a frown. "It's not for me to say."

"Sure it is," Trew said.

"No, it's not. This is Brandon's simulation. Thorn warned that the rest of us were not to interfere in how it was being played. Doing so could ruin everything Brandon has accomplished up until now."

"Maybe before, but things are different where you're concerned."

Cooper thought about it for a few moments. Trew saw his eyes register with understanding as he nodded.

"You think I'm allowed to weigh in now because I'm here full time," Cooper said.

"That's right," Trew agreed. "I think Brandon paid the price to put you into play. He's not here, but having you inside the Sim allows you to use your considerable experience and talents to assist us."

"He is here, you know."

"He is?" Trew sounded confused by the statement.

Cooper leaned forward and tapped Trew on the centre of the chest. "It's taken him decades, but he was able to breed and groom an individual from this planet to emulate him. There are moments when I swear that you are him."

"Really?" Trew asked.

"Without a doubt. Most of the time, you're a confident young man who knows exactly how to move forward. Still, there are rare moments of hesitation when I see you wondering what Brandon would do."

"Yes," Trew confirmed.

"Well, don't," Cooper said. "Know that you and he are the same. There will likely be some areas where you are even better than him."

"I doubt that," Trew laughed.

"I don't." Cooper nodded seriously.

"What makes you say that?"

"Because I know that boy," Cooper said. "The only way he would leave this simulation in the hands of someone else is if he was absolutely certain that he was leaving it to someone better than he was."

Trew thought about it for a moment. "So he's stacking the deck of cards," he said. "He knew it would increase his chances of success to have you here with him, and so he brings you in."

"Leaving you behind as a version of himself because he knows he has to exit to get me in," Cooper says. "Very clever."

"Very sweet, boys," Sylvia's voice spoke up. "Cooper is absolutely correct, by the way. Brandon had been working for decades to produce someone who might exceed his qualifications, and he was convinced that you are that person, Trew."

You mean NPC, Trew wanted to say, but he didn't. Serious soul searching and internal debate had led Trew to put that dilemma aside — for the moment anyway. Finding out that the base elements of his cells were digital bits instead of carbon changed nothing. Everything broken down to its smallest unit was the same material.

"I have some interesting news to share," Sylvia said.

"What is it?" Trew asked.

"There is one monitor on Tygon which is receiving a live feed of events occurring inside the Game."

"What?" Trew jumped out of his seat excitedly. "How were you able to determine that?"

"Since 'the Day' occurred, I've been testing all sources on the planet for connectivity. There are an incredible number of feeds to check, so it's taken me days to complete the process."

Cooper chuckled. "One of the last feeds you checked was the live one?" he guessed. "Isn't that always the way? The last place you look is where the treasure is so often hidden."

"Not at all," Sylvia said. "It was the first place I looked, but it wasn't live the first time I checked it. There must have been a program in place to force me to check the entire complex system before it became active. It's as if there was a built in factor which forced us to be in the dark for exactly forty-eight hours of our time, and almost three years of Game time."

"Brandon," Cooper guessed.

"Most likely," Sylvia agreed.

"Where is the feed?" Trew asked. "Can you patch it to me here?"

"I can't redirect it to any other location. You'll have to go to the terminal itself."

"Brandon's penthouse?" Trew guessed.

"Yes," Sylvia said. "Although it's your penthouse now, Trew."

Trew was already walking towards the door with Cooper close on his heels.

11

Angelica landed flat on her back with a loud thud.

She lay there for a moment, blinking her eyes as the numbness faded and the pain spread like liquid fire throughout her frame. She gauged the messages being sent to her brain, waiting to see if there were any indicators of serious damage. She moved her head slowly from side to side and wiggled her fingers and toes.

"You're trying to kill me," she announced to the air above her.

Samantha's smiling face appeared overhead, her hand coming into view. Angelica grabbed it and stood up, looking around to see if anyone was watching. Of course they had an audience. A small crowd always formed when Eternals gathered to train in the yard.

"I may not be Carl," Samantha said, "But I am over two hundred years old, sugar. If I meant to kill you, you'd be dead."

Angelica nodded as she stood and slowly stretched her arms behind her back. She felt a heavy throbbing near her right eye and reached up to touch the spot. She pulled her hand away and showed Samantha the blood. "Is it bad?" she asked.

Samantha came closer and inspected the wound. "It could use some attention," she nodded and raised her hand close to the wound, holding it there as warmth began to emanate from her palm.

Angelica sat quietly, feeling the warmth spread into her cheek and down her body. After a few moments the pulsing and pain subsided. A minute later Samantha removed her hand and inspected the area.

"There," she announced. "Good as new."

Angelica nodded and bent down to tie her shoes. "When do I get that skill?" she asked.

Samantha shrugged. "Reiki? You already possess that skill, girl."

"I can't do that with it."

Samantha laughed and shook her head. "Of course you can't," she said. "Keep practicing and you'll grow in all abilities. You're just a young one, A. Stick with it, and in a few decades it will come to you."

"I thought I would have more powers to start off with."

"Then somebody gave you the wrong info," Samantha said.

"She was a Timeless," Angelica walked back into the middle of the sparring area and stood five feet away from Samantha.

"An old one?" Samantha guessed.

"Yeah, I think so."

"It's different for each of us, A, but no one ever gets all the skills to start. What would be the fun in that?"

"I guess you're right," Angelica said.

"You have serious skills in the area of damage. There's no way you can be equally as good at healing as you are at hurting. It just doesn't work that way."

"You're beating me easily, which makes you better at hurting than healing," Angelica countered. "Yet you can hold your hand over my cut and make it disappear in seconds."

Samantha shrugged. "You know my real strength is healing. The only reason I can beat you is because I'm a Timeless with over two hundred years' experience. A regular person couldn't best you in combat."

"Is that true?"

"It is if you want it to be," Samantha tapped her head. "The one thing we have that normals don't is the knowledge that this is a

Game. Knowing that allows us to manipulate the world, and the people living in it. At first we aren't very good at it. But we get better as time goes on, while normal players die and come back to start from scratch."

"Is that why Danielle is as skilled as a Timeless?"

"Absolutely," Samantha nodded. "Because she knows this is a Game." Samantha stepped close to Angelica and whispered. "If normal avatars believed the truth, most of them could do more incredible things than any Timeless. Danielle and Melissa, and the others who have jumped straight down the hole to find reality are anomalies that Timeless have never seen in the entire history of the Game. Exciting things are happening, Angelica, and you are here at the best time ever."

"We don't have long."

Samantha waved her hand absently. "You're not on Tygon anymore, girl. You will live for thousands of years in here if you learn what we're trying to teach you."

Angelica froze and looked slowly towards Samantha.

"What's wrong with you? You look as if I have a second head sprouting from my neck."

They don't know, Angelica thought. The Timeless don't know this all ends in just a few Earth years. She shook her head and smiled to break the tension. "Nothing's wrong," she said. "Just thought I felt a chill run up my spine."

A voice from the other side of the area interrupted their conversation.

"You can feel it too?" the voice rumbled.

Angelica didn't bother to face the newcomer. "Feel what, Carl?" she asked.

"Your slow, painful, embarrassing death," he said with a hungry grin.

"You can't do that now," Angelica said. "We're on the same side."

Carl walked over to a nearby picnic table and sat down. "Tell her, Sam," he said.

Samantha winced and looked at Angelica with sympathy. "Thing is, that sometimes Timeless kill each other. It doesn't matter if they're on the same side or not. It doesn't occur often, but if they really hate each other, then it can happen."

Angelica laughed and looked over at Carl. "So you're just gonna kill me?" she asked.

"Eventually," he nodded, "but now that you're one of us, there's not such a rush. Last time I tried it was because I knew you were leaving the Game and you wouldn't be coming back to play again. Now that I know you're here for longer, I'm willing to wait and give you a fighting chance."

"That's mighty nice of you," she said.

"Not really," Carl laughed. "I could snap you in seconds. You can't even beat our worst fighter in hand to hand combat yet."

"Worst fighter?" Angelica looked at Samantha who blushed. "Samantha has been easily putting me on my back for the past two years."

"I really am a very bad fighter," Samantha admitted. "For a Timeless."

"Don't beat yourself up about it, darlin'," Carl said. "No one can heal like you, and you have other considerable talents. Just cause you can't fight well doesn't mean much. Especially when you don't have to fight very often." He smiled mockingly. "Plus it gives us a member who can help the young ones learn the basics."

"Ahh, look at you, being so sweet to me!" Samantha ran over and kissed Carl on the cheek, ignoring his attempts to push her away. Then she looked back at Angelica. "But seriously, girl, he could kill you super easy. I'm surprised he hasn't done it already. Actually, check yourself; you might be dead and just not realize it yet."

Angelica couldn't help but laugh. Samantha was always able to make people laugh, and her laughter was a treat to hear. "Stop it! You're making me feel bad about myself."

Samantha pushed Carl playfully. "Make her feel a little better, Carl. Give her a compliment."

Carl frowned, but nodded his head. "At the two year mark we all suck," he confided. "If I had to rate you against the thousands of recruits I've seen over the centuries, only the sisters were better than you are at this stage of the Game."

Angelica was surprised and encouraged by the compliment. She hadn't expected to hear a kind word from Carl today. For the past two years, they had both gone to special lengths to stay out of each other's way. "Why thank you, Carl. That must have been painful for you to admit. I appreciate it."

"It was," he agreed. "Just hurry up and improve. When you can give Raphael or someone decently skilled a run for their money, then I might decide to kill you."

Angelica ignored the threat. "What two sisters are you talking about? Real sisters? Or Sisters in the Timeless sense?"

Samantha answered. "Real sisters. They were sisters on Tygon who both became Timeless here. They're pretty famous in our circles. I'm sure you'll hear their story someday."

"She knows them," Carl said. "Don't let Angelica play the poor new Timeless, Sam. She was one of the best players to ever be in the Game." He looked at Angelica and watched her closely for a reaction.

"The Timeless sisters that Sam is referring to are old friends of yours, Angelica."

"I have no idea who you're talking about, Carl," Angelica said.

"Skylar and Courtney," Carl said.

Angelica gasped in surprise as Carl chuckled and nodded.

12

"**We need more flyers**, Danni."

Danielle sat in her office chair and poured a small taste of Timeless wine into a single glass which she pushed towards her guest.

Melissa picked up the glass and held it up to the light. "What is this?" she asked. "It looks like antifreeze."

"It's a gift. Go ahead and take a sip."

Melissa took a small drink and smiled as a dozen smells and flavours flooded her senses.

"What do you think of that?" Danielle asked.

"Wow!" she said "Where did you get this stuff?"

"The Devil hand delivered it to me for a birthday present."

"What? When was he here?"

"On my birthday," Danielle winked. "I snuck out to meet him."

Melissa shrugged her shoulders and took another tiny sip. "Okay," she said. "Dani, we need more flyers."

Danielle smiled. There were many in the Colony who were protective of her, but Melissa wasn't one of them. The two women had been through a lot together, and neither would ever insult the other by questioning their judgment. "What do you need more flyers for?" Danielle asked.

"To fly," Melissa smiled. After 'the Day,' people were isolated and forced to use old and slow methods of travelling. To be able to fly meant covering phenomenal distances in short periods of time; the few who could do so in the Colony were kept extremely busy. As their tribe had grown, new demands were placed on many of the flyers which resulted in them being grounded to look after other matters. Melissa had been kept in the air, but Danni knew she was becoming tired of the grind.

"How many full time flyers remain?"

"Counting me?" Melissa asked. "One."

Danni smiled. "Hmm, yes, I see what you're getting at. Why don't you go recruit some more and start training them?"

"How many years did it take to get you into the air?"

"I don't remember exactly," Danni said.

"Too long, and we don't have that kind of luxury anymore." Melissa finished the wine and put the glass down on the desk. "Thank you so much. That was incredible."

"No problem," Dani said. "There might be a quicker way."

"I'm interested in what you're saying..." Melissa leaned forward.

"The old man introduced me to a very promising new Colony member,"

Melissa frowned. "Why do you still call him the 'old man'?"

"You have a better name for him?"

"Yes, I do," Melissa grinned. "We've started calling him Grandpa,"

Danni laughed and then nodded. "He is old, and he brings us treats from time to time like a grandfather would."

"And it doesn't sound cold and impersonal like calling him 'old man' does."

"There's that, too," Danni admitted. "Okay, Grandpa introduced me to a very interesting new member. His name is Thirteen, and he's a genius when it comes to quantum mechanics and physics. I think he might be able to watch what you do and help break it down to help others learn more quickly."

Melissa nodded. "I'm certainly up for trying. If we could get just a few more of us birds into the air, life would be better."

"You know the old man —" Danni paused to correct herself, "Grandpa, I mean — can fly?"

"No, I didn't," Melissa said. "Although I should have guessed he could, since he opens those portals so easily."

"What?" it was Dani's turn to be surprised. "I had no idea he could do that!"

"Looks like he keeps different secrets depending on who it is he's spending time with. Is he still here?"

Danni paused and stared into space for a moment before shaking her head. "I don't sense him. That doesn't mean he's gone, though."

"When can I meet this Thirteen?" Melissa asked.

"I'll find him and arrange to introduce you," Danni said.

"It will be good to meet another number. I hope he's as friendly as the other one."

"What do you mean?" Danni frowned her eyebrows in puzzlement.

"Miranda," Melissa said. "Wasn't she called Three by that nut job Shane when he captured her before the Day?"

Danni stood up quickly and grabbed her jacket. "I'd totally forgotten about that. Come with me, quickly."

"We're going to find Miranda, then hunt for Thirteen?" Melissa guessed.

"Yes," Danni said grimly. "Then we're going to find out if Thirteen is here to help... or harm us."

13

Trew and Cooper sat beside each other and watched the live feed of the Game.

Cooper had offered to let Trew watch it alone, but Trew simply shook his head and pulled up an extra chair. They'd sat down and tuned into the feed, eager to see what was occurring in the Game.

Two hours passed.

Finally Trew looked over at Cooper. "This isn't what I was hoping it would be," he said.

"I agree," Cooper said. "It keeps switching perspectives every few minutes. Is there no way to control who we're viewing?"

"I tried everything when we first started watching," the frustration could be heard in Trew's voice. "No matter what I do, the feed continues to switch to different players."

"Let's talk about what we're seeing," Cooper suggested.

"It's a mess in there," Trew shook his head. "Every view has been full of pain, fear, and misery. Most players are hiding in small groups, struggling just to find warmth, food, and shelter to get them through the next day. Maybe it's better if people can't watch what's going on in there right now. I don't know if the fans would tune in."

"You know they'd tune in," Cooper said. "This is exactly the kind of thing they want to see."

"It shouldn't be," Trew said.

"Yet it is."

The telephone rang, and both men looked towards it deliberately. Trew walked to it and pushed a button to answer it on speaker. There was a series of clicks and beeps, followed by a hollow popping noise.

"Are you watching the feed?" Thorn asked.

"Yes," Trew said. "Although I'm not sure what we're supposed to do with the information."

"It's the best feed I could provide. I don't intend for you to sit in front of it for days on end; that would accomplish nothing. The feed will go dead in two more hours, so sit and watch it until the signal fades."

"And then get back to work," Cooper said.

"Exactly," Thorn agreed. "It's bad in there, and it's getting much worse as time goes on. Millions are going to die to meet the number Brandon set with the Timeless."

"Five hundred million?"

"Yes," Thorn said. "The Gamer culling took out about one million, one hundred fifty thousand, give or take. That leaves over three hundred fifty million more to be ejected; and that's what's happening with this event."

"Brandon wants to save as many of the children as he can," Trew guessed. If they were caught inside the Game when Danni died, then they would die permanently on Tygon.

"What?" Thorn sounded confused.

"He wants to save as many lives as he can by ejecting them early," Trew said again.

"That doesn't even make sense," Thorn said. "What would he care for the lives of NPCs outside of the Game? He needs them to wake up inside the Game, to realize they are in a simulation and break free from it. Ejecting them from the Game and leaving them to sit on Tygon makes no sense for achieving the goal."

"He seemed to care for some of the NPCs," Trew snapped. "Much more than you do, it sounds like."

Cooper shook his head and looked into the air. There was a moment of silence as Thorn understood that he wasn't talking to Trew anymore; he was speaking with an NPC.

"I'm sorry, Trew. I didn't mean to sound cold or uncaring."

"It's fine." Trew cut him off. "I don't think NPCs would have any care for you or your kind either if they learned the truth."

"Oh," Thorn said. "I never thought I'd hear a phrase like that voiced."

"I can see why so many people were sent to the camps with very little remorse on Brandon's part," Trew said. "None of us are real to him, so he didn't give it a thought when millions failed out of his project and were exiled to finish their days in pain, fear, and humiliation."

Thorn responded softly. The compassion in his voice was noticeable. "You're right, he didn't, and neither did I as I watched it. Most of the time, it was like working with bacteria in a lab. When one colony failed, we would dispose of it and work with a new batch. It's no excuse, but we never imagined NPCs would become so... real."

Trew walked back to look at the monitor, as people — his people — struggled to survive. "This conversation is a waste of time," he announced. "We will do what we were programmed to do. We'll save our lives, and maybe show you how to save your own in the process."

"That's the goal," Thorn said.

"Is he there?"

"Who?"

"Brandon. Is he with you right now, listening in on this?"

Thorn paused. "No, he isn't. Things are getting worse here, and he's..."

"I don't care how bad it is there." Trew cut him off. "Your problems don't concern me."

Thorn was silent for a few moments. Trew watched the monitor intently as Cooper sat and observed him with an amused look on his face.

"I'll leave you alone for now," Thorn said. "The monitor will go blank in two hours. Pay close attention to this last bit of time. You will start to see people familiar to you now. For small snippets."

Trew said nothing and watched the screen until he heard the speakerphone click and the line went dead. Cooper got up to end the call from this end.

"This whole NPC thing is strange," Trew said.

Cooper laughed and nodded. "It sure is, boy. There was a time when all an NPC could do was stand in one spot and perform one simple task. Your race has caught up to ours, it would seem, and my opinion of what you are has changed completely."

"How so?" Trew asked.

"I can no longer discern any difference between you and me," Cooper replied. "For me to say that... well, it's a big deal."

Trew started to speak, but his eyes caught something on the monitor and his head spun back to the viewscreen. "Quiet," he commanded.

"I see her," Cooper whispered.

The two men sat silently for the remaining time, occasionally catching glimpses of Danni and her Colony.

Exactly two hours later, the feed went dead.

Cooper said nothing, staring first at the monitor, and then at Trew.

Trew looked at the blank monitor. Another hour passed as they sat silently and considered the situation. Finally Trew stood up and nodded at Cooper.

"I know what we need to do next," he announced.

14

"**I don't recognize** him."

"Are you sure, Miranda? If you can remember anything, even the smallest detail, it could help us."

Miranda continued to look at the man sitting across the street and down the block. Danielle had chosen her base carefully; Cambridge was once three smaller towns that had grown over decades to become a single city, even though the three areas remained slightly distinctive. Three small urban centres separated by only a few miles and connected by a river made for a very pleasant living area, something that early settlers of the land had no doubt considered. Thirteen had moved into one of the areas and was doing his best to get settled in. It was challenging for an intellectual to fit into this new world where a strong back was required more than the ability to program a computer or conduct thought experiments.

"He doesn't look familiar, Danni," Miranda shook her head again. "Most of my time spent in the Zoo was hazy. Maybe if Sparx were here, she would recall something..." Miranda still missed her nanocompanion and wondered if she had ceased to exist when the rest of technology stopped functioning. In her mind, Miranda told herself that it was still possible for Sparx to be operational. The nanocomputer's composition and functioning resembled living cells more than it did computer technology. Most of the time she was optimistic that Sparx was out there somewhere, trying to find its way back to her.

"Okay, thanks for trying. Come over and meet him with me; maybe he will remember you."

"Of course," Miranda nodded, her gold-flecked eyes glittering in the morning light. When 'the Day' had occurred, Miranda's eyes had changed from the Infernal crimson to the gold of the Eternals. Danni had been relieved to see the change; she hadn't wanted to bring an Infernal with them on their journey, even if it was one that appeared to be friendly.

Danni took a step into the street when she heard a raspy voice from behind her call out a greeting.

"He's safe, Danni. I would never bring a dangerous creature into your home."

Danni turned around and saw the old man leaning against a building. She wondered why he continued to wear garbage bags. Attempts to clothe him had proven futile; Danni had given up when she'd placed fresh clothes beside him while he was eating lunch and he'd used them to wipe his hands and mouth clean.

"Good morning, Grandpa," she smiled.

"Grandpa?" he scowled as if tasting something sour. "Why on earth would you call me Grandpa? Save that vile title for someone old, if you please." He nodded his head towards Raphael who stood a block down the street watching them casually. "Call that old fart Grandpa and see how well it goes over. I'm not that much older than him." He paused to consider his statement, then he nodded confidently. "Okay, maybe in some places I'm older than him, but here I think he's actually older than me."

He leaned into the street and waved his arms flamboyantly to get Raphael's attention. "GOOD MORNING, GRANDPA!" he shouted. "OUT FOR A LITTLE WALK THIS MORNING?"

Raphael tried to ignore the shouts, but those nearby began to look first down the street and then at him, smirking at the humor of the situation. After a moment Raphael looked skyward and moved to join Danielle.

"Oh, look at him go!" the old man said, clapping his hands in delight. "He sure is spry for an old fella!"

Raphael scowled at the old man as he reached them. "How many times is that you've blown my cover?" he asked.

The old man raised his eyebrows and covered his face with his hands, pretending to be upset. "I'm insulted that you would accuse me of doing such a thing. If I blew your cover, then it was by accident, and this must be the first time it's occurred." He held up eight fingers to indicate the actual number of times, winking at Raphael playfully.

"So what do you want us to call you?" Danni put a hand on Raphael's shoulder. He chuckled at the old man's antics and looked down the road to keep an eye on Thirteen.

The old man shrugged. "Names have never much mattered to me. I've always liked the name Brandon — perhaps you would like to call me that?"

In unison, everyone in the group snapped their heads to look at the old man.

He saw their looks and laughed gently. "All right, fine," he said. "Not a very funny joke, perhaps. The truth is, Danni, that I don't really care what name you call me. 'Old man' fits me just fine. Once I'm gone, no one will remember me anyway."

"I want to know who you are," Danni said.

"So do I, dear," He looked at her soberly, all traces of mischief gone from his eyes. "So do I."

He raised his hand and made a tight circular motion. A bright white doorway of light appeared in the alley behind them. "I have to head out for a while. You go have a chat with Thirteen and see what the two of you can come up with. He's a very good boy, Danni. Please look after him."

Danni nodded and the old man walked towards the doorway.

He paused at the entrance and looked at Stephanie, who had just joined the group. "Keep an eye on that one, Danni," he said pointing towards Stephanie. You may think spending your entire life with someone counts for something, but to a Timeless, a few short decades doesn't guarantee lifelong loyalty." He stepped into the doorway and it faded from sight.

Danni looked at Stephanie. Her eyes were sad and there were signs of tears on her cheeks. Before Danni could ask what the problem was, she looked closer and shook her head sadly. "Oh, no, Steph," she groaned.

"He's wrong, Danni," Stephanie sobbed. "I won't ever betray you or Trew, I swear it."

Raphael reached out to touch Stephanie's face and gently turned it towards him. "I'm sorry, sweet girl," he said. "Your eyes are telling us that it's time for you to leave."

Stephanie nodded and blinked away the tears. She took a step toward Danni with her arms extended to hug her, but Danni shook her head and stepped backwards defensively as her own eyes reflected the sadness of the group.

The crimson flecks in Stephanie's eyes flashed in anger at being denied a parting embrace, but she closed them and nodded in understanding.

"Love you all," she whispered. "I won't let them use me against you, I promise."

Stephanie knelt quickly and exploded upwards into the sky. The group watched her go until she faded in the distance.

Finally Danni broke the silence. "Is that a promise she can keep?" she asked.

"No," Raphael answered sadly. "She may be able to resist it for a while, but eventually a Timeless has to follow their eyes."

Danni pursed her lips and looked at the group grimly.

"Then let's hope she can resist until they turn gold again."

15

Two weeks later, Stephanie sat alone in front of a fire. It was a small blaze that she'd built for warmth, thirty feet from the main road. A rabbit roasted over the flames, and she warmed her hands as she waited patiently for her meal to finish cooking.

Stephanie had flown far away from Danielle and her friends, not stopping until she was almost halfway around the world, somewhere in Russia. She'd covered a considerable distance during her flight, but had spotted no significant outposts or large groups of people along the way.

Stephanie felt a slight disturbance in the energy field and raised her head to look into the nearby darkness. A Timeless approached her. She recognized the energy signature as it got closer, and she reached out with her hands to grab the rabbit from the spit to let it cool. "Just in time for a free meal. You never change, Daniel."

"Just my good fortune, darlin'," the Devil chuckled from the edge of the firelight. "Is that your fancy way of inviting me to dinner, then?"

She nodded and pointed to a small chair on the other side of the fire. "Be my guest," she said.

The Devil sauntered over and dropped down lightly into the offered chair, taking off his long, black leather trench coat and laying it beside him on the ground. "You've led me on a bit of a chase these past few days," he said.

"I didn't know you were looking for me," Stephanie began to cut the rabbit in half, placing one steaming piece of golden brown meat on a tin plate and handing it to her guest.

Daniel flashed her a grin as he took the plate. "Look at you," he said. "You've been an Infernal for just a few days, and already you lie like a pro." He took a big bite and began to chew, nodding enthusiastically as he savoured the flavour of fresh grilled meat.

Stephanie watched him eat, holding her plate in her lap as she sat, looking tired and dejected.

"I've got big plans for you, girl," Daniel said as he continued to attack the rabbit, juice dripping slowly down his chin. Hunks of meat were visible in his mouth as he spoke. "This is your first time being an Infernal. Young little thing like you is gonna learn a lot of nasty and useful skills on this side of the fence. It's important to find the right mentor your first time, and I think I have just the person in mind for you."

"Really?" Stephanie asked sarcastically.

"Oh, yes," Daniel nodded. "I know you likely don't want to be involved with any plans that I have for Danielle and her bunch, which is fine with me. For the first couple of years it's best to keep you away from them, anyway. That way it will be more effective when they finally do see you and get to experience the horrific creature that you've become."

"I've met many Infernals," Stephanie said. "They aren't horrific creatures."

"First time they see crimson, they are," Daniel tossed a bare leg bone into the fire. "The purpose of being an Infernal is to spread pain and confusion across the world. The first time our eyes go crimson, it can take decades, if not hundreds, of years to calm down enough to appear civilized and sane again."

"Really?" Stephanie's eyes betrayed concern at the thought of losing control and becoming a violent bringer of pain to those she'd always worked so hard to protect.

"With the right mentor, we could cut that cycle into just a few short weeks." Daniel stared hungrily at Stephanie's untouched meal and she quietly passed it over to him. She felt nauseous anyway. Daniel nodded and snatched the rabbit from her plate.

"Then why let it stretch out so long?" Stephanie pleaded. "I don't want to become a psychotic madwoman."

"If it were up to me alone, I would agree with you." It was obvious from his grin that it was up to him, and he was choosing not to help her. "It's not often that we get to put a brand new Infernal into action, and since the Day we haven't had a single one. If there's one thing this world needs right now, it's a crazy woman with powers roaming around killing at random. Heck, you might even build a reputation to rival Carl's, and let me tell you, he was a very energetic first timer when he came to the party."

Stephanie stood up, grabbed another log, and threw it onto the fire.

"Maybe I'll just kill you and become the new leader of the Infernals," she said casually.

Daniel threw his head back and laughed loudly. One short bark turned into more, until eventually, he was laughing hysterically at the idea. Stephanie grinned at him the entire time, saying nothing while he hooted and hollered at the thought of a fresh recruit toppling him from his role as the Devil.

Finally his laughter began to lessen. Daniel wiped tears from his eyes and took large breaths of air to regain his composure. He looked over at Stephanie. "I have to thank you, darlin'. I haven't laughed like that in centuries. The thought of someone as weak and young as you attempting something so... well, so diabolical her first time as an Infernal... I'm gonna treasure that for months to come."

Stephanie continued to smile sweetly as she shook her head. "No, Daniel, I'm afraid you won't."

Something about the way she smiled made Daniel pause. He narrowed his eyes to look at her carefully, and he noticed that she wasn't looking at him.

She was looking at his empty plate.

He tried to stand up, but for some reason his body was slower than it should be. Sluggish.

In a flash, Stephanie moved from her seat to a position behind Daniel, holding his head in an iron grip. He struggled to stand, but the intense force she was exerting held him in place.

"So careless, Daniel," Stephanie purred into his ear. "So many years secure in your position. All immediate Infernal threats identified and neutralized to make certain you were safe. Your reign was impressive, but it's time for a new Devil to run the show."

Daniel tried to say something, but the poison from the food was coursing solidly through his veins, sapping him of the majority of his strength. He knew he had only one chance, if he could just get his mouth open to speak three words. He tried to make his jaws work, but Stephanie's hands clamped his mouth securely shut.

"Oh, no, you don't." Her voice dripped like golden honey. "I've been fully prepped for this little meeting for years. We've been waiting for one of us to turn, and hoping it would be me."

Daniel's eyes blazed with fury. He knew the words she would say next, and his blood boiled in rage as she spoke them.

"Carl sends his regards," she whispered.

With a sharp twist, the Devil's neck snapped like an ancient tree being shattered by a tornado.

Stephanie held him for the count of ten, and then she lowly let him sag to the ground.

"Quickly," Raphael materialized from the darkness and strode purposefully towards her. "Make the mark and transfer the power."

Stephanie nodded, and with a forceful punch, she tore into Daniel's chest cavity, removing his heart from his body. She took the blood from it and smeared a mark, first on his forehead, and then on her own.

"One bite," Raphael said, his face a grim mask of purpose as he watched the scene unfold like the director of a Broadway play.

Stephanie nodded and raised the heart to her mouth, tasting coppery blood and feeling the thick toughness of heart muscle as her teeth ripped into it. She chewed quickly and swallowed, dropping the heart onto Daniel's chest.

Instantly, red lightning streaked from the sky. In the space of a heartbeat, the crimson bolt pierced Daniel's head at the mark, and leapt into Stephanie's matching symbol.

Stephanie was thrown off her feet and lay on her back, a small trail of smoke rising from the middle of her forehead. She opened her eyes and blinked, then stood up and looked at Raphael questioningly.

Raphael nodded grimly, then his face broke into a smile. "That's it, then. You're the Devil."

Stephanie started to smile, but it quickly became a worried frown. "Was he right, Raph? Am I going to turn into an insane creature of destruction?"

"Yes, but not for long, if you stick with the plan."

"What if I do something horrible?" she asked.

"Sweet girl, you are now the Devil. You're going to do many horrible things. Remember the next part of the plan?"

"Yes. I find the sisters and rely on them for help."

"I've found them for you and brought them here," Raphael pointed his finger down the road. "They're inside the first house in that direction, waiting for you. Do as they say and you will get through the tough part quickly."

"I wish you could do this," Stephanie said.

"I couldn't have pulled it off. He would have been ready for me. You can do this, Sister. Be strong, and know that you are loved, no matter what happens."

"Better the Devil you know..." Stephanie said.

"Exactly," Raphael smiled.

16

'As day three of the Game blackout fades, fans remain in the dark. Experts, computer programmers, analysts, ex-players, Patrons...no one can give us any explanation as to what's happening.

The biggest question fans are asking is; since the Game is still operational, who has blocked the feed and for what purpose?

Trew is addressing the world tonight in less than half an hour.

I am certain everyone is interested in hearing what he has to say...'

Lisa Rohansen

Trew walked to the centre of the stage. The muffled rumble and buzz that builds when any large group assembles was quickly replaced with absolute silence.

Trew stood on the giant stage and looked out at his audience. Despite the bright, hot lights and darkness that lay beyond, Trew could sense the immense crowd that was gathered to hear his address. Cooper had told him there were over two million people assembled, making this the largest speaking event of his many lives.

Years of practice and experience kicked in, banishing any nerves that he might have about this speech. Trew smiled and looked directly into the audience. It was a look that made each person feel as if he was looking directly at them. Leaning slightly into the podium with his hands resting on each side, he began to speak.

"I've spoken on this topic so many times over the years that perhaps you'll become bored and tune me out." He paused and raised a hand, turning his head to the side while still focusing straight forward. "I urge you to resist such a temptation. I think most of you will find this talk very... memorable."

Trew pushed himself away from the podium and began to stroll back and forth slowly across the stage; a classic orator's technique, but effective.

"Thoughts... are real."

He paused in mid-stride, looking out into the audience and locking eyes with a middle-aged man wearing round, gold-coloured glasses. Trew's look became puzzled, as if the small sentence didn't make sense. "Can that be true? Can thoughts be real?"

He resumed his pacing, looking down and nodding. "Inside the Game it is very true. Fans of the Game have caught small glimpses of this truth over the years, if they were very lucky and happened to be watching the right feed at the precise moment a miracle occurred."

He turned to face the audience squarely, standing still and casually crossing his arms. "And we have certainly seen some incredible things during this Thirtieth Anniversary Celebration year so far, haven't we?"

Trew knew the crowd would acknowledge this fact, but he wasn't sure if they would cheer or simply nod quietly. He smiled inwardly as tens of thousands of heads nodded. Perfect, he thought, they are following where I am leading them.

"We've learned of the existence of powerful beings inside the Game. I've spent a lifetime living with Eternals, and I can tell you first hand of the awesome things that they can do."

He resumed his stroll, moving towards the right edge of the stage.

"I've witnessed powerful energy that can heal the avatars we inhabit inside the Game. We've all seen a very beautiful woman retain her youth and beauty well beyond the accepted normal period of years. My Game wife is as gorgeous at 64 as she was at 35."

Trew nodded at his own words, knowing the crowd was mirroring his agreement. He had reached the steps at the edge of the stage and began to slowly descend, speaking as he did so.

"We have seen people levitate items into the air, using only their will and thought." A small dais, five feet in diameter, began to rise from the ground a few paces in front of him. It rose 10 feet into the air before it stopped its motion. Trew climbed the stairs in silence before coming to a halt in the middle of it; again above the crowd.

He spread his arms and the spotlight snapped onto him, this time a bit brighter with a bluish tinge to it. "We've even witnessed individuals who can fly!" he looked around in amazement at this fact, shaking his head in wonder. By this time the energy had built in the stadium, and people began to cheer and applaud the accomplishments Trew was listing.

He paused and nodded until the applause died down a few moments later.

"It's easy to watch an avatar playing inside the Game and think it's actually them doing these incredible things," he said. "Yet when you think about what is truly happening, it's nothing more than a young child, lying comatose on a bed, sending their thoughts into a simulation."

Trew scanned the closest members of the audience. It was clear by their expressions that many had forgotten this fact. "Thoughts are powering a virtual world populated and existed in by billions of children." He shook his head slowly. "How can so many miss the lesson in that truth?"

It was so silent that Trew could hear individuals breathing around him.

"We see it's possible to fly in the Game, yet Tygon's skies are empty of people flying." He rotated slowly in a circle as he looked out. "We see it's possible to levitate objects in the Game, yet nothing floats above our palms here."

He took a silver coloured bar from his pocket and held it flat in his hand as he continued to slowly rotate. "Many of you say the Game isn't real. Many maintain that things work differently inside the Game, even though since day one we were told that Game conditions exactly mirror our own universe."

With a dour frown, Trew stopped moving and looked at the bar in his hand. "Many of you will say that there is nothing you can do. About anything. And because you believe it, you are absolutely correct."

Trew paused for a moment, and then he threw the silver bar straight up into the air. As it came spinning down towards his hand, he knew what the crowd was hoping to see. He knew everyone held their breaths in anticipation of him catching the bar with his will, allowing it to float lazily above him; Trew the leader, showing everyone what the mind could truly accomplish.

As it came rushing towards his flattened palm, Trew moved his hand out of the way and the silver bar hit the stage with a loud clanging ring that echoed to the furthest corner of the silent arena.

Trew watched it until it had come to rest, and then he raised his eyes to scan the crowd with a pleasant smile on his face. "Most of you will ask what I'm trying to prove with this demonstration. Some might even ask if it's possible to levitate matter. The answer is yes." Trew walked down the steps so that all but a few of the closest onlookers could see him. His voice continued to ring out loudly. "If you all really want to know what's happening inside the

Game, if you truly want to see the feeds again, then stop hiding in your homes like powerless blankets and waiting for life to come to you. The truth is, if enough of you think about it happening, it will happen. That's the secret; I hope that enough of you believe me."

Trew stopped moving and knelt down slightly. "For those of you that lack belief, I will do what I can to help you change your way of thinking."

He pushed up mightily and propelled himself into the air, floating fifteen feet above the ground while the stadium erupted into excited shouting and cheering. With arms crossed and feet together, Trew floated slowly towards the main stage, gently touching the wooden surface and walking towards the exit.

"As for the bar," he raised his hand slightly and the silver bar shot swiftly upwards into the air, stopping four feet off the dais. It began to spin slowly, the light reflecting off of it as it did so. "When one of you believes enough to pull it from the air, bring it to me."

Trew stopped at the edge of the stage and looked out over the crowd. "That's all I have for tonight, Folks. Please go home and think about what I've shown you. I need you all to do one simple thing."

He scanned the crowd one last time, giving them his best motivating posture and smile.

"Stop wondering when the Game feed will come back on, and start believing that it will come back on now."

Trew exited the stage as two million people sprang to their feet and loudly began to cheer and chant two simple words.

"We believe!"

Trew took a drink of water and smiled confidently.

17

"She just killed Daniel," Brandon's eyes widened in surprise as he watched the scene unfold.

"Indeed," Thorn agreed.

"How does that work, then? Wesley has no viable body on Tygon, so does he come out of the Sim now?"

Thorn didn't answer, which caused Brandon to look up from the monitor in concern.

"I want to see them," Brandon stood up.

"See who?"

"My Hand."

Thorn didn't move from his chair.

"Take me to them," Brandon said with authority. "Now."

"Brandon," Thorn said gently, "I explained the situation to you already. We are running extremely low on power. Every spare ounce is being diverted to the Simulation to give us as much time as possible."

"You told me you had to unplug the other teams," Brandon's voice was icy, "you didn't mention my Hand."

"They're not dead," Thorn said, "exactly."

"Exactly? What in the name of all that is digital does that even mean, exactly?"

"Calm yourself. We had to unplug them just like the others," he raised his hand before Brandon could interrupt him, "but we were able to put them in cold stasis. Their bodies are in suspended animation. The power required for that process was available at the time."

"But you don't have the power to bring them out of stasis," Brandon guessed.

"Correct," Thorn said.

"So when Wesley just died in the Game, did his consciousness zip back here into the skull of his frozen body?"

Thorn raised his eyebrows and grimaced uncomfortably. "So much of this is happening for the first time, son. We've never experimented with this type of thing before."

"You have no idea," Brandon shook his head.

"I have no idea," Thorn admitted.

Brandon returned to his seat, his attention returning to the monitor.

"I want back in, Father, and I think the correct time is now."

"You've been out for only a few hours," Thorn said. "You've done your part, Brandon. Let it play out now. The chances of success look extremely promising right now."

"I did one part," Brandon said. "I'm still needed in there. Trew and Cooper are doing well. Danielle is doing better I'd hoped. The rest of the players are doing their part, but Stephanie becoming the Devil is a wild card, and there are other wild cards. I must go back in, and the time is now."

Thorn looked at Brandon sadly. "Time is running out, my boy. Life support is not an option, and even if it was, your body cannot withstand the stress of full immersion again so soon. I told you already, going back in is very likely a one-way trip for you. Do what you can from out here. Talk to the men on the phone if you must."

Brandon looked at Thorn and his eyes took on a faraway, serious tone. "I know how it will play out here, Father, but I have no choice. We are in the home stretch, and my plan has been to go back in for some time now, no matter the cost." The boy put his hand on Thorn's shoulder and squeezed it reassuringly. "This is my choice. Put me back in."

Thorn stared at Brandon for a long moment, and then nodded. "All right," he said. "Let's get you back to Tygon."

18

Carl touched down in the middle of the empty city street. He looked around slowly, searching with his eyes as well as his other senses to determine if anyone was nearby. A few moments passed and he nodded to himself, satisfied that the hooded person standing in front of him was the only individual within at least a one-mile radius.

"You're lookin' good, sugar," Carl drawled.

"I feel like garbage," the robed figure said in a husky, ragged voice, "unless I'm killing or causing pain to others."

"I know the feeling," Carl nodded. "Let's take a good look at you, then."

She raised her hands and slowly removed the hood covering her face.

Carl scrutinized Stephanie's overall appearance. The beautiful young Hispanic girl was still there, but she no longer appeared healthy and vibrant; her features had become narrower and darker. The energetic, glowing girl had been replaced with a sullen, darker version of her old self.

"I know old crack whores who would be glad they didn't look like you right now, Steph," Carl said.

"There are days when I look even better than I used to." She wasn't pleased that Carl seemed happy to see her looking like this.

"Yes, I'm sure there are," Carl chuckled. "When you're elbow deep in blood and misery I bet you look absolutely stunning."

She looked at him with a cruel smile, the crimson in her eyes flashing brightly as they swirled rapidly.

"The girls say I'm almost out of the initial phase of the change," she said.

"They are good at what they do," Carl nodded. "I'm glad they've been able to keep you alive. I can't recall the last time a brand new Infernal became their leader."

"It's never happened before. It wouldn't have happened now if not for the help I received from you and Raphael."

A thought occurred to Carl and he looked around the open area, again searching for the presence of others.

"To fast track this change you need to kill a powerful Eternal. Is that why you called me here, girl?"

Stephanie looked at Carl with a fierce grin; it was evident that she struggled to control her new urges and impulses. Carl knew he'd guessed correctly, she was looking at him like he was the sheep and she was a hungry tiger. Carl chuckled to himself and took off his trench coat.

Before his coat hit the ground she closed the distance between them, screaming in rage with a cruel looking dagger in her right hand, thrusting powerfully towards his eye.

If anyone had been present to watch, they would have missed the entire charge; the attack was simply too fast for the eye to follow.

With the slightest sideways movement Carl shifted to avoid her attack. As she streaked past him he grabbed the blade from her hand and hit her on the back of the head with the flat of it. Hard.

In the space of a breath, Stephanie was lying on the ground stunned, while Carl looked at her with amusement, examining the blade that he now held in his hand.

Stephanie groaned and moved slightly. Carl streaked downwards and jabbed her with iron fingers in the back of the neck, at her kidneys, a spot on either leg, and between her shoulder blades. Then he flipped her roughly onto her back and stood up.

His strikes had hit pressure points, she couldn't move at all.

"Over the past few years I really started to take a shine to you, girl," Carl bounced the dagger lightly on his shoulder as he looked down at her. "For that reason, I haven't killed you. Everyone who knows me — including you — would say that selecting me as your prey isn't smart."

The rage in Stephanie's eyes melted away, and was replaced with anguish and suffering. Tears began to flow as forceful sobs wracked her body. Carl looked at her blankly.

After a few moments Stephanie calmed down and regained her composure. Carl retrieved a handkerchief from his jacket and bent down to gently wipe her eyes.

"I know it was stupid to challenge you," she said. "I convinced the sisters that I could beat you like I had Daniel, and they reluctantly agreed to let me try. I knew there was no way that I could beat you, though."

Carl stood up and nodded with understanding. "You wanted me to kill you," he said.

"Yes," she agreed. "I can't do this, Carl. I know you and Raph told me this would be difficult, but I had no idea just how hard it would be. I've killed so many, and it has been so..."

"Pleasurable." Carl finished her sentence.

She nodded slightly and blinked as tears came to her eyes.

"If I let you go, are you gonna try being stupid again?"

Stephanie continued to cry, shaking her head that no, she wouldn't.

Carl reached down and restored control to her body. She sat up and brushed dust off the front of her clothes.

Carl sat down beside her.

"You can do this, sugar," he said. "So you've had to do some unpleasant things. We all have to do unpleasant things from time to time. If the Game is about balance, and it is, then I expect you have quite a bit more evil to do before you come close to balancing it out with all the good you've accomplished."

"How can I continue to do this?" she asked.

"See that tower over there?" Carl asked.

Stephanie nodded.

"Before the Day, that tower was a fun place full of children and laughing families. Everyone from miles around came to spend time in that building. There were treats and entertaining events held there that made other entertainment destinations seem dull in comparison. I haven't had many good days over the centuries, but my absolute best memory is from spending time in that tower."

"Wow, really?" Stephanie looked at the ruined tower with interest, trying to imagine the good times that Carl was describing.

"No, not really," Carl said. "I lied. That tower was actually one of the worst places in the world. People who went inside never came out alive. Residents who lived close by would wake up in the middle of the night from the screams of pain and terror emanating from inside. I went into that tower once and experienced the worst pain I've ever felt in my life. To this day, I have nightmares about being in there."

Stephanie looked at Carl with a frown. "Is that true, Carl?" she asked.

"Neither story is true, girl," Carl said. "I've never seen that tower before in my life."

"Oh." Stephanie looked confused.

"My point is this. Nothing is inherently good nor bad in this or any other universe. It is the thinking that makes it so."

"I know that."

"You thought you knew that," Carl said. "This new experience has either made you question it, or you realize that your definition was good up to a certain point. I'm here to tell you that taking lives inside this Game is just as important as saving them."

"You are condoning killing," she said.

"The Devil does not make butterflies and throw parties for little children," Carl said. "You must become the worst demon in the world so that you can prevent the other demons from doing what even I would consider evil."

"I see."

"I don't think you do, but I hope that you start to, and soon, because the other demons have felt the change in power. They know Daniel is gone, and they will come to take his place. You must either fight them all, or make them so scared of you that they won't bother to challenge you."

"Which I do by killing."

"Yes," Carl agreed. "You do that by killing... both players and NPCs."

"Players and NPCs...?" Stephanie said. "You're right, Carl. I forgot."

"Don't ever forget, girl. This is a Game. Play it to win."

The two of them stood up and Stephanie hugged Carl fiercely. Carl laughed in surprise, but after a moment he returned the hug.

"You'll be close to your normal self when the initial phase has passed," Carl assured her.

"I want that to be soon," she said.

"It will be," he smiled, "but until it is you must do your best to get out there and show the Infernals what the new Devil is made of."

Stephanie stood straighter and nodded.

Carl winked at her. "Players need to be ejected, sugar. Do your part."

19

"**How are you** finding life in our Colony so far?"

Thirteen looked up from his bowl of soup and met the eyes of his lunch host. He couldn't believe that she was sixty-three years old; she looked decades younger. The spoon in his hand paused close to his mouth as he answered her.

"Life is good, even in this new world in which we find ourselves." He quickly put the spoon in his mouth to finish his last taste of soup and then he politely placed it on the table beside the bowl, then he smiled politely and waited for Danielle to ask her next question.

"Did you seek us out, or did the winds of fortune just drop you at our doorstep?"

Thirteen looked around the table as he considered how to answer. He was surrounded by very powerful creatures; Eternals. He'd been in the camp for less than a month but others had been quick to talk about them. Now that he was sitting so closely to them he observed that they looked much like normal people. The stories from others had been anything but normal, though. Thirteen decided that it would be in his best interest to answer each question truthfully if he wanted to stay in the Colony, and he did want to stay here — for the moment, at least.

"No, I never intended to come to live here," he answered. "At first I just wanted to join a group where I could be safe. I wish I'd had more time living in the world when technology existed. I think I would have done better in that reality."

"In that reality?" Daniel asked. "You're in the same reality as before the Day, Thirteen."

"Not really," he shrugged. "Reality has changed. Even though the stage appears the same as it once did, the rules and props are not the same as they were."

"Interesting way to think of it," Raphael said from beside him.

"I suppose so," Thirteen shrugged.

"Why do you want to stay?" Miranda asked.

"Safety," he replied. "I'm not strong, or skilled at combat. This world has become lawless. If you can't fight back, then the odds are good you'll be beaten down, a slave to others." He reached for a piece of bread and tore off a chunk, popping it into his mouth and chewing. "The basics are like treasure. Warmth, food, and safety. I will do whatever I can to prove my usefulness in this community so that I can stay."

"What do you think of the Gamer philosophy?" Danielle asked as she poured coffee for everyone at the table. Coffee was becoming scarce; it was a treat Thirteen hadn't had for quite some time.

"It's an interesting theory," Thirteen said. "From a quantum point of view, it makes a lot of sense."

"Before the Day, most quantum scientists said the theory didn't make sense," Danielle said.

"That's because most quantum scientists were still too far behind in their knowledge," Thirteen explained.

"You're from the Zoo, right?" Miranda asked.

Thirteen's mouth became dry and his skin felt as if a warm sweat were forming on his arms and chest. Slowly he looked at Miranda and nodded. "Were you there too?"

It was Miranda's turn to nod. "Do you recognize me?"

Thirteen shook his head slightly. "No, but the old man told me there was another in the Colony who'd been there. He said Three was in the camp. I don't remember anyone from there." He looked at Miranda hopefully. "Do you remember me?"

"No," Miranda admitted. "The only one I would recognize is the boy called Seven."

"His pet," Thirteen said. "I would recognize him too. He was often present when the Man would talk with me."

"What would the Man talk to you about?" Raphael asked.

"Advanced quantum mechanics and computer theory. It was refreshing to speak with someone who seemed to understand what I was talking about. After I was freed and before the Day, even the best scientists didn't seem to understand what I was speaking about."

"He did, though?" Danielle confirmed.

"Absolutely," Thirteen confirmed. "I think he knew even more than I do. Some of his calculations and hypotheses were beyond my scope of comprehension. The Man was brilliant."

"Do you think he could have done this?" Danielle asked.

"Done what?"

"This," Danielle spread her arms to indicate the world as it currently was. Could he have caused the Day?

"Of course he did," Thirteen confirmed. He looked at Miranda with a puzzled expression. "You must have known this; why haven't you told them?"

Everyone at the table was shocked. The question had seemed small and insignificant, just part of the conversation with Thirteen. Danielle had just stumbled onto the answer to the most important question everyone had been asking for the past three years. Possibilities and ideas began to tumble through her head.

Miranda recovered first and answered Thirteen. "I wasn't there when it occurred. He ejected me from the Zoo weeks before the Day."

"I wasn't there when this happened either," Thirteen said. "One day we all woke up from the Haze and found ourselves standing outside of our cells," he explained. "Somehow the Man had reintegrated our broken halves. He told us we were no longer either a genius or a disconnected regular. He told us that we were whole, and then he gave each of us a bag of money and supplies and told us that we were free."

"Then how do you know he's responsible?" Danielle asked.

"He informed us that we could go anywhere and do anything that we wanted, but that we had best get to where we wanted to be within thirteen days."

"On day thirteen," Raphael said. "What happened?"

Thirteen spread his arms to mimic Danielle's earlier symbol for the current state of the world.

"This happened," he said.

20

An hour later, Danni and her Eternals concluded their meeting with Thirteen. Miranda, Raphael, and Danni travelled to one of Danni's houses which overlooked the rest of Galt, one area of the city. They assembled in the great room. Carl, Angelica, and Samantha arrived before long and Raphael filled them in on the information they'd learned.

"We thought it might be Shane," Carl said. He reclined in one of the chairs with a water glass full of dark amber coloured alcohol. They had all seen him drink, but no one could recall ever seeing him get drunk.

"Guessed," Danni corrected, "but now we know for certain that it was him."

"What do we do with this knowledge?" Samantha asked.

"We find Shane and make him turn things back on."

The room erupted into laughter. Danni looked around the room; apparently everyone but her and Angelica found the idea funny.

"I didn't say it would be easy," she said.

"What you should have said is that it's impossible," Raphael said. "Eternals have been hunting him for thousands of years, Danni. There are squads whose only purpose for being inside the Game is to find Shane." He shook his head in frustration, "The squads are augmented and trained specifically to find this creature, but no one has ever done it. Finding Shane is, for the most part, a key Timeless goal. Except for Daniel and a few other Devils along the way, finding and subduing Shane is a Timeless Alpha order."

"What's an Alpha order?" Danni asked.

Raphael nodded at Angelica and she spoke up. "No matter what operation or task is being performed at any given moment, Alpha orders require the Timeless to abandon everything else in order to complete them."

"So, if someone is three steps away and about to plunge a knife into me and you're rushing to save me from certain death, if you see Shane you abandon me and take off after him?" Danni asked.

"Absolutely," Angelica said with a sly grin.

"In most every case," Samantha corrected. "Using your example, Danni, we would still rush to save you. That's because you come with a complete set of very concise Alpha orders that focus on you."

Danni nodded and looked at Miranda. "You almost had him," she said.

Miranda shook her head. "I saw him, but there was no way I ever had a chance at him. The plan there was for me to get a location and Sparx would report back to a larger force that would come in to neutralize him. I didn't find him, though. We guessed that he liked to fish for broken avatars, so I volunteered to be broken and dangled out there as bait on the hook. It took a long time to get him to bite, then it ended up failing."

"I don't know about that," Raphael said. "He may have slipped the trap, but if not for your time spent in the Zoo, we wouldn't know what we do today."

"Why did he release them?" Carl asked. "Why not just kill them when he was done?"

"Not everyone plays that way," Danni said.

"Shane does," Carl assured her.

"Then he must have a plan for them," Raphael said.

"I think we need to find them, and bring them here," Angelica said.

Everyone considered her idea. Heads slowly began to nod in agreement.

"Any chance they give off a distinct energy signature?" Carl asked.

"There's always a chance," Samantha said. "I'll examine Miranda and Thirteen to see if I can come up with anything."

"Good," Danni stood up and walked to the window. "Any suggestions on how to start looking for them?"

"Even if they have signatures, it will be like finding a specific grain of sand on a large windy beach," Raphael said. "I don't know if this is the best use of our time, Danni."

"I know who would be willing to do it," Carl said.

"Who?"

"Tracker squads," he said. "If you can convince them it's the best chance of finding Shane, I don't think you'll have a problem getting them to agree to it."

"Great idea," Raph said. "That raises another problem, though. The only one who can locate and give new orders to Trackers is our leader. I haven't had any luck locating Gabriel since the Day."

"The old man still around? Maybe he could locate him."

"He's not here," Danni said, "but we can put the word out that he's needed and he might pop up."

"What if the Infernals are looking for these thirteen individuals as well?" Angelica asked.

"Then we'll have to be sure and find them first," Danni said. "We know Daniel is around, perhaps we can ask for his help in finding either Gabriel or the Trackers. Maybe we can even convince him to set his own squads to look."

Carl chuckled and shook his head slightly. Danni frowned. "It's not a terrible idea. You just said all Timeless want to find Shane."

"Look as hard as you want. Daniel isn't gonna be found," Carl said.

"Why not?" Danni asked.

"Danni, there's something we should share with you," Raphael said.

"Okay."

"It's about the Devil," Raphael poured her a drink. "You might want to sit down for this one..."

21

One thing Danni missed was knowing the exact time.

It was something that she'd taken for granted; all of them took the simple things for granted back then. Once technology stopped working, she'd quickly lost track of the time. Not the days, months, and years; they were always able to keep track of that. It was the smaller increments that presented the challenge. Right now was a perfect example; she knew it was late, but not wasn't exactly sure how late. Was it midnight? 2 a.m.?

Danni shouldered her backpack and adjusted her gear. Whatever the time, it was late enough to execute her plan.

She left the house through the back door, careful to make as little noise as possible. She'd chosen the back door because it had been oiled recently and opened and closed without a sound. Perhaps her shoes would have made a creaking or some other betraying noise on the back porch, but she was floating just a fraction of an inch above the ground. She smiled to herself as she reached the back gate and quickly disappeared from view in the brush of the gully that led towards the dark town centre.

Danni touched down and began to walk when a chuckle from above made her start with surprise.

"Where you goin', girl?"

Danni frowned and looked above her head. The old man floated in the air, his black garbage bag clothes billowing in the soft wind and his hair moving about as if it were a white scraggly fire.

"I'm glad you tie those garbage bags at the legs," she whispered. "I would get a shocking view from this angle if you didn't."

The old man slowly descended to the ground beside her. To reward her for the lewd comment, he flashed her a grin, his teeth reflecting patches of brown and white in the dim light. "Looks like you're plannin' on taking a hike of some sort."

"Might be that I am." She began to walk again, and the old man began to walk alongside her.

"Want some company?" he asked.

Danni stopped and shook her head wearily. "I haven't been alone for many moments during my entire life, and frankly I'm tired of it." She pointed back towards the house she had just left. "I've had protectors and shadows and others with me since I was a little girl. It's not that I resent that fact..."

"Sounds a little bit like you do resent it," the old man observed.

"Well, I don't," Danni said. "But I do think it's overdue for me to spend some time on my own. This has all become very complicated."

"How do you figure? Since the Day, most people would say things have become much less complicated. Life now is mostly about eating and surviving the day."

"You must be able to guess what constitutes a normal day in my life," Danni said. "If you can't, then believe me when I tell you that things for me have become much busier and stressful since the Day occurred."

The old man nodded and put his hand sympathetically on Danni's shoulder. "I know for you it has, girl," he said. "You've taken it upon yourself to save as many of these fine folk as you can. It's an admirable endeavour, truly it is, but the weight on your shoulders is significant."

"It is," Danni agreed.

"So you're just gonna run away," he nodded. "Maybe find a nice mountain cave and become a hermit lady. You don't read about many female hermits in the history books. I wonder why that is?" he scratched his beard reflectively.

"I'll come back," she said, "but I intend to make things... less complicated for a while."

The old man looked out over the dark city centre for a time, then nodded his head and looked back at Danni. "Okay," he said. "Where you going?"

Danni hiked her backpack up onto her shoulder and began walking once again. "I'm going to make things right with the world," she said. "I'm going to find Shane and make him turn the power back on."

"Not a good idea," he said. "I've met that boy a time or two, and let me tell you, he is not someone you want to spend time with. He'll eat you alive, girl."

"I don't think he will," Danni said confidently. "He might be surprised to find a meeting between us does not end well for him if he doesn't behave."

The old man chuckled again as he looked at Danni. "I imagine you could be right, Danni," he said with a shake of his head. "Maybe he's met his match when it comes to you."

Danni nodded and the two walked in silence for a time.

"How you gonna find him?" the old man asked.

"I have no idea," Danni admitted. "It's more important to search than it is to find him."

The old man stopped walking and looked at her seriously. "What do you mean by that?" he asked.

Danni looked over her shoulder and turned to face him. "I mean that everyone else wants to sit and tell me why it's pointless to go look for him. I say you'll never find anything sitting on your arse in a house making excuses or reasons to fail. So I don't know how I'm going to do it, but I do know that the only way to find what you're looking for in life, and by that I mean anything, is to get up and go look for it."

The old man rubbed his face with a dirty hand, massaging his forehead and eyes slowly. He looked up and nodded at her. "That's pure wisdom in the words you just said, girl."

"Likely," Danni agreed.

"Okay, then. Let's go," he said.

"Go where?"

The old man winked, then adjusted his course to avoid the town as he began to walk.

"To go see Shane," he said.

"You know where he is?" Danni asked.

The old man snorted. "Of course I know where he is. That's no surprise to you, though, is it?"

"I had a hunch," she admitted.

"Then let's get going. We have a long journey ahead of us."

"How long will it take us to fly there?" Danni asked.

The old man looked at her and shook his head. His eyes twinkled as he answered her. "We won't be able to fly there, girl. If you want to do this, then it has to be on foot. Let me assure you before we even get started, it's gonna be a long, tough trip."

Danni looked at him for a moment and then nodded. "Lead the way, old man," she said.

Danni followed him out of town and into the dark wilderness.

22

"**Have you seen** Danni today?"

Carl didn't bother to look up from his task of smearing honey onto a thick piece of warm bread. "Saw her last night, same as you, Raphael. Let the girl sleep in. I don't think she was too happy with the news we shared."

Raphael grabbed the loaf of bread, sawed off a large slice, and spread fresh butter onto it, plopping the knife back into the bowl where he'd found it. "No, she wasn't," he agreed as he moved to sit at the dining table.

"I wouldn't worry about it," Carl joined him and took a bite of his bread, savoring the taste. "She might fret and mope around for a while, but the girl has to realize that we're with her not because she's in charge of us, but because our goals coincide for the most part."

"Agreed," Raphael said. "She's just so damned easy to follow. She has an air of authority that is rarely seen... for a mortal."

"Maybe she's had multiple lives leading," Carl shrugged. "Perhaps she played Napoleon and Caesar in past lives. We've run into stranger things than that before. Doesn't really matter. Making a play on the Devil was our call, and it's working out as well as we hoped it would."

"Is it?" Raphael asked. "You know better than anyone what the crimson eyes do to us. Stephanie might not be able to hold on to enough of her Eternal essence to help us accomplish the goal."

"The girl's a pro," Carl said. "She'll do fine. She needs to get into her groove, that's all. Give her a few years and she'll have the reins on her dark side enough to do what we want her to."

"We may not have a few years," Raphael said.

Carl shook his head disgustedly and snorted. "You're kidding me, right? Time is exactly what we have."

"This scenario is wiping out millions, even billions of humans," Raphael said. "We might not have enough to work with before she's ready."

"Then we wait a few centuries until the population rises again," Carl took another bite of honeyed bread. "We've seen big dips in the numbers before. They will just allow more players to flood the field. Now stop whining like a recruit. You're making me want to puke up my breakfast, and if I do that, I'm gonna get angry."

Raphael ate his bread in silence. When he finished, he reached for another slice.

"She's not in her room," he said calmly as he scooped honey from the bowl.

"What?" Carl looked at him with a frown. "Why didn't you say so in the first place?"

Raphael blinked his eyes slowly at Carl as he took a bite of his second piece of bread.

Carl pursed his lips in thought, then closed his eyes. His face became calm and detached as he entered a meditative state.

After a few moments he opened his eyes. "She's not in the city," he scowled.

Raphael continued to eat his bread.

"Well?" Carl snapped.

Raphael finished chewing his mouthful and swallowed deliberately. Then he slowly wiped his mouth with a napkin. "Yeah," he said, "that's what I was saying when I came in here."

Carl stood up quickly, the sudden motion sweeping his chair loudly out of the way behind him. "Well, you didn't say it right," he muttered. "We should take to the air and scan for her from the corners of the Colony." He paused suddenly and tilted his head to look at Raphael. "You're her protector, right?"

Raphael nodded.

"What's your range? For detecting her?"

"Two hundred kilometres."

Carl swore under his breath. Flying to the edges of the Colony would do them no good. Raphael knew she was nowhere close. "Who's our best tracker?" he asked.

"Normally it's you or Miranda," Raphael said, "but since I have protector range on her, it would be me."

"Why are you still sitting here for, then?" Carl asked. "Go look for her."

"I did," Raphael said. "For the past three hours I've flown all over. That's why I came in here wondering if you'd seen her."

"You're driving me nuts, Raph," Carl snarled. "Your brain isn't firing right. If you could sense she wasn't here, why come asking me if I'd seen her?"

Raphael shrugged. "Thought maybe you'd opened a portal for her."

The thought made Carl nod grudgingly; that actually made sense. He sat back down and grabbed his glass of water, taking a sip while his mind raced through ideas for finding her. Finally, he sat back and put his feet up on the chair beside him.

"So she's gone, then," he announced.

"Looks like it," Raphael said.

"That good or bad?"

"Likely one or the other," Raphael agreed. "Let's hope it's good."

"Well, let her be and see how it turns out."

"I would, except there's that whole issue where if she dies then the entire reality we now call our home comes crashing down around us."

Carl looked at Raphael for a moment, then his eyebrows raised in understanding. "Ahh, yes, I'd forgotten about that."

"Seriously?" Raphael asked. "You forgot about that?"

Carl shrugged. "I have a lot on my mind. Besides, Danni can take care of herself. Even I would have a difficult time killing her now; she's very lethal."

"What if she's with the old man?" Raphael asked.

Carl thought about the possibility and looked at the ceiling, contemplating. "Yeah, he might just be able to harm her," he agreed. "Do you think he would want to, though?"

"I have no idea, which worries me."

"Me, too," Carl agreed. "Want me to come with you?"

"No," Raphael shook his head. "I'll take Miranda. We have another concern I'd like you to handle in the Colony."

"What's that?"

"I think we might have an assassin ejecting players from the Game in our midst."

"Really?" Carl's eyes lit up with interest. "Anyone we might know?"

"I don't know," Raphael said. "Can you find them for us?"

Carl grinned, his concern for Danni forgotten for the moment. "I'll get right on it. When I finish up, I'll come join you in your hunt for Danni."

"Good idea," Raphael agreed.

23

"Five days have passed on Tygon as fans continue to stare at static on their viewers. Trew has thrown down the gauntlet and challenged the masses to use what he calls 'the very real power of thought' to influence events and bring the feeds back up.

Initial reaction to Trew's mandate brought skepticism, but ejected Gamers around the globe got behind their leader and began to rally others to the cause.

Round the clock rallies, meditation sessions, and inspirational gatherings are occurring simultaneously all around the world in hopes that thoughts truly are real, and the combined will and intent of billions can do the impossible; bring the Game feeds back online..."

Game Channel 72

"**What if the** Game feeds don't come back online?"

Trew looked up from the report he was reading and looked at Michelle.

"It's only been a few days, Michelle. Don't give up so easily. I have a feeling they'll come back online in just a few days."

"Why do you say that?" Lilith asked.

Trew shook his head. "I just have a hunch, is all," he looked back down at the report.

"I hope you're right, Trew," Lilith said. "The world has become dependent on the Game. There's no telling how much damage a prolonged blackout would do to the economy."

Trew held the report up and waved it gently. "I'm reading about the current state of the economy right now, Lilith."

"And?" she asked.

He laughed and let the report fall gently onto the table. "Business is booming," he said. "People love to try to fill in the gaps, and the Game has certainly created a very large gap in everyone's lives since the Day occurred."

"Numbers are up?" Michelle was surprised to hear such a thing.

"Across the board," Trew nodded. "Michelle, how many have been ejected from the Game since the Day?"

Michelle typed a command into her tablet. "Two hundred eighty million," she said.

"Adding the Gamers that were ejected before that... we are getting close to four hundred million, are my numbers correct?"

Michelle nodded.

"Okay, then," Trew said. "That means one hundred million more to be ejected to reach the magic number."

"What magic number?" Lilith asked.

Trew stood up and stretched, raising his arms over his head and groaning loudly as he turned his neck from side to side. "Brandon instructed the Timeless to eject half a billion players from the Game."

"What? Why would he want to do that?"

"I'm sure he had his reasons," Trew said. "I can even guess at a few of them. The more I sit in his place, the more reasons that I can come up with for doing something like that."

"What's your best guess, then?" Cooper asked. He'd been sitting silently in the corner for so long that Trew had almost forgotten he was present.

"He wanted them out here for me," Trew said.

The group quietly considered the idea for a few moments, and then they began to nod in agreement.

"They followed you devoutly inside the Game," Cooper said, "and the hundred million Gamers are absolutely following you on Tygon."

"Perhaps the others being ejected have had experiences since the Day that will help them to believe my message better than they could before the event occurred."

"Interesting thought," Cooper said.

"Thank you," Trew smiled.

"So when do we worry that the feeds won't come back up?" Michelle asked.

"Even if they never come back up, I'll keep you on the payroll, Michelle," Trew flashed her a grin.

"I'm not so worried about that," she said.

"I know," Trew gave Cooper a signal and moved towards the door. Cooper nodded as he stood up and followed.

"If kids start dying on their tables, then we can get worried." Trew paused with his hand on the door knob. "Otherwise, we get ready for when the feeds come back on, because it's going to be a scramble like we've never experienced in the history of the Game."

Before Trew could exit the room, the phone rang. He paused while Michelle answered it and spoke with the person on the other end.

"Just a minute, I'll tell him," she looked towards Trew with a slight frown on her face.

"That's security," she said. "Seems they've found a young kid sitting in your penthouse apartment. They have no idea how he got through security, but he's smiling away and asking to see you. He had no weapons on him."

Trew's eyes narrowed in concern at the announcement. He looked at Cooper who shrugged his shoulders and quickly looked away, not quite quick enough to hide the grin forming on his face.

"How old is the kid?" Trew asked.

"He's claiming to be thirteen," Michelle said.

"Tell security I'll be right there, and not to let him out of their sight for a second!"

Cooper looked back at the doorway and swore softly under his breath, then sprinted quickly to catch up with Trew, who was already halfway to the elevator.

24

"Happy birthday, sleepyhead!"

Danni opened her eyes and raised her head. The morning light was just beginning to peek over the horizon, spilling softly over her campsite. She scanned the area to make sure everything was in order. Her campfire had died; white ash rested like a small round cat's blanket surrounded by rough stones. Danni felt a light pressure and added warmth against her right leg. She reached down to gently pat the body of her constant companion, a large, dark brown German Shepherd that had joined her on her quest.

"Good morning, Zeus," she said, feeling his body nuzzle into hers at the mention of his name. "Some guard dog you turn out to be, letting dangerous strangers come into camp unannounced."

She looked across the fire pit at the newcomer. The old man rummaged through a wool knapsack in search of something.

"You've been gone a while," she said. "Find anything interesting?"

The old man looked up and grinned. "I found you a birthday present," he returned to his task of searching the overflowing bag. "I hope I remembered to bring it with me. I had to make a hasty exit from the last town I passed through; people aren't getting any nicer to strangers over time, I can tell you that for certain."

Danni didn't bother to ask him what town he was talking about. She'd learned that the only information he shared about his trips away from her was the information he decided to give. Danni had learned a lot on this adventure with the old man. When she'd left with him to find Shane, she had been sixty-three. It hadn't turned out to be the short adventure she'd envisioned.

"You sure it's my birthday?" Danni sat up in her sleeping bag, feeling the bumps and small stones that lay beneath her despite a thorough cleaning of the area before she'd put her bed down for the night.

"Absolutely," he confirmed. "Here it is!" he pulled a small package out of the bag wrapped in what looked like an old magazine cover with a piece of bailer twine encircling it and tied in a bow. He hefted the package in his hand, gently tossing it a few inches into the air and letting it land lightly in his palm. He walked over to her and extended his hand ceremoniously, making an extravagant flourish as he bowed to her. His garbage bag outfit crinkled noisily and the red pop bottle cap gloves clinked with a special music of their own as they opened to reveal Danni's gift.

"Thank you," she took the small package and turned it over in her hands. "How old am I today? The number in my head must be incorrect."

The old man blinked a couple of times, and he leaned forward to peer into her eyes intently. He smiled and nodded, stepping back and chuckling to himself. "You're playing with me, girl. You know exactly how old you are."

Danni nodded. "Sixty-seven." She held the gift up and raised an eyebrow questioningly. "Is it a map telling me where to find Shane? You must know that after almost four years on the road with you, that's the only gift I want."

The old man shrugged, and waved his hands for her to open the little package. Only on rare occasions would he respond to complaints of being so long on the road. "There are many things in life that cannot be rushed, young lady," was his common response, and Danni had almost stopped mentioning it. Almost. She'd learned how this game of life seemed to work best; to struggle and fight for an outcome was to deny the outcome from occurring. In every aspect of her experience, Danni knew that the best way to achieve anything was through acceptance — specifically, acceptance that the thing you wanted would either happen... or it wouldn't. Countless were the times that Danni had finally accepted the futility of a situation and then, suddenly as if by magic, the exact situation she had made peace with never attaining would suddenly manifest.

Danni knew that the best way — perhaps the only way — to find Shane was to accept that she might never find him. She couldn't do it, though. With every fiber of her being, she held onto the goal of confronting Shane and forcing him to fix the power issue in the world.

The old man seemed content to watch her struggle, sometimes talking about it and coaching her, or saying nothing and smiling quietly, and yet other times leaving her to walk the road alone until he would reappear unannounced, as he'd done today.

Danni sighed and examined her present. She untied the string and gently unfolded the crude wrapping paper until she'd exposed the gift contained.

"It's beautiful," she said. Lifting the delicate silver chain into the air she inspected the oval-shaped, blue cut stone the size of her thumbnail. It was set in an ornate silver pendant.

"Is it sapphire?" she asked, admiring the gem as it caught and reflected the morning rays of sunlight.

"No," the old man snorted as if Danni had said something funny. "Sapphire is too easy to find, and serves no real purpose for you at this time, girl. It's taken me two years to find this stone for you."

"Really?"

"Yes, really," he smiled. "It's called Kyanite."

"Kyanite," Danni repeated. She had an interest in gemstones and believed in their ability to help a person amplify energies. "I don't recall learning about Kyanite."

"Gemstones are funny like that," the old man admitted. "There are so many and their properties vary and sometimes overlap. I have a theory that some gemstones hide and make their appearance when they are most needed to assist a person in their journey."

Danni nodded. She didn't need to clarify what he meant by 'journey.' She knew that he was referring to the journey that every person took — the journey of a lifetime. "What does it do?"

"It does many things, but I thought three of its properties would suit you." The old man held up three fingers and began to tick them off as he talked.

"One, it will align all of your Chakras and help you refocus and gain your spiritual energy."

Danni nodded quietly.

"Two, it will help to strengthen your abilities. You haven't flown in years; I can't remember the last time you healed or recharged yourself with Reiki energy. You've stopped working out from a psychic point of view." His mouth turned upwards into a faint grin. "Psychically, you're getting flabby!"

Danni made a wry face, but nodded in agreement.

"Three," he continued, "Kyanite helps to quiet the mind, dissolving emotional, mental, or spiritual confusion, and letting go of anxiety." He stopped talking and looked at her with a pleasant expression, allowing Danni to receive his subtle message.

Danni knew that she needed to let go of her anxiety and accept that she would find Shane if and when the time was right.

"Thank you," she said sincerely. "It's the nicest thing anyone has given me... this year. Come to think of it, no one else has even bothered to even wish me a happy birthday!"

The old man chuckled and sat down by the cold fire pit, pulling his bag close. He reached into it and produced two energy bars, handing one to Danni and opening the other. They sat eating their bars, Danni broke off a small piece and fed it to Zeus, who lifted his head from the old man's feet to accept the treat.

"That dog loves you," Danni said.

"All dogs love me!" he exclaimed. "Kids seem fond of me as well. I'm sure the two are related. Filthy little beasts... all of them."

Danni laughed at his mock gruffness. All it took for the old man to become a kid himself was the eager presence of an animal or child. Within minutes he would be the silliest of the bunch, entertaining either barking dogs or laughing children at every opportunity.

They sat in content silence for some time, both lost in their own thoughts as the morning sun rose on a new day.

Finally the old man spoke up, startling Danni from her thoughts.

"We're close," he looked at his bar with interest and attacked it, ripping another small piece off and chewing slowly.

Danni looked at him out of the corner of her eye. "You said that two years ago."

He looked at her and winked slyly. "We're closer than that," he said with a grin.

"Dare I ask how close?"

"Not a good question, girl," he reached down to scratch Zeus behind his ears. "Won't be much longer, though. So begin to prepare yourself."

"For what?"

He looked back up at her and his gaze was serious. "For everything, girl. I already told you that boy is not stable. Be ready for everything."

25

The Devil had a recurring dream...

I'm walking. Most often through cities, but sometimes it can be a country town or even a lone, empty road.

I look towards the top of a tall building... there's always a tall building within sight, and there's always someone standing on top of it, looking sad and depressed, as if they want to jump.

I try to stop them but I'm too far away. I yell as loudly as I can to get their attention; they never hear me.

Then I remember I have powers that can save them.

Before I can reach out to hold them up, they step off the ledge and fall to earth. I watch in horror as they hit the ground, and when I look back up again, there are dozens more, standing on multiple buildings.

They all begin to jump, as I watch in horror.

In this dream, there's only one girl, dressed in a frilly purple dress that flares at the bottom. She's pretty and her skin is covered in black snakelike tattoos. She goes through the same sort of pre-jump ritual as the others do in this type of dream. I watch as she falls towards the ground, waiting for her to thud wetly to the pavement like they always do.

Instead of smashing into the pavement, she stops suddenly just as she reaches the ground, landing softly on her feet and bending her knees slightly to absorb the tiny impact. I'm so surprised that I can't move; I can't speak.

She looks at me, and her gaze is like nothing I've ever felt before. She stares at me calmly while my panic and fear slowly rises like steam in a boiling kettle. She stares pointedly, even hatefully at me for what feels like an eternity.

Eventually my mouth opens and I begin to scream. The sound is blood curdling and disturbing. I wonder at first where it's coming from, until I realize it's me. Which makes me scream even louder.

And then I wake up.

===

"You shouldn't be sleeping by yourself out in the open," Carl's voice rumbled from beyond the light of the fire.

Stephanie quickly scanned the energy field that surrounded her at all times, testing to make certain no one had tried to breach it.

"I've learned how to protect myself, Carl," she sat up in her sleeping bag. Sap in one of the logs touched the flames, causing it to snap and crackle loudly.

Carl emerged from the blackness of night and sat down beside her, leaning against a log and reaching for a plate of half-finished food.

"You've learned a lot these past few years, girl," he said.

"How am I doing so far?" she asked sincerely.

Carl stopped eating and looked at her with an amused expression.

"If I still had your colour eyes, I would kneel before you and call you mistress," he said, "and I would likely only think about killing you fifty percent of the time, which is a compliment from me, darlin'."

Stephanie nodded curtly, although she wanted to smile at the kind words.

"It's a horrible life," she said.

"Of course it is," Carl snorted. "That's how you know you're doing it correctly. I don't hear the regret in your voice that was there when you first changed four years ago."

"I've become... accustomed to the lifestyle," she said.

"I bet you have. It's stupid not to have protection close by, though. You're too still young to travel alone."

"I'm not alone," she smiled sweetly.

Carl paused and looked around, tilting his head like an animal to listen to the sounds around him.

"The girls?" he nodded. "They are very good. I hope you're using them to their full potential."

"Absolutely. Once it became known they were loyal to me, the rest of the organization quickly came to heel. I only had to kill three Infernals to deliver a proper lesson."

"Kill two more, and do it soon," Carl shook his head. "I can't believe the girls haven't guided you better in some areas of the Lore. Five is your lucky number, and it will send a proper message to Infernals everywhere."

Stephanie smiled cruelly. "The girls are doing fine, Carl. We will hit five on the anniversary of my fifth year in power. No one knows who it will be, which has the entire group on pins and needles. I learned well from Raph over the years. I am strong in my position, yet not so arrogant as to believe there aren't multiple threats to me at all times."

Carl nodded and finished his meal, then grabbed the canteen and drank deeply from it.

"How is everyone?" Stephanie asked.

Carl shrugged as he leaned back to stare into the fire. "Everyone's fine, Steph. The Colony has doubled in size and continues to be a royal pain in the ass. The rest send their love."

"Tell them I send it back."

The two sat quietly and watched the fire.

"I'm not sure what to do about your Colony," Steph said finally.

"Don't do anything," Carl advised. "You have the whole world full of scattered and fearful people, Stephanie. Look in another direction and do your thing."

"How many of the Thirteen do you have?"

"Six," Carl looked at her. "How many do you have?"

"Five."

"When can we collect them from you?"

Stephanie frowned at him and shook her head slightly. "I'm not sure you can," she said.

Carl continued to gaze into the fire. "That wasn't the deal, Steph."

"There are some who don't want to turn them over to you."

"So?" he asked.

"So, I'm not strong enough to go against their objections yet."

"Then get strong enough," Carl snapped. "We need them together, and we need it sooner rather than later."

"Don't take that tone with me," Stephanie warned.

"My tone doesn't matter, darlin'," Carl whispered. "My actions do. If you need me to go hunting for Infernals to help you get support, then just say the word at this lonely campfire in the middle of nowhere and I'll get to it."

"You would do that?" she asked.

"We need the Thirteen in our camp," Carl said. "That's been my order since you became the Devil. The way I figure it, that allows me to do your dirty work in good conscience."

Stephanie held her hands to the fire for warmth. "I have four names," she said.

"Speak them," Carl told her.

Stephanie gave him the names, as well as their locations in the world.

"They die and we get the five numbered people," Carl said.

Stephanie considered the deal for a moment, then nodded slowly.

Carl stood up and began to walk towards the shadows. "I'll let you know when it's done."

26

"**You look pretty** comfortable sitting in that chair," Trew called out as he entered the penthouse apartment. Across the room Trew and Cooper could see the boy sitting in the plush leather chair. He looked up from the computer monitor and smiled, spinning the chair around and flashing them a genuine smile of delight.

"It seems a lot bigger than I remember," he hopped down and walked towards the living area, plopping comfortably onto a black leather couch. His smiling eyes flitted to Cooper and he nodded. "Enjoying a full time gig in the Game, Cooper?" he asked.

"I've only been here a few days, boy," Cooper sat down with an amused look. "Trew's kept me busy so far."

"Excellent," the boy said. "Let's chat for a bit, shall we, gentlemen?"

Trew sat down and looked closely at the boy. He looked to be around thirteen or fourteen years old, with short brown hair and bright blue eyes. He wore comfortable fitting clothes that matched the current teen style on Tygon, along with black running shoes. He looked like any normal boy his age on Tygon, except for his eyes.

Children who played the Game began to display a 'look' shortly after they began to play incarnations as humans. The more lives they lived, the more of a presence they displayed. Between the ages of sixteen to eighteen it was impossible not to recognize a

Gamer entirely by their bearing and presence. Younger children didn't show it so acutely; to see the presence so strong in a boy this age was, to say the least, remarkable.

"Brandon?" Trew asked, just to make it official.

"What?" the boy asked seriously, then winked and beamed a huge smile.

"Just confirming what we all knew," Trew said. "Didn't take you long to get back in here."

"You shouldn't be back in here," Cooper frowned.

"Says who?" Brandon asked.

"It's too soon, Brandon," Cooper began. "There are rules and procedures for re-entry..."

The boy held his hand up and made a clicking sound with his tongue. "The rules have been changed," he announced. "I was needed here now, so I came."

"You know what could happen because of your choice," Cooper said.

"Better than anyone," Brandon nodded. "Yet here I am."

"What is it you need to do here?" Trew asked.

"We'll get to that in a few moments," Brandon said. "First, you two need to fill me in on what's happening here. How is Tygon?"

"You know about the Game, right?"

"Uh, yeah," Brandon said. "I invented it."

Trew looked at the boy, trying to understand why he was joking around. Brandon shook his head and raised a hand in apology. "Sorry 'bout that," he said. "I'm new to this body. It's immature and I'll need a bit more time for my personality to fully take control. Ignore most of my adolescent outbursts."

Trew paused as he recalled what he'd witnessed on the video Thorn had shown him. Rather than being born, Brandon had transferred his consciousness into an existing NPC avatar. He wasn't sure what happened to the NPCs consciousness, but he had a feeling that was a question for a different conversation.

"The Game feeds are down," Trew said.

"Ahh, yes. The Game feeds are down," Brandon said. "How's that working for everyone so far? It's shaking things up properly, I bet?"

Cooper chuckled and Trew made a wry face. "Yes," Trew confirmed, "it's shaking things up very nicely. I'm guessing that it's intentional?"

"It is," Brandon said. "My old body drops, the feeds go down."

"For a preset amount of time?" Trew asked.

"Kind of."

"What do you mean, kind of?"

"How many Gamers are on Tygon now? Not players of the Game, but members of the Gamer movement from Earth."

"Over a hundred million," Trew said.

"Closer to four hundred million," Cooper said.

"Really?" Trew looked surprised. "Only one hundred million were culled."

"I've been making inquiries," Cooper smiled. "Turns out that most of the players who exit their plays are joining the movement."

"Good," Brandon said. "I hope you've been encouraging them to help bring the feeds back up?"

"I was right, then," Trew nodded. "If enough of us focus our intentions on that outcome, it will happen."

"That's always been the truth of the matter," Brandon said. "I tried to do it by making the Game a spectator sport, but it wasn't enough to unite the masses. It took you and Danni to join enough minds to the same focus point."

"Did you set the feeds to come back up at a set time?" Cooper asked.

"No, I couldn't make it work like that," Brandon said. "We need to know for certain that it's the thoughts of millions producing the result."

"So the feeds come back up sometime, but we aren't sure when. What purpose does that serve?"

"It's a demonstration, an exercise to show the masses what they can accomplish when they put their collective minds to it. When the feeds come back up, everyone will know that thoughts are real in this world and they have the power to alter reality," Brandon said.

"What do we do after that happens?" Trew asked.

"Oh, no, you don't," Brandon smiled, and shook his head. "This part of the game is yours to play, Trew. I'm not here to take your spot; I've already been the leader of this world. The job belongs to you now, and you will be better at it than I was."

"Why are you here, then?" Trew asked. "Just to answer a few questions and live life anonymously?"

Brandon laughed out loud. "I might be young, but I've lived long enough to have had my fill of vacations and roaming around with no purpose. That's fun for a while, but it becomes boring."

"How old are you?"

Brandon arched an eyebrow at Trew and gave him a serious look. "Thorn showed you my story; you do the math. I'm older than thirteen, but I don't intend to grow up into an old man inside this skull." He tapped his head with one hand and knocked the table with the other to make a hard rapping noise.

"So what's your plan, then?" Cooper asked.

The boy smiled. "I'm gonna spend a few days with you and answer whatever questions I can. I have to be very careful; I don't want to give Trew, here, any info that might change how he proceeds. When the Game feeds come back up, I'm going in."

"Into the Game?" Trew asked.

"Yes, into the Game," Brandon laughed. "There are things that need doing in there that only I can do."

"You need to talk with your Hand," Cooper guessed.

Brandon gave him a sideways look and a quick nod. "Yeah, that's one thing I need to do."

"You made me to be like you, didn't you?" Trew asked.

Brandon nodded. "For decades I've been running the simulation and putting NPCs through a grinder to churn out one who would be as much like me as possible. I thought it would be difficult, and then I began to think it was impossible." He looked at Trew with the fondness of a parent. "My whole plan rested on producing you, Trew. I'm glad we still have a shot at fixing all of this."

"Of waking your people up? The ones dying in the Dream?"

"Yes."

Trew nodded thoughtfully. "So we have you with us until the feeds come back online."

"That's right," Brandon said.

"It could be any time?" Cooper asked.

"It could."

"If you had to guess, how long would you say you'll be with us before you go back into the Game?" Trew asked.

"You're a clever lad. I like that," Brandon smiled. "I guess there's no harm in answering that question, since it's just a guess."

Brandon walked got up and walked to the bar, grabbed a fruit juice and returned to the couch.

"If I had to make a guess, I would say in three days I could be heading into the Game."

27

"You've been in a bad mood lately."

Danni looked up and glared at the old man. The heat was heavy and uncomfortable, like a woolen blanket piled on top of her when she already had a fever. The sun burned through the sky and prickled at her skin, though the years of walking had toughened her to its attacking fierceness. They'd been plodding along the highway silently for most of the day. This had become their routine, and it had lasted for what seemed like an eternity.

"This is ridiculous," her tone was both angry and bitter. "I should never have agreed to follow you! I certainly should have stopped by now."

The old man turned to face her. His face was pleasant and he seemed genuinely surprised by her outburst. "We've had some fun times, Danni. Surely you can admit that."

Danni shuffled to the side of the road and sat down on the hood of an abandoned car. She reached down to pat Zeus on the head, remembering as she did that Zeus was no longer with her. She missed that dog; he'd died bravely protecting her that night.

"We've had many adventures," she conceded. "More than I would like to recall, if you ask me."

"Good." The old man nodded in satisfaction and joined her beside the car. He reached into his backpack and pulled out two energy bars and a bottle of cool, fresh water. She reached for one;

she'd long ago stopped wondering how he always seemed to have a supply of energy bars and cold water at hand when he reached for them in that pack of his. "For a moment there I thought you were going to tell me that the only thing you recall about this journey is the moments spent walking down the road towards our destination."

Danni drank as much from the bottle of water as she could, and handed the rest back to him. Then she opened her energy bar and took a bite. "It's my birthday again, I think."

The old man shook his head. "No, ma'am, it is not."

"It's soon, then."

He chuckled and ate his own energy bar, not bothering to remove the wrapping as he took a big bite from it. "Yes, girl, it is soon. I have a very big present for you this year."

Her eyes were flat as she stared at him. "I'm about to turn seventy years old," she said.

"Really?" he looked impressed. "I would guess maybe forty at most. You are a very fit and attractive woman, Danielle Radfield."

"I was sixty-three when we started this farce."

"Danni," the old man's eyes softened with sympathy. "I know you think this has taken too long. I know there have been times when you wanted to give up. Look at all that we've accomplished, though. We've covered a considerable distance in the past seven years. The lives we have touched, the memories made, and the people saved... you have no idea how important this journey has been to the world, but let me assure you, the feats you've accomplished will echo across time and affect more lives than you will ever know."

Danni said nothing. She looked at him tiredly. "I've decided that I no longer believe a word you say," she said.

The old man smiled. "That's okay," he assured her. "Perhaps you'll believe me when I give you your birthday present. I can tell you what it is now, if you'd like? It's tomorrow, by the way; your birthday."

She took another bite from her bar and shrugged indifferently.

"You look like you could use a pick-me-up, so I'm gonna tell you, even though you don't seem too interested."

Her eyes drifted back to rest on his as she waited expectantly.

"We're gonna meet with Shane on your birthday, girl!" he exclaimed. "Tomorrow we finally reach our destination!"

28

"Any time now." Brandon sat in what Trew referred to as 'Sylvia's office' and strummed his fingers in boredom as he watched the static on the main viewer.

Trew looked up from writing notes. "You've been saying that for the past three hours."

Brandon grimaced, not bothering to look in Trew's direction.

"I'm impatient," he said. "Sitting in boring offices and watching grownups work hard to accomplish little is not why I came back here."

"You've shared much information with me," Trew said, "and I've enjoyed spending time with you again."

Brandon looked at Trew; he forgot that he was the only father figure Trew had ever had. He smiled and walked over to Trew, nudging him in the shoulder.

"Want to go outside and play catch for a bit?"

Trew smiled. "There's no time. I never did get to do that... in this life."

"We made sure you didn't miss out on the experience, Trew," Sylvia said. "There were multiple lives where you enjoyed those things in the Game."

"That's true," Brandon said.

"She turns seventy today," Trew said, changing the subject to wonder about Danielle.

"I wonder if she's still hot?" Brandon asked. He laughed and shook his head. "Sorry, thirteen-year-old boys sure do have simple thoughts in their heads."

Trew smiled. "I can't wait to see her. I hope you're right about the feeds coming back up today."

"Everything was on track when I saw things last," Brandon confirmed.

"What do you mean by that?" Trew asked.

"Um..."

"You could see the Game when you were in the Dream? You were able to watch what was happening in there?"

Brandon walked back to the monitor and looked deeply into it as if searching for detail behind the static. "Yeah, we could see into the Game."

"Why didn't you tell me?"

"I just did."

Trew took a deep breath and sighed. He knew Brandon couldn't reveal much. There was a master plan, and he could understand the need for keeping secrets. Still, a part of him wanted to learn more from Brandon's mind before he departed. Trew controlled the impulse to begin interrogating the boy with questions that both knew couldn't be answered.

Minutes passed as the two went about their own activities.

"I met him the other night," Brandon announced. "In my dreams."

"Who?" Trew asked. "The old man?"

"What old man?" Brandon looked at Trew sharply.

"Dirty old man with crazy white hair all sticking up," Trew said. "Dressed in black garbage bags and heavy military boots with no laces. Has the most interesting gloves I've ever seen; made from red pop bottle caps somehow laced together."

"I'd forgotten about him," Brandon said.

"That's not who you're talking about?" Trew asked.

"No," Brandon waved his hand, "but that's who I want to talk about now. Did you find out his name?"

Trew shook his head.

"What did he say to you?" Brandon asked. "Have you only met him once? How many times have you seen him? Is it always in a dream? Do you remember ever seeing him here on Tygon? Or in the Game?" Brandon held up his hand to stop himself from firing out any more questions. "This is strange — I had totally forgotten about him, yet he is somehow in the simulation."

"Sylvia? Have you ever heard of this old man? Have you seen him in the Game?"

Sylvia didn't reply.

"Sylvia?" Trew asked.

"Yes, Trew?" she said.

"Did you hear Brandon's question?"

"I did."

"Why didn't you answer him?"

"I'm trying to recall such a person inside the Game from the description you provided. Searching databases now."

"That's odd," Brandon said. "Your answers are usually immediate."

"I'm searching for more than just a grain of sand on the planet, Brandon. I'm searching for what was a grain of sand a hundred thousand years ago and has changed to become hundreds if not thousands of different things since then. That kind of search takes some time."

"Okay, I understand," Brandon smirked. "You have limitations. It was bound to manifest eventually. You're a thirty-year-old computer, after all... they usually go out of date every couple of years or so."

"I'm not even going to entertain your attempt to bait me into a reaction," she said. "I'm as aware of my age as you are. I also know that you keep me updated with every new piece of technology as it becomes available, which makes me the most up-to-date technology on this planet. Good try, though."

"Thanks, old gal," Brandon smiled.

"My pleasure, young boy," she said.

"Still no luck?" Trew asked.

"Putting an image up on the main screen now," she said. "Is this who you're talking about?"

Both looked at the screen and nodded their heads.

"Yep, that's him," Trew said.

"Incredible," Brandon said. "How did he get into the Game?"

"No player is inhabiting him, Brandon," Sylvia said. "Whoa, wait just a minute!"

"What?" both men asked in unison.

"Give me a minute," she became quiet while Trew and Brandon looked at each other curiously.

"You didn't put him in there?" Trew asked.

"I haven't seen him since I was a kid," Brandon smiled wryly at the humour in the statement. "I mean, I met him once, before Thorn began the simulations. He was in my own dream."

"When you were a child on your home world? The one you call the Dream?"

"Yes, sorry, it gets confusing. On my home world... when I was dreaming... I saw him in there."

"I've only seen him in my dreams since I exited the Game," Trew offered.

"Let me write this down," Brandon got a piece of blank paper and pencil.

"I saw him as a boy in the dreams of my reality. You saw him in your dreams in this reality. Sylvia says he's been inside the Game." Brandon looked at the information on the paper and held it up for Trew to examine.

"Looks like he can move into any reality he chooses," Trew said. "I don't see a reference to him walking in your world, or on Tygon, but my guess is that he has."

"He's old," Sylvia announced. "Now that I know what to look for, I see him making appearances in the Game from the very beginning."

Brandon moved to the computer at the main desk. "That's not possible," he said. "For the first ten years of the Game there were no Timeless. Only my Hand and some of the Twelve were inside the Game during that time. It's not possible for him to have been there; we would have noticed it."

"He was there," Sylvia confirmed, "and none of us saw him, not even me."

Brandon sat with his brow furrowed together in thought.

"Who is he?" Trew asked.

"I don't know," Brandon said with a serious look, "but I will be sure to look him up when I get in there."

Brandon went back to watching the static feed of the Game while Trew looked to his plans on a tablet.

A brief time later Trew looked at Brandon. "If it wasn't the old man you saw in your dreams, then who were you talking about?"

Brandon nodded his head at the reminder and flashed a grin. "Yeah, that's right. I met Tygon's version of Sylvia."

"What did he have to say?" Sylvia asked quickly. She was always interested in discussing the mainly quiet spirit of Tygon.

"Some thoughts, tips, and recommendations for me," Brandon said. "Nothing I can discuss yet, but I was glad to finally meet him."

"You never met him before?" Trew had always assumed Brandon had.

"What was it like?" Sylvia asked.

"Like nothing I've experienced in any of my lives," Brandon smiled. "It was incredible."

"Perhaps I will meet him someday," Sylvia said wistfully.

Trew could tell from Brandon's body language that he knew more than he was able to say.

"Perhaps you will, Sylvia," Brandon said. "With faith and belief... anything is possible."

29

Danielle heard a hissing to her right. She turned her head to look in the direction of the sound, knowing what she would see.

The bright white outline of a doorway appeared in the air. The white spread from the outside inwards, until there was a large rectangular doorway of light suspended in middle of the green field.

Danielle stood straighter as first the old man and then another individual emerged.

The old man walked calmly to stand beside her, while the other stopped a respectable distance away and stood facing her with an amused look on his face.

"I hear birthday wishes are in order," he said with a smile. "You look very good for your age, Danielle. It's a shame the old man didn't teach you how to halt the aging process altogether; you could look even better."

"That's not the purpose of my life, Shane," she said. "I don't want to be Timeless; I just want to show the average person that they can live longer, happier, healthier lives."

Shane grinned and his eyes looked at her with a mixture of cruel amusement and mocking humour. "Happy, Danielle? I think anyone who has followed your life wouldn't rush to the front of the line to get the small amount of happiness that has trickled your way."

Danielle smiled in return. "I don't expect a monster like you to understand what happiness truly is, Shane. I would guess that for all your millennia of living, you haven't experienced a fraction of the happiness I've enjoyed in my short life."

"Agree to disagree." Shane waved a hand. "Your friend here," he indicated the old man with a nod of his head, "tells me that you've been searching for me for some time. He claims that you walked the entire way here?"

"That's right," Danielle confirmed. "It was his condition for finding you."

"I'm amazed that you made it almost to my doorstep undetected," he said. "It's definitely because you didn't use any significant energy. Good plan, old fella."

The old man nodded curtly at Shane's comment, but remained silent.

"Must have been some tough times during the walk, though," Shane said. "Specifically, walking across the ocean."

"What do you mean?" Danielle asked, shooting a glance at the old man who suddenly seemed intent on examining his gloves.

"You walked across the Atlantic Ocean to get to me," Shane said.

"What? There's no way that's true..." but somehow, she knew that it was.

She looked at the old man. "How?" she asked.

"Tricky," he admitted, "but possible. Anything's possible, Danni, you know that better than anyone. I've had lots of experience doing things that are impossible. This wasn't even one of the more difficult feats I've pulled off."

"So you're here," Shane said. "What do you want?"

"I want you to turn it back on," Danielle said.

Shane considered her for a moment, then smiled.

"What if I say no?" he asked. "Then you'll try to fight me? Force me to do what you want?"

"No," Danielle shook her head calmly. "If you refuse, then I will kill you."

Shane gauged the seriousness of her comment, then nodded. "I'm afraid the old man has lied to you if he led you to believe you could kill me, Danielle. You made this trip for no reason. I hope it didn't take up much of your time."

Danielle wasn't sure what to do. If he refused to do as she asked, then she would fail. Standing across from him, in this open field on a green peaceful morning surrounded by the sights, sounds, and smells of nature all around her, Danielle couldn't remember why she had agreed to come on this journey at all.

"There is one certain way for you to die, Shane."

Danielle and Shane both looked at the old man. He was now sitting on a large tree stump, although Danielle couldn't remember it being there a few moments ago. His legs swung lazily back and forth, the loose tongues of his laceless boots making a gentle clicking sound as the flapped upwards and then down. He looked calm and peaceful, sure of himself in a way that was strangely threatening.

"The Game stops, you die," the old man winked at Shane knowingly, then his eyes flicked quickly to look at Danielle. "The power has been off for ten years, boy, and I'm sure you've had some very fun times during this little episode. Enough is enough, however. It's time to restart the system and get power flowing into the world again. If you're not prepared to do that — right here, right now — then it's Game Over."

Shane looked from the old man to Danielle. He understood the mistake he'd made. He thought Danielle was coming to force him to do something that she couldn't possibly accomplish. Now he knew that the old man was threatening to kill Danielle and end the Game if Shane did not comply.

"That kills you, too," Shane said. He knew he was trapped and he was stalling in hopes of finding a way out of the mess he'd willingly walked into.

"After all these years you don't really know anything about me, Shane," the old man said. "There are lots of places I can go. But for you, this is it."

Shane laughed. "This isn't it for me. I would go home."

"Oh, my poor boy." The old man shook his head sadly. "It seems you have not been kept up to date on events in all realities. There is no other place for you to return to."

Danielle nodded, wondering how Shane could not know his body was dead on Tygon after all this time. She didn't understand that the two men were talking about an entirely different reality called the Dream.

Shane's jaw ticked methodically as he considered the situation. Danielle could almost hear his mind working despite the twenty-foot gap between them.

"I never said I'd kill the girl," Shane said.

"I never expected you would," the old man replied.

Danielle turned her head to look at the old man. Had he just implied that he was going to kill her if Shane didn't agree to restore power to the world? Why would he make such a threat? She wondered. Shane doesn't care if I live or die? Why would he?

The old man kept his unflinching stare on Shane, even though Shane wasn't returning the look. Instead, Shane looked at Danielle with a frown on his face.

"What is it that you're not telling me?" Danielle asked. "I didn't come all this way for you to threaten my life, old man."

"Hush, girl," the old man said softly. "I'm getting you what you came for."

Danielle began to say something, but she decided not to interrupt whatever seemed to be going on. She could ask questions later, unless the old man attacked her, then she would do her best to defend herself.

"Time's running out, Shane," the old man said. "Give me your answer. Do you turn the power back on? Or does the Game end now?"

30

"Okay," **Brandon entered** the room and dropped down onto the couch beside Trew. "I think it's go time. Let's get me hooked up and into the Game."

Trew looked at Brandon curiously. "Seriously? The feeds are about to come back on?"

The boy they had come to know as Brandon had taken on a very businesslike air. Some of his old mannerisms had begun to show through this young body in the past three days, and it was clear that he wasn't kidding around.

"I can feel something," he said. "My best guess is that the time is close."

Trew reached for his phone on the table and sent a broadcast message to Danielle's team, instructing them to make their way to the command centre. "Do you want me to come with you?" he asked as he stood up.

Brandon shook his head and walked to the door, opening it and waiting for Trew to join him. "No need to come with me. I'm not a frightened child who needs an adult's hand as I make my way into the Game for the first time." They began to walk towards the elevator. "You need to get to the Command Centre. It's gonna be crazy for the first few hours while everyone tries to piece together what's going on with all the players of interest. Ten years have passed inside the Game since fans were able to view it. They'll be shocked and surprised at the changes that have occurred."

"Viewership will swell," Trew said.

Brandon laughed and entered the elevator as the door opened. "That's an understatement. I would guess that every pair of eyes on Tygon will be watching the Game. You will have the one thing I dreamed of for years... total focus on the Game."

Trew's hand hovered over the elevator button as the implications of Brandon's statement sunk in. "That's what you wanted all along, wasn't it?" he asked.

Brandon looked both old and young as he winked at Trew knowingly. "It's definitely part of the master plan, young man," he said. "Double your money if you guess which channel almost everyone will be watching when they tune back in."

Trew didn't need to answer. He knew as well as Brandon did that the world would be tuning in to watch Danni.

===

Shane looked back and forth between Danielle and the old man. They all knew how he would respond, but it was obvious from the look on his face that he wasn't pleased about it.

Finally his eyes became calm, his posture relaxed, and he shrugged his shoulders nonchalantly. "All right," he said. "I'll restore things to how they were before. Things were getting boring this way, anyhow."

"That's a good lad," the old man said. He stood up on the stump and clapped his hands three times slowly. "Doing the right thing is never easy, especially for you, Shane."

Shane smiled. He raised his hand as if to snap his fingers, then paused and cocked his head as if a thought had just occurred to him. "I must insist on one condition."

The old man chuckled. "There will be no conditions; you're in no position to make bargains."

Shane lowered his hand to his chest, wiping it smoothly against the breast of his shirt. "I've stated I will comply. If you won't agree to my condition, then you can end the Game right now and the blame for it will fall on your shoulders, not mine."

The old man pursed his lips in annoyance; he knew Shane was right. By agreeing to restore power, Shane would not technically be to blame if the Game ended. Both the old man and Shane understood the ramifications for causing the Game to end, and neither wanted to be blamed for causing that to happen from a universal perspective. "So you take defeat and manage to slide in a small victory before you concede?" the old man said. "Name your condition, and I will consider it."

"It's a small demand," Shane said, "and it will be simple for you both to agree to."

"What is it?" Danielle asked.

"Neither of you can reveal what I've done."

The old man laughed, slapping his knee with one hand and waving the index finger of his other in Shane's direction. "That is clever! Absolutely brilliant, boy!" he sat back down and laughed loudly again.

"I'm glad you like it," Shane said.

"It's not really that big of a deal," Danielle couldn't understand why Shane had asked for something so trivial and the old man thought it was so clever.

"So you agree to my condition?" Shane smiled sweetly.

"Yes."

"I do too," the old man said.

Shane nodded and snapped his fingers and announced, "Then it's done."

"Just like that?" Danielle asked.

"Just like that."

Danielle shook her head. "I've travelled this world on foot for seven years to find you."

"Yeah, you mentioned that already," Shane said.

"Faced countless dangers."

"Mmhmm."

"Taken lives, and saved others."

"All right."

"I can't remember the number of times I almost died trying to find you."

"Eight," the old man offered helpfully.

Danielle ignored him. "And now, after we finally find you, a short conversation is all it takes to persuade you to reverse what is likely the most devastating event in the last hundred years?"

"Thank you," Shane nodded.

"I expected more."

"What more could you have wanted?" Shane asked. "You got what you came for."

"I expected a fight."

Shane looked at the old man and shook his head. "Why do they always want to fight?"

"She did sacrifice considerable time and effort," the old man said.

"Fine," Shane sighed and untucked his shirt. "Since it's your birthday. Show me what you got."

"This isn't a joke," Danielle said. "If we fight, I intend to kill you."

"I understand."

"You're underestimating me, Shane."

"Likely," Shane rolled his head from side to side and then nodded. "Whenever you're ready, pumpkin."

Danielle returned his nod and slowly reached behind her back.

===

"It's live!" Michelle yelled. The command centre erupted into loud cheers and celebration.

Trew gazed at the main viewer and immediately saw Danni. "Quiet down and let's figure this out as quickly as we can!" he shouted.

The room became quiet and all attention centred on the viewscreen.

"What's she doing?" someone asked.

"Who's that?" another voice inquired. "Standing across from her?"

"It looks as if she's going to fight him."

"Who is it?" Michelle looked at Trew.

Before Trew could guess, they heard Danni speak. "You're underestimating me, Shane."

"Oh, no," Lilith said.

"Likely," Shane rolled his head from side to side and then he nodded. "Whenever you're ready, pumpkin."

No one moved in the Command Centre as Danni slowly reached behind her back.

===

Brandon lay on the table and smiled confidently. The static on the viewscreen in his room had just disappeared, and clear images were being received from inside the Game. He saw Danielle standing across from Shane and he chuckled. It looked like fans would return to viewing the Game with a bang.

"Are you ready?" the doctor asked. Only Trew, Cooper, and Sylvia knew who he really was, but the doctor and nurses guessed that he must be someone important to get a private luxury room like this.

Brandon watched the scene in the Game unfold for a moment, then he looked at the doctor. "Yes, I'm ready to get in there, Doc," he said.

The doctor nodded and began to lower the mask over Brandon's face. Before he settled it into place, Brandon spoke one more time.

"Please deliver a message to Trew for me once I'm in?" he asked.

"Of course," the doctor said.

"Tell him to keep a very close eye on Melissa."

"I'll tell him."

Brandon smiled. "Then let's play," he said.

31

"We are halfway through day seven of the blackout and there's nothing new for us to report. Despite the outpouring of positive thoughts and intentions being focused by most of the adult population, Game feeds are still down. People are not giving up, however, as efforts across the planet increase in the hopes of... One moment please, I'm getting new information here...

"The feeds are coming back up! I repeat, the Game feeds are coming online all over the world at this very instant!

"I'm sure no one is watching me any longer...Barry? Can we stop transmission, please? I want to see Danielle's feed immediately!"

    Lisa Rohansen - reporting day seven of the Game Blackout on Tygon.

Danielle - 70

As I slowly reach for the first of four knives sheathed behind my back, my primary thought is that I likely shouldn't be doing this.

I got what I came for; there's no real purpose in fighting one of the most powerful beings on the planet. The odds are good that he will kill me, but for some reason I don't seem to care at this moment.

I've gone through so much, travelled such a long distance, and seen horrible painful things that are all because of this creature's actions. Thousands of thoughts rush through my mind in the brief seconds that it takes to put my hand on the handle of the throwing knife, but one thought is foremost in my brain: Seventy years is good enough. Let's see if I can make this monster pay for some of the crimes he's committed over the millennia.

I see him smirk and my mind is made up; my hand grips the throwing knife comfortably, and quicker than most eyes could follow, I pull the blade from its sheath and whip it forward as hard as I can. No more time for thought... there is only action.

My first blade streaks in a straight line towards his left side. He begins moving to the right, but my next blade is already sailing in that direction, cutting off escape. Quicker than thought he begins to prepare himself to rush towards me, but my third blade is now in the air and halfway towards him following the straight path, making an advance to me impossible.

With knives flying at him from all directions, there is only one way he can go, and he launches himself upwards like a lightning bolt leaving the ground.

He gets three feet into the air before I close the distance and intercept him. I have become fast, and my arm encircles his neck as I begin to turn and twist it in a way that will break his spine as close to instantly as exists in this fast-paced dance. With my other hand I begin to plunge my fourth knife straight towards his exposed eye, just in case he manages to break my wrenching grip.

Shane grunts in surprise as all three knives whistle by below us and we drop to the ground with heavy force. His neck is strong, and instead of resisting my attempt to bend his neck and break it, he allows his body to move with the motion which reduces the force exerted and allows him to break my grip. I grin as my knife continues on course for his exposed eye, but my triumph fades as he gently bats the blade away to the side with the momentum of his right hand.

I land on top of him as we hit the ground with a heavy thud, both of us still and panting from the exertion that has taken place in the span of less than five seconds.

He shoves me with a powerful heave of his arms and I'm sent rolling a few feet away from him. I stop my spinning and spring up to stand on my feet in a battle stance, knife at the ready to either defend or attack as required by his next move.

His smile is broad and it looks like he's genuinely pleased with me. "Is that it?" he asks. "I would imagine the first rush was the best you can do. I have to admit that it was a wonderful attempt, Danni. To see that calibre of skill from a mortal... hell, I've rarely seen that kind of skill and speed from most Timeless, and they have centuries to perfect their skills. Bravo, Danni, bravo!"

I stand there, uncertain how to proceed. It was my best attack, and now that I've had a chance to gauge his abilities, I don't think I want to try again. He seems to be giving me an out, so I decide to take it.

"That's the best I could do," I say. "I wish it'd been good enough to end your miserable life, Shane, but I guess that will have to be accomplished by someone better than me." I stay in my defensive pose, ready in case he decides to strike, but he doesn't.

"Don't be too hard on yourself," he says. "I've been at this Game for thousands of years. I hate to admit this, but if you had trailed me into some dark alley and somehow managed to avoid me detecting you, I think that move could have very well ended my life. I am sincerely and deeply impressed with your skills."

"Thanks." I look at the old man; he's watching us with a bored look on his face. "So now what?" I ask him.

The old man stands up and hops down from the stump. He nods at Shane and uses his hand to make the outline of a rectangle in the air. It immediately begins to shimmer and fill with the familiar white light of a portal. "Now it's time to go home, girl," he says.

"Just like that?" I say.

"Yes," he nods solemnly. "Sometimes things happen in life 'just like that.' This is one of those times."

I look at Shane. "I hope to never see you again," I say.

He smiles and raises one eyebrow. "If you do your job right, then perhaps we won't need to meet again."

I open my mouth to ask him what he means, but he smirks and summons a doorway of his own. He quickly turns and disappears through it.

I look at the old man, and he motions to the doorway with his arm. "Let's go, Danni," he says. "You've been on the road long enough. It's time to go home."

I nod and enter the doorway, feeling its hot rush of speed as, in an instant, we travel the distance that it took seven long years for us to walk.

32

Danielle - 70

I step out of the doorway and onto a hard packed, well-travelled dirt road with woods on either side. The old man appears out of the light beside me and the sound of hissing disappears, signaling that the doorway is gone.

I look around slowly; the woods are thicker than I remember them being but that's not a surprise. I've been gone from this place for seven years.

I look down the road to my right, and off in the distance I see the front gate of the Colony. When I left there were over forty thousand people living there. I wonder how much it has grown. From here, everything appears normal; the wall is intact, and there are people standing guard on top. I begin to walk towards home.

"Danni," the old man says from behind me. "Before we get any closer, I think there are a few things you should know."

I feel a tightening in my stomach. The old man rarely tells me anything, and when he does it's usually bad news. I turn to look at him, and his face confirms that I'm not going to like what I hear. "What is it?" I ask.

"Things have changed here," he says. "Since you've been gone."

"I would imagine they have," I say. "Give me the highlights."

His expression becomes pinched and uncomfortable. "I wouldn't exactly call them highlights..." he says.

"Quit being cryptic," I snap. "Tell me what you have to say."

"It's very difficult to run and maintain a colony of this size, especially when you were the big draw... and you were no longer present."

"That makes sense," I agree.

"A couple of years after you left, things started to become... strained."

I look at him, waiting for him to finish telling me what he has to say.

He sighs and shrugs his shoulders. "Okay, then, there's no easy way to say this, so I'll just come right to the point."

"I'll be surprised if you can do that."

He looks at me and nods. "Yeah, I deserved that. The Colony has a new leader, and not one that is very friendly towards you."

"Who is it?" I snap impatiently.

I hear rustling in the brush and turn to see Raphael appear. From his gear and appearance it looks like he's been out in the wilderness for more than a few days. He also looks like he's stepped out of a scene from a fantasy book. He's wearing a chain mail shirt with its hood hanging against his back. His arms have plates of steel strapped on to provide forearm protection, and his boots and leggings finish the outfit, making him look like some elven ranger from The Lord of the Rings. Behind his right shoulder I can see the ornate hilt of his favourite long blade poking up from its sheath.

His eyes are grim as he approaches. He stops in front of me and I can see a mixture of relief and curiosity in his eyes. He opens his mouth to say something, I can tell he's going to scold me or yell at me, but then he shakes his head and pulls me close to hug me.

Suddenly I feel as if I'm a little girl again being pulled out of the way of danger into his strong protective arms. I begin to weep, letting out all the tension and stress of years on the road. He stokes my head and rocks me gently as I sob and hug him tight.

After a few moments I feel much better. He loosens his grip to hold me at arms' length and examines me with his gaze. I can see tears in his eyes as well.

"You don't look a day older than when you left," he says.

"That's kind of you." I wipe my eyes with my sleeve. "I know for a fact I look at least a week or two older than that."

He chuckles and relaxes his grip. "Come on, let's get off the road. It's not safe to be standing here."

He starts to walk back towards the forest. I look around for the old man, but as is so often the case, he has quietly disappeared.

"Why isn't it safe?" I ask. "What's going on, Raph? Who's in charge of the Colony?"

He looks over his shoulder as he continues to walk. "Stephanie," he says. "While you were gone, the Devil came in and took over."

===

"What the hell is he talking about?" Michelle looked at Trew.

"Stephanie must have become an Infernal," Trew said, "and somehow she's aiding Daniel. Looks like she's high in the organization, if she's working directly against Danni."

"That doesn't sound right," Nadine said. "How can one of her closest protectors for decades suddenly become an enemy?"

Trew looked at the others around the table. "Timeless are a real wild card in the Game," he said. "I've learned a bit about them, and the truth of the matter is that they follow their allegiance above all else. When their eyes turn colour, they have no choice but to follow that path."

The room considered the implications of having Stephanie as an enemy working for the Devil.

"What about that fight she was in? With Shane?"

Trew shook his head. "Forget Shane for the moment. We have no idea where she was or even where to begin looking for him. Let's focus on the Colony first."

People nodded and began to type commands into their tablets.

Trew stood up. "Find out whatever you can," he said. "Start scanning all the feeds to view people who are in the Colony. Many of them were likely low ranked players before the Day. It's going to be crazy for the first few hours here. It will take some time for the computer to update all the rankings as information floods in. Once we get knowledge of the newest rankings, start viewing channels with players inside the Colony. I want to know what Stephanie is up to. I also want to know where the Devil is right now. Find me Daniel."

33

Danielle - 70

We hike a few kilometres into the woods until we come to an opening. Raphael stops and turns to look at me.

"We fly from here," he says.

I sigh. "It's been so long since I've flown, I wonder if I'll still be able to."

He frowns at me. "Why haven't you flown?"

I shake my head. "Long story short, the old man wouldn't allow it. It was the only way we could find..." I clamp my mouth shut. I don't think I'm supposed to tell anyone about meeting with Shane. Something tells me bad things will happen if I break my vow and tell others that the power is back on. Not that it should make a difference; it won't take long for someone to discover the truth of the matter. I will honour my word, which means telling no one about the finale to my long trip abroad. "He just wouldn't let me fly," I say.

"It's like riding a bike," he assures me. "I'll go slow at first. When you're comfortable, give me a sign by passing me in the air and I'll speed things up a bit."

"Okay," I say.

He nods and jumps into the air, hovering ten feet above the ground.

I close my eyes and summon the glow. It's still there, as strong as ever, and I feel its warm embrace as I jump into the air and drift up to float beside him.

"Excellent," he says. "Now follow me."

I bask in the sensations that come with flying; the cold wind in my face, contrasted by the warm sun, and the crisp feeling of the air as it rushes over my nostrils and around my eyes; I'd forgotten how incredible this feeling is! I swear we were made to fly through the skies; I wish everyone could do it. Correction — everyone can. I wish they would.

It only takes a few moments for me to feel comfortable enough to increase my speed. I fly past Raphael and he laughs and nods, increasing the pace so that we can travel more quickly. I follow him and soon guess where he's taking us. What used to be a 40-minute drive from the Colony, there is a large stone bluff called Rattlesnake Point. It looks like he's heading for that.

We reach the bluffs about fifteen minutes later and land at the top of the escarpment. Raph sits down and swings his legs over the edge, and I quickly join him, glancing down at the jagged rocks over a hundred feet below.

"I've always loved this place," I say.

Raphael nods. "Rattlesnake Point. Over ten kilometres of cliffs surrounded by woods and nature on all sides. We've begun to spot the odd rattlesnake, and they were gone from the area for decades."

I begin to say something and he nods his head. "I know the point wasn't named for them — it was called Rattlesnake Point because it looks like a snake from the air. Still, it's interesting to see nature return to the old ways since the Day."

I nod in agreement. "You said 'we' a moment ago. How many are here? Can you tell me what happened?"

"We tempted fate and tried to do something that we all knew was risky," Raphael said. He looked out at the sun as it was setting on the horizon. "We made a deal with the Devil, and eventually the Devil had to renege on that deal."

"You never did tell me how you helped her overthrow Daniel," I say, "or how you managed to turn Stephanie in the first place."

"We didn't know that it would be Stephanie," Raphael admits. "We guessed that one of us would turn eventually, and we made a binding agreement between all of us that when the time came, whoever turned would take a shot at eliminating Daniel. When it ended up being Steph... well, she had the best chance of surprising him. We knew our odds were excellent when we saw that her eyes had changed."

"How were you so certain someone would become an Infernal?"

"We know the Game. In Africa there is a frog that sometimes suffers from a disease that kills only males. Sometimes it is so deadly that it can leave a population with no males at all, leaving the entire group without any hope of procreating," Raphael says.

"Sounds nasty," I say.

"The nasty thing is what nature does to correct the situation," he says. "Some of the females spontaneously become male, allowing the frogs to mate and the species to continue to exist."

"Is that true?" I can't believe such a thing could happen.

"Absolutely," he assures me. "It's the same with everything in this world. Nature, or the mainframe, or whatever you want to call it, can perform miracles to restore balance to the world. We knew that we were upsetting the balance. So many Eternals in a concentrated area couldn't go unnoticed by the system forever. We knew that eventually one or more of us would experience the change, so we made a bold plan to take advantage of the situation when it occurred."

"Daniel's dead?" I ask. "Gone forever, because he no longer has a body to return to on Tygon?"

Raphael pauses and his expression tells me something different from the words that come out of his mouth. "Yes," he says. "Daniel is gone."

"You don't sound so sure," I say.

He opens his mouth to say something, but shakes his head instead. "He's gone," he assures me.

"What did you want Stephanie to do?" I ask. "If she succeeded in becoming the Devil?"

Raphael looks thankful for the change in subject. "We wanted to bring Shane's released people together. Many of us felt this would enable us to figure out how to turn things back on. If Shane gathered and used these individuals to cause the problem, we guessed they could help us to reverse it. We gathered over half of them, and the Infernals had managed to acquire the other half."

"So you wanted Stephanie to take over and bring you the numbered people that the Infernals had in their clutches," I guess.

"Yes," he says. "We wanted her to do that, and one other thing."

"Which was?" I ask.

"Leave you and the Colony alone," Raphael answered. "We knew the Colony was a big target for Daniel, and we'd put him off repeatedly by convincing him that too many would die if he tried to take over. We also knew that eventually he would tire of our stall tactics and attack us like a rabid dog. Putting one of us in the Infernal leadership spot would help increase the chances that you would be left alone."

"Looks like that plan backfired," I say.

"They both backfired," he says. "She stalled when it came to turning over the numbered people. I convinced her to give me two of them, but then she dragged her heels and even tried to give us an imposter who'd been trained to lie very convincingly. When we figured out this new person hadn't been one of the original numbered, we knew things were going to get messy. We planned a raid and stole the remaining numbered individuals out from under her nose."

"She retaliated by invading the Colony?" I guess.

"Yes," he answers. "She took her time and built a network inside the Colony. Three years after you had gone, the population of the Colony was well over a hundred thousand. It was impossible for us to detect every traitor or agent in a community of that size. Two years ago, a new mayor and governing body were elected. Turns out, Stephanie had slowly and cleverly recruited and aided them. When they took power, one of the first things they did was convince the regular population that Eternals had been taking advantage of everyone for years; sitting around doing nothing while the rest of the Colony worked to provide us with our lifestyle."

"Oh, no," I say.

"Yes," he says. "In no time they were asking us to leave, and then when we refused, they began to threaten us. Rather than start a physical confrontation, which they were all too eager to do, we decided to go."

"They wouldn't let you take the numbered group, though?"

"That's right. The thirteen stayed in the colony."

"Now you live here."

"Yes. The old man came to us and assured us that you would return in a few years. We decided to stay close enough to keep an eye on the colony and see if they would rise up against Stephanie and her minions. Most of the followers are allowed to live normal lives; Stephanie caused very few ripples when she took over. She even lets them retain their faith and following as Gamers."

"Well, I don't like it," I say. "There's no way I'm gonna allow my people to live with Infernals running the place. I'll give everything that's in me to kick Stephanie's scrawny ass out of the colony and leave my people alone."

Raphael smiles. "I was hoping you would say that," he says. "Let's go meet the others and see if we can't mount an effective eviction operation."

34

Trew

Trew looked up as the door slid open. Cooper sauntered in, looking comfortable — he always appeared comfortable and relaxed — but Trew had seen him spring into action enough times to know that this was how he lulled opponents into underestimating him.

"Slight concern," Cooper announced as he sat down.

"I can't wait to hear it," Trew said. "The feeds have been live for a few hours and I expected problems to be pouring in by now."

"I'm sure you'll get your wish sooner or later."

Trew shook his head. "It's a realistic expectation under the circumstances."

"Maybe," Cooper said. "I think this one will keep us busy for a while on its own."

"Okay, I'll bite. What is it?"

"Brandon has disappeared."

Trew frowned. "How?"

"His signal should have fed into channel 445. That channel is showing another player."

"Are you certain?" Trew asked. "It's a private channel. Only two terminals will view that channel; the viewer in Angelica's apartment, which now belongs to you, and here in Sylvia's office."

"It's not appearing correctly in my apartment," Cooper said.

"Sylvia, can you bring up that feed on this monitor, please?"

"Certainly, Trew," Sylvia answered.

The view materialized and Trew watched it for a few moments before nodding in agreement with Cooper. "Okay, I see what you mean. This definitely isn't Brandon."

"Of course it is," Sylvia said.

"If it were Brandon, we should be seeing the first person view of a newborn baby," Trew said.

"Why would you assume that?" she asked.

"Because that's how you enter the Game."

"No," the men could hear the amusement in Sylvia's tone. "That's how players enter the Game. I think we all know Brandon well enough to know he wouldn't waste time inside the Game as a young child."

"He came back to Tygon that way," Trew said.

"Because he had to," Cooper explained. "When entering this Sim from the Dream, you come in at the same age you are in real life. That's why you see me as I am and not younger."

"You enter the Game by being born as an infant... unless he went in as a Timeless?" Trew guessed.

"Good guess," Sylvia said, "but not quite right either. Brandon designed the simulation. He can enter at whatever age he desires."

"Have you been monitoring him, Sylvia?" Cooper asked.

"Yes."

"Give us a quick update, please."

"He entered as a twenty-year-old man. He looks the same as he did at that age on Tygon." In the corner of the screen a picture appeared of a good looking young man with an athletic build, sandy brown hair and brown eyes.

"Crisis averted," Trew said. "Brandon is found; right where we expected him to be."

"It looks like he found Melissa already," Sylvia said.

Trew looked back to the monitor and saw Melissa in his view. Brandon was observing her, unseen, from a distance. "Brandon told me to keep a close eye on Melissa." He looked over at a second monitor that was showing the Game from Melissa's point of view. Watching through her eyes, Trew saw Brandon approaching her from an inconspicuous angle.

"It looks like this might be an interesting feed to observe for the next few minutes," Cooper said.

"How long has he been near Melissa, Sylvia?" Trew asked.

"Twenty-six minutes."

Trew turned the monitor so Cooper could see it as well. "Let's watch the feed for a few moments. If nothing develops, then you can go back to your apartment to observe for a few hours, until my next address to the nation."

Cooper nodded and watched the monitor.

===

Melissa

I'm walking through a small village, inspecting the produce for sale at one of the stalls. They usually have delicious apples, so I stop by whenever I'm in the area.

A voice speaks up from behind me. "I remember you from before the Day," it says. "You're the flying girl, right? Melissa?"

I turn around and see a young man standing close to me. He looks to be nineteen or twenty, with the athletic build of a rugby or lacrosse player. Lacrosse has become popular again in most of the small settlements, likely because it's easy to gear up for and play on an open field. This kid must play; he looks sharp and quick. I can't see his face, because he's wearing a light black hoodie with the hood pulled up to cover his features. I can see his eyes, though, and they almost glow. It must be a trick of the light at this hour of the day.

I glance around to see if anyone else has noticed me. There are no other eyes lingering or suddenly looking away from me. I look back at the young man and nod. "Yeah, I'm Melissa," I say. "What's your name, kid?"

He walks towards me and raises both hands, lowering the hood so that I can get a better look at him. Wow, he's an attractive young man. His hair is dirty blonde, with sharp, angular features, yet soft enough to be attractive. His smile reveals perfect, white teeth, and the rest of him looks... angelic. His eyes are striking; they're brown, but they still appear to glow, with a silvery tint to them, almost like Danni's.

"My name is Azrael," he extends his hand and we shake.

"Like the archangel?" I ask.

He releases my hand and shrugs as he looks around casually. "I guess," he says.

"He's the archangel of death," I say. "I'm sure people must have mentioned that to you before?"

The smile on his face transfers to immediately to his eyes. The silvery colour makes them look like they're sparkling. "I've heard that from time to time," he admits. "I prefer to think of him as the angel who guides souls back to their homes."

"What home would that be?" I ask.

"Their original home." He looks around and raises his hand. "This is just a place we visit for a while. I think he helps them return to where they truly reside."

"Sounds cryptic," I say.

His eyes lock onto mine and touch me deeply. I feel the glow begin to emanate from my core, like a light bulb being lit from proximity to powerful electricity.

"You don't belong here anymore, Melissa," he says.

I try to take a step backwards, but I can't move. I've never felt the glow like this before, not even when I'm flying; it's intense. "What are you doing?" I manage to ask in a whisper.

"I'm helping you," his voice is gentle and soothing, like a parent would speak to a frightened child. I realize that I am frightened.

I feel myself sitting down on the ground. The people around us begin to shimmer and fade. The entire scene begins to flicker, at first slowly, and then more quickly. "What's happening?" I ask again.

"Close your eyes and calm your mind," he says. "I want to show you something."

I feel very strange, but my instincts tell me that he's trying to help me. I close my eyes and take deep breaths. I can move again, and I cross my legs and rest my hands on my knees. I enter a light meditative state, which is something I've become very good at over the years. "Show me what?" I ask.

"Where you really come from," I hear his voice say. "Time is running out, Melissa, and I need you to wake up soon. In a moment you will see the real world. Please don't panic when you do."

The clear darkness melts away to be replaced with a golden, pulsing glow — the common view for me when I'm meditating. I can feel another presence in the glow; I think it's the young man. Instinct tells me to open my eyes, and although I'm not sure what that means at first, I open my inner eyes for the first time to view deeper into my meditation.

The glow disappears and I see a world around me. It's different from Tygon. I'm lying on my back, and there isn't much that I can see, so I turn my head slowly from side to side. After a few moments it becomes tiring to look around and I close my eyes again.

The glow returns, and I again hear Azrael's voice.

"That's long enough, Melissa," he says. "Slowly open your eyes and come out of your meditation."

I open my eyes. I'm sitting on the hard dirt ground in the middle of the small village again. It feels strange to be here. Before I closed my eyes it felt like home, but now it feels as if I'm a stranger visiting a foreign land.

I look at Azrael, who nods. "Very good," he says. "I knew you could do it."

"Where did I just go?"

"You went to your reality, Melissa,"

"It felt like a dream," I say.

"It will, at first," Azrael nods.

"At first?" I ask. "I'm going back there again?"

"Oh, yes," he assures me. "Soon you will be going back there for good."

"How?"

He smiles and offers me his hand to help me stand. "Simple," he says. "You'll wake up. You already know how to do it. I just have to help you with the final part."

35

"Game fans pulled themselves away from their monitors briefly to listen to Trew address the world. He kept his address brief and thanked us all for our positive thoughts and efforts, which he assures us caused the feeds to come back online. Trew also counseled everyone to watch the Game more closely than ever before; he reminded us that the Game mirrors our own world in every way.

"Does that mean we will soon see Tygon citizens flying around the skies? Or healing each other with mysterious and invisible energy such as Reiki? Trew assures us that all of these things are possible, and more...

"Trew then caused a major buzz by ending his speech with an announcement.

"For the next three months, no players will reenter the Game. This has evoked an outcry of protest from fans and players around the world.

"What is Trew up to, and why has he made this decision?

"We continue to watch the Game in hopes of learning answers to these questions and more."

Lisa Rohansen reporting

Danielle - 70

Raphael and the others have spent years carving a detailed cave system into the bluff.

I spent the first couple of days reuniting with the others and learning where all the entrances were and how to find them.

Our numbers are few. Less than two hundred retreated to the caves to wait for my return.

Now that I'm here, they all look at me as if I know what to do, but I don't.

I'm trying my best to catch up on the seven years that I missed, making certain to speak with everyone, discussing their ideas and thoughts, trying to figure out if anyone has any insight that might help me decide on a course of action.

One hundred eighty-five humans and fifteen Eternals. Our options are limited, and I can think of only one scenario that will work. I stand before the group in the main eating hall. I doubt anyone will like what I'm about to say.

"I walk up to the front gates and deal with Stephanie," I say.

They wait for me to expand on the plan. After a few moments I nod my head. "That's it," I say. "That's the strategy."

Carl speaks first. "I like it," he nods.

"Really?" I ask.

"It could use some fine tuning," he admits. "Rather than approach through the front gates, instead you sneak in and slide a blade into her eye, but I think the general idea is sound. You face her and take the Colony back."

"She doesn't need to die," I shake my head.

"Oops," Carl folds his arms and leans against the rough wall behind him. "You just lost me."

"I agree with Carl," Raphael says. "Her death would result in chaos for the Infernals. They would begin to fight each other to select a new leader."

"We put her there," I say.

"To do a job," Carl snarls. "Which she failed to do, and seems to have no intention of completing. She's useless to us. Worse than useless, because she's in our way."

"We need the Thirteen," Samantha says.

"What for?" I ask.

Samantha frowns, then looks at Raphael with a puzzled look on her face. "Did she suffer from memory loss while she was away?"

I look at Raphael and catch the worried look on his face before he manages to hide it. "We need the power back on, Danni, that's still our main goal."

I nod and close my eyes. I can almost hear Shane laughing from wherever he's hiding. How long will it take the world to realize the power is back on? I wonder silently. Will they even bother to check the generators? I realize that this power outage could go on for another decade because of false assumptions. Perhaps the Thirteen will be able to ascertain that the power is working and fast track things back to normal.

"Okay, then," I say. "We need to get the Thirteen so they can help us bring the power back online."

Raphael nods grimly. "We need to do it soon, Danni. Time is running out."

"I understand," I say.

"I don't think you do." He looks at the Timeless, and they each nod in turn.

"You need to come with me," Raphael says. "There's something you must see."

The meeting concludes and I follow Raphael. Carl joins us, silently assuming a position at my right side. I find it comforting; I've missed him.

We go down a long stone hallway that slopes downwards. After a few minutes the air becomes colder and damper than normal.

Eventually we stop at a narrow doorway cut into the end of the hall. Water trickles down the sides of the walls like tears.

There's a small pile of two-foot-long sticks lying to one side. Raphael grabs one and wraps some dry cloth around it. He focuses his will on the end and a small, bright flame appears.

"We found this about a year ago," Raphael says. "I've been a Timeless for over four thousand years, Danni, and I've never seen anything like it inside the Game."

That gets my attention. I feel a mixture of fear and excitement as I ask him, "What is it?"

"Things are more complicated in the Game than the average person can understand," he says. "I won't overwhelm you with the details, but Timeless know with absolute certainty that we are living in a computer construct. Your faith and belief have led you to form the same conclusions, but after you see what lies beyond this door, you will never again doubt that we are living inside a computer simulation. You must be prepared to accept this, Danni. I have not asked this of a mortal before, but time is running out."

I consider his words seriously because it feels like the proper thing to do. I have no clue what he's about to show me, but I can't wait to see it. Finally I nod. "I am prepared, Raphael. Show me what's in there."

His lips purse together firmly and he glances at Carl who shrugs his shoulders and nods.

He hands me the torch and takes a step backwards. "Do not go more than five steps in," he warns me. "Do not step off the path. You will be tempted to stay in there, but you must come back out, Danni. Please do as I have instructed."

I look at the two men one more time. Both refuse to meet my eyes. I shrug and duck down as I stick the torch into the hole and step through...

Immediately I feel strong winds and loud, jarring sounds all around me. I have no idea how, but my torch remains lit, guttering slightly without seeming to feel the major effects of the winds buffeting me. I look at the ground first to make sure of my footing. I'm standing on a narrow ledge, no wider than three feet. Below is pure blackness; I begin to feel vertigo and force my eyes back to the stone pathway to resist the urge to jump into the great void below. A quick glance behind confirms that a doorway remains, but I can't see Raph or Carl on the other side. Raph said no more than five steps, and so I take only three. I look around and my breath catches in my throat.

I'm in a tremendously large cavern. The walls aren't made out of stone; portions are, but the majority of it is... what is this?

Everywhere I look, there is a great lattice of energy. Strings of purple, and green, and blue, and red, and gold. Great beams of energy in crisscrossing lines, with intersecting colours. The strings are various sizes and diameters, ranging in thickness from the size of wool string to the thickness of my arm.

It's a giant grid of colourful energy strings, and it's absolutely beautiful!

I take a few moments to stare at the centre of the cavern in wonder, marveling at how the lines vary in size and how they intersect with each other. As I begin to look at the lines nearer to me, I can hear them making buzzing and hissing noises where they intersect. Along the edges closest to me, I can see that matter is attached to the lines, like cement stuck to rebar as it clings to give a structure form and shape.

I stand gaping in awe at the sights before me.

After only a few moments, something nags at me, and I wonder if I should go check with Raph. He said that I must return to him, and I decide to go out and ask for clarification about how long I can stay in here. Only a few minutes have passed, but I don't want to overdo it.

I turn around and exit the cavern, smiling as I see Carl and Raphael standing right where I left them.

"See, told you she would be back," Carl says.

Raphael takes the torch gently from my hands and hugs me tightly.

I laugh and hug him back. "You look so relieved, Raph. What's the big deal? I was only in there for a couple of minutes. I came back out to ask if I could stay in for a bit longer."

Raph nods and touches my face fondly. "You were in there for over three hours, Danni," he says.

"What? That's not possible."

"It's true," Carl confirms. "What did you think of the view in there?"

"It was magnificent," I say. "What is it?"

"It's trouble," Raphael says. "This world is built on the framework of a supercomputer matrix. There shouldn't be a cavern in there, it should be solid rock."

"It's a huge cavern, full of amazing colours and lines."

"Yes," Raph says. "Matter is disappearing. What you saw in there is the simulation unravelling. Matter and form are coming undone from the inside out."

"The Game we live in is shutting down, Danni," Carl says.

"How?" I ask. "Why?"

"Excellent questions," Raphael says. "More reasons why we need the Thirteen. Maybe they can help us understand it, and reverse or at least slow down the process."

36

It's difficult to piece together what we've missed this past week inside the Game. The screens have come back on and suddenly we're seeing an Earth that is entirely different from the one we all knew. Civilization has been reduced to small groups of people trying their best to simply survive. All advancement has disappeared, and Earth seems like a very depressing place.

When we focus on everyone's most followed player, Danielle, the questions come fast and furious. What's Danielle been doing for these past ten years inside the Game? Who was she battling as the feeds came back up? What's this talk of Stephanie becoming the Devil and how will that affect the rest of the population?

Most alarming is what fans witnessed when Danielle entered the cave and saw the very matrix of the Game beginning to unravel and shut down.

What does it all mean? Is this all part of the Thirtieth Anniversary celebration events, or is it something more serious than that? Is the Game falling apart, and if it is, what does that mean for our world economy and the lives of our children who are trapped inside while the framework that keeps them alive begins to crumble all around them?

The Game Fan Channel 22

Trew

Danielle's team sat in the Command Centre waiting for Trew to arrive. Everyone had spent the last few hours watching every live feed they could, specifically Danielle and those around her.

The door opened and Trew strode in. He moved directly to the head of the table and sat down.

"Here's how we handle things," he began. "Earth is in utter chaos and we don't have time to do everything that needs doing. I want the world to watch the Game without me having to hold their hands and answer every little question about what's going on. The best way to get them off our backs is for me to do a quick press release. I will tell them that yes, this is all part of the Thirtieth Anniversary celebrations and they have nothing to worry about." He looked around the table and everyone nodded.

"Next, I want as much information as quickly as we can get it. We only have a few weeks with Danni in the Game, and I have no clue how long until the Game comes unravelled. We make sure our girl finishes number one and piece together the other puzzle chunks as we go. Primary focus should be this; we need to make contact with our Timeless on the inside immediately," Trew said.

"From what we've seen so far, that's not gonna happen, boss," Michelle said. "They don't meditate much anymore as far as we can tell, which is how we contacted them. The other avenues aren't available to us since the news and media outlets remain dead on Earth. There's no way to contact anyone in the Game right now."

"This isn't good," Cooper announced from his seat. Trew threw him a glare but said nothing. His statement was correct; this was not good at all.

"Then tap into the social network feeds, blogs and Game update programs," Trew said. "It looks like the best way for us to get up to speed is the same way the fans are doing it... become immersed in the glut of information pouring in and sort it as best we can."

"What about Stephanie taking over the Colony?" Lilith asked.

"I'd love to know how she became the Devil," Trew said. "I can't believe it's true, but it is. Without being able to make contact, all we can do is watch and hope the right talent is in place for Danni to do well."

"What if the Game ends before we get them all out?" Nadine asked.

Trew looked at her and shook his head. "That's not going to happen," he assured the group. "Keep your focus, people, and let's spend the next couple of weeks doing our absolute best to win this."

Trew nodded to Cooper and started to move towards the exit. Cooper followed him out; the two said nothing until they entered the elevator.

"I need to contact Thorn," Trew said.

"Easy enough," Cooper kept his gaze on the numbers as they counted down on the elevator wall. "He's sitting in Sylvia's office at the moment, waiting for you."

Trew made a wry face and nodded.

===

"I didn't realize you knew about Sylvia," Trew said as he entered the office and saw Thorn sitting at his desk.

"There is very little going on in this simulation that I don't know about," Thorn said.

"You know what's going on inside the Game as well."

"Yes," Thorn nodded.

"It would've been handy to get updates along the way," Trew snapped. He was frustrated by lack of information and the snowballing events both inside the Game and out.

"That's not allowed, Trew."

"Fine." Trew slashed his hand dismissively. He knew Thorn only stayed in this reality for limited amounts of time and he had no intention of wasting it on pointless small talk. "Sylvia, what's Thorn doing here?"

"Asking me for random Earth measurements and figures, specifically regarding areas that are disintegrating into the base matrix structure."

"What can you tell me?" Trew asked as he looked at Thorn.

Thorn scanned the information he'd compiled. "I can tell you that Brandon shouldn't have gone into the Game."

"Why?"

"His energy signature is uniquely measured by the simulation called Tygon," Thorn explained. "It was constructed for him."

"So?"

"It's complicated," Thorn shook his head. "The easy answer is this; the energy used to power this simulation is linked with Brandon's position inside of it. When he is on Tygon there's a certain amount of power being used by the computers running the simulation. When he's out of the simulation, it takes considerably less power to run it."

"So when he died and returned to the Dream, that gave Tygon more time before power is lost and the simulation ends?" Cooper asked.

"Yes," Thorn nodded, "but he negated that benefit by coming back in. That didn't matter too much because we were still operating on the same timeline. Now that he's entered the Game, however, it's accelerated the power usage. Going into a simulation within a simulation draws exponentially more power from the grid. Since we only have a limited amount of power left in the Dream to run this simulation..."

"Brandon has shortened the overall life of the entire project," Trew finished Thorn's sentence.

"Exactly."

"Did he know this would happen?" Trew asked.

Thorn nodded.

"How much time remains?" Cooper asked.

"That's what I'm trying to determine," Thorn said. "I'm having Sylvia report all incidences of Matrix break down inside Earth and using the information to calculate how much time is left."

"Any luck?" Trew asked.

Thorn barked out a bitter laugh. "If luck is what you can call it," he said. "I have a reasonable idea of how long things will last at the current pace."

"And...?"

"Danni intended to live to the age of one hundred and forty years inside the Game, and for whatever reason, Sylvia was willing to allow it to happen."

Trew nodded.

"That meant seven Tygon weeks remained to her inside the Game, or seven more weeks before the Game ended for good. With Brandon entering the Game, the number has been reduced... drastically."

"How long?" Trew asked.

Thorn looked uncomfortable. "Thanks to Brandon's decision to head in, the Game will cease to exist in less than three weeks. Instead of seventy years, they now have less than thirty to reach their goal."

37

Danielle

I look at Raphael and wink. He smiles back and nods.

We're waiting at the Colony's front gate. When we first strolled up, it took only a few moments for guards to shout down and ask our business. Both young men, likely no older than eighteen, they didn't seem to recognize me as they scanned us with bored looks. Giving them my name and announcing who I wished to speak with seemed to wake them up. They told us to wait here, and that's what we've been doing for the past fifteen minutes.

The doors screech open and two women stroll out to meet us. They appear strong, limber, and confident in their movements. As they get closer I can see them smiling at Raphael with excitement. Both women are red haired and beautiful, the woman in the lead is about two inches shorter than the other, but other than the height difference they could be twins.

They are fair-skinned, with smooth white complexions. The shorter one has bouncy, curly hair that rests lightly on her shoulders, while the other's matching auburn locks hang midway down her back. They both possess lean, muscular builds and their bearing matches that of martial artists who've been training all their lives. They wear black leather leggings, vests, and comfortable looking thigh-high boots. Blade hilts are visible at various places on their bodies; the shorter one has one in her boot and another on a sheath attached to her left arm, with the handle pointing downwards to allow for a quick draw. The taller of the two has a small throwing knife on her left shoulder and a longer blade sheathed cleverly on her right thigh. I can see what looks like the same pattern on the ornate silver hilt of a long blade that must be similar to my own peeking up behind each of their left shoulders. As they get close I notice bright crimson flecks swimming lazily in their eyes. These must be the sisters that Raphael spoke of.

"Raphael, you old dog, look at you! I swear he gets more handsome as the years go on, doesn't he, sister?" The tall one spreads her arms widely and Raphael embraces her with a hearty laugh.

The shorter one grins and watches me with a friendly smile on her face until Raphael releases the first woman and hugs her.

"Hello, Sisters," Raph says. "It looks as if nothing can take the smiles from your faces, even all of this pain and strife that we now see in the world."

The shorter woman laughs and slaps him on the back lightly before disengaging from his arms. "We are Infernals, Brother. The worse things get, the bigger our smiles become."

"Then the two of you must be joyous all the time," he says.

The taller woman shakes her head slightly as she looks my way and meets my eyes. "That's not the case, Raphael. There are always challenges to face, but we are happy to see you today, that's for certain. Are you going to introduce us to your friend? The guards claim that she's Danielle. Is it true the leader of the Gamers has returned after being away for so long?"

Raphael smiles and walks over to put his hand on my shoulder. "That's right, ladies, the prodigal daughter returns to claim her flock. I'm pleased to introduce you to Danielle Radfield. Danielle, the shorter of these two beauties is Skylar, and the taller is her baby sister Courtney."

Both women offer their hands in greeting, and I smile pleasantly as I shake each one in turn. "These are the two who can't seem to control the leader that they helped make?" I ask.

Courtney, the taller of the two laughs at my comment and nods her head. "Of course we can't control our leader, darling. What kind of leader would Stephanie be if others could force their will on her?"

"Exactly," Skylar agrees. "Are you going to tell us that Raphael can get you to do anything that isn't in your head already?"

I grin and nod. "I suppose she wouldn't last long if she was seen as weak," I admit.

"Exactly," Courtney admitted. "I'm proud to say that among the Infernals, Stephanie is being hailed as one of the strongest leaders to take the position of Devil in ages."

"I'm happy to hear that," I say. "I will wish her continued prosperity in her role... as soon as she agrees to move on and leave my people alone."

Skylar giggles and looks at Raphael playfully. "This girl is a treat to listen to, Brother," she says. "She's like a baby kitten, convinced that it's a mighty hunter."

Raphael raises his eyebrows and nods. I wonder what game they're playing at. Neither woman seems impressed by me in the slightest. I guess that's no surprise, considering I'm a young mortal and these women have centuries of experience under their belts.

"We aren't here to discuss details, Sky," Courtney says. She walks over and grabs her shorter, older sister gently by the arm. "Let's escort them to the rendezvous point as instructed."

Skylar nods in agreement. "Of course, Sister. If the two of you would be so kind as to follow us, we will take you to Stephanie. She looks forward to seeing you again after all these years apart."

Raph and I start to follow the two women, expecting them to head for the front gate. They guess our thoughts and shake their heads in unison.

"She isn't in the city," Courtney says. "We will take you to her, but first we must show you something on the way."

"You have to see it for yourself." Skylar's tone echoes the seriousness of her sister's. "We're going to fly over certain portions of the city. You have to understand that we're not responsible for what you're going to see."

"What is it?" I can tell from their faces that it isn't good.

"People are dying," Courtney says. "Not just a few; tens of thousands of people."

"What?" I ask in alarm. "How? Why?"

"We don't know," Skylar says. "It started only a short time ago. At first we thought there was a disease or plague going through the Colony, so we began to quarantine the sick from the healthy. We have healers as good as Samantha here, and they haven't been able to cure the sick."

"What are the symptoms?" Raphael asks.

"First, they get tired and weak," Courtney says. "Then they stop eating and their complexion becomes grey. A couple days later they simply lie down and die."

"No coughing, fever, visible signs of illness?" I ask.

The women shake their heads.

"Curious," Raphael says.

"It gets worse," Skylar says. "We started hearing from the other colonies around the globe."

"What other colonies?" I ask.

"Stephanie will tell you more about that," Courtney says. "In a nutshell, she's set up colonies all over the world to enable people to live safely."

"That doesn't sound like any Devil I know," Raphael says.

"Steph had a couple ideas that required bodies and souls," Skylar flashes him a grin. "That doesn't matter at the moment. Reports are telling us that the same thing is happening all over the world."

"Do the victims have anything in common?" I have a feeling that she's going to nod.

Both women nod and a chill comes over me.

"All the people who are dying," Courtney says, "are NPCs."

===

Trew

"Not one single player is dying from this plague?" Trew looked away from the monitor where Danielle was meeting with the Sisters.

"That must be the case," Michelle said. "Almost no players are being ejected from the Game. Just the normal number of old avatars who are dying from old age and a few accidental deaths from bad luck."

Trew felt his chest tighten in panic. The rest of the people in the room didn't understand that every single person living on Tygon was an NPC as well!

What if it's a digital plague that can jump to our reality? He thought.

"We need to find a solution to this," Trew said. "We need to help them."

"Why?" Michelle asked. "Shouldn't we be glad it's only affecting computer code? If it crosses over and starts killing players, then we have a concern, but it's only killing NPCs."

Trew's pulse hammered loudly in his head. The sounds in the room faded away as thoughts and feelings overwhelmed him the same way they had when he'd first watched the video of

Brandon's life and learned the truth about NPCs. He wanted to stand up and scream at the top of his lungs. He wanted to tell everyone in the room there was no such thing as 'just an NPC!' He wanted to share this incredible burden that had been thrust upon him so he wouldn't have to carry it alone.

With wild eyes he looked at Cooper who was watching him intently as if he could hear the struggle going on inside of him. Cooper nodded softly and held his palm flat and lowered it gently towards the floor.

He's telling me to calm down, Trew thought. I can't lose it, especially not over something like this. There's no way anyone will believe me anyway. Memories of being George Knight inside the Game surfaced. Believing with absolute certainty that he was living inside a computer simulation, while no one believed him. The looks and ridicule that had resulted from his attempts to share what he knew to be true, while being believed by no one.

For some reason Trew knew the same thing was happening again, only this time it was the knowledge that Tygon was populated entirely by NPCs.

Trew closed his eyes and tried to slow his breathing. He summoned the golden glow, letting it bathe him in its calming embrace. Eventually the anxiety began to fade. When the waves of terror, fear, and loneliness had subsided to a faint pulse, he opened his eyes.

Everyone in the room stared at him with concern. He stole a quick glance at Cooper who nodded slowly and smiled encouragingly. It had passed. Everything was okay.

"There must be a reason for this," Trew said out loud.

He looked at the monitor again and watched as Danni took flight with Raphael and the sisters. In silence he watched as they flew over large areas of the Colony. Once vibrant sections of living subdivisions were now empty, dark areas along the outer edges of the settlement. Immense burial sites had been excavated, and people worked slowly to place the bodies of the dead into the gigantic pits they had dug.

Trew looked around the room at the faces of Danni's team. They watched with curious interest, but it was obvious that they didn't mourn for the loss of these NPCs. It was apparent that they felt no connection with the empty, digitally manufactured avatars that were being buried in mass graves.

Trew felt something, though.

He knew that if his friends and family died, he would be crushed. He knew that perhaps in the Dream, viewers would watch with detached interest as NPCs lived and died on Tygon, but to Trew and every other citizen, the losses would be very real.

His mind began to race, wondering why he'd been shown the truth of something that no one else could know, first in the Game as George Knight, and now on Tygon as Trew. His mind worked furiously to put the pieces of a puzzle together that only he seemed capable of seeing.

And then, in a flash, he had it.

"Oh, my God!" he said.

The others looked at him with curiosity.

Lilith thought she saw tears in his eyes and wondered at what was making him act this way. "What is it, Trew?" she asked in concern.

"I think I just figured it out," he whispered in awe.

"Figured what out? Why the NPCs are dying off?"

"No." Trew looked seriously at Cooper, who scrutinized him closely and raised his eyebrows in surprise at what he saw.

"I think I just figured out the entire purpose of the Game."

38

Danielle

After the Sisters do a flyby of the Colony, they hover in the air for a moment to speak with us.

"Not good." Courtney meets my eyes and can read the agreement in them. "Let's take you to see Steph now. She's camped a short distance from here. Follow us."

The women turn and begin to fly toward the east. Twenty minutes later we reach the bluffs where Raphael's group has been holed up. There's a large clearing surrounded by old trees below. On a flat, rocky surface in the middle of the clearing are three tables with chairs arranged around them.

We drop to the ground and Stephanie stands from her seat at the centre table. She's holding a glass of pale golden liquid, which she raises as we draw near.

"The favoured leader has returned," she says with a smile. Her expression looks as kind and loving as it always did, but somehow I have trouble buying it.

"Stephanie," I say coolly. "You look better than ever. It would seem that being the queen of all that is evil in the world agrees with you."

Stephanie nods and continues to smile. Her eyes flit questioningly to Raph, revealing more vulnerability than I would have expected. I look at Raph in time to see him smile and nod. She returns his grin and walks towards him as the two embrace warmly.

"It's good to see you again, little Sister," he says. "I'm glad that you survived the succession."

"Thanks, Raph," she says. "I couldn't have done it without help from all of my friends."

"I'm glad you've done well for yourself, Steph," I say, "although I would be a lot happier if you hadn't taken over the Colony. Before I left, Daniel expressed an interest in doing the same thing, and I would have gone to war to prevent it. For some reason, Raph, Carl, and the others let you walk right in and take over. Raph said there were valid reasons and assured me that when the time was right, you would explain things to me."

"Let's enjoy a meal first," Stephanie says, "then we can get down to business."

I shake my head. "How many are dead?" I ask.

She looks at me for a moment and then sighs heavily. "You always were business first, pleasure if there was enough time for it. So often there wasn't enough time for pleasure with you, Danni. How much life you missed out on over the years..."

I smile and shake my head. "Some lives are for pleasure," I reply. "Other lives require different results. I guess it's easy for you to lose track of that, since life is just one long episode for you, Stephanie. I kind of like how us players do it. Besides," I say, "I did have a significant amount of pleasure during this life."

"I guess that's true," she admits. "Let's take a seat and I'll fill you in on what's been happening."

We move to the centre table and sit down. The sisters sit on either side of Stephanie and we sit across from them.

Stephanie pours drinks for everyone and raises her glass to make a toast. "Welcome home, Danni," she says.

I clink glasses with the others and take a drink of the light, fruity wine. No one speaks at the table; I'm not sure if they're waiting for me to speak, but I'm still waiting for the answer to my first question.

Stephanie chuckles and nods. She's known me since I was a young girl and I haven't changed that much.

"Danni, it's absolutely boring being in charge of a large colony of mortals. You know that better than anyone here."

A slight grin forms against my will. She's right, it's a nightmare. Of all the things I ever did in my life, governing the Colony was the most arduous task I experienced.

"Yeah, I thought so," Stephanie says. "To keep things brief, there are many things that Infernals do to spread confusion and discord across the world, but there's one very important rule that all Timeless must follow."

"Maintaining the balance," Raphael says and the others nod in agreement.

"Exactly," Stephanie agrees. "The balance must be maintained. There have been times throughout the history of the world when severe events have happened which forced the Timeless to abandon their traditional roles and work together for a common cause. If chaos becomes too widespread, then Infernals tone it back. If order threatens to take over, then the Eternals begin to do nasty things." She shrugs. "The simple answer to your question is this; the Day made things too chaotic, so Infernals were called on to help add a little bit of order."

"As simple as that?" I ask.

Stephanie laughs. "Of course it wasn't as simple as that. Horrible events have occurred, but years have passed and the dust has settled, leaving me solidly in place as the Infernal leader. I surrounded myself with powerful allies," — she motions to the two sisters — "so that I could implement changes to help further the cause of order and assist with restoring the balance." Her eyes flash with an evil look. "The sooner we get things back on track, the quicker we can get back to doing what our crimson eyes really want us to do... start breaking things again."

"You expect me to believe that you took over leadership of the Colony to help?"

Stephanie shrugs. "At this point I don't really care what you think, Danni. I left things to the status quo, for the most part; I think you'll find that the majority of the population still belongs to the Gamer movement. Ask Raphael if you don't believe me."

"Why did Raphael and the other Eternals leave, then?" I challenge.

Stephanie chuckles. "I bet you haven't even asked him that question, have you?"

My cheeks flush with embarrassment which confirms the truth of her statement. "Oh, Danni," Stephanie says. "You must learn to find out all the facts before you go storming into a situation. One of the follies of youth, I suppose. Do try to remember this lesson when you return to your home world."

"You're willing to leave the Colony, then?" I ask.

"I've already left." She spreads her arms to remind me that we aren't in the settlement. "If you're that keen about reclaiming the job, then I'm glad to hand the reins back to you."

"What about the Thirteen?" I ask.

Stephanie raises her drink and looks at me over the edge of her glass. "What about them?"

"Where are they?"

"Gone." She finishes her drink and sets it down on the table.

"What do you mean, gone?" I ask.

Stephanie glances at Raphael. "Did you show her the cavern?"

Raphael nods and Stephanie looks back at me. "They weren't helping here, Danni. We sent them on."

I turn to Raphael with a look of confusion on my face. "What is she talking about?"

"The Thirteen are important for another game, Danni," Stephanie says. "I don't think you'll get to see how that one turns out... but we sent them to a different part of the world. They will be safe there until the opportunity comes for them to be put into play."

"What about the power outage?" I was really hoping they would confirm to the rest that things were back online. Why did I ever agree to Shane's ridiculous condition?

"I'm not certain that it's important anymore," Stephanie says.

"Of course it's important," I say. I spent seven years looking for the solution to that problem. There's no way I will believe it was all a waste of time, although I did accomplish many positive outcomes for people along the way. I shake my head and continue to talk. "The world needs power, Stephanie. The past ten years have been hell for everyone who was lucky enough to survive."

"Do you think everything will suddenly be all right if people can text each other again?" she asks. "Perhaps e-mail will make the world's considerable problems just melt away?"

"There's more to it than that and you know it."

Stephanie runs her hand through her hair and rubs her eyes. "Look, I'm willing to do whatever you like. If you want me to take my group and go live on the other side of the world, then I'll head out. If you want our help, then I'll help. I know you find it hard to trust the Devil, and I don't blame you, sweetie, really I don't." She looks at Raphael and then the Sisters. "This world seems to be unravelling. I think we should try our best to find out if we can stop that from happening. In my humble opinion, that's more important than getting video games and soap operas functioning again."

I sigh and shake my head. "I really don't know what to do at this point," I say.

"Perhaps some time to consider things will help," Raphael offers.

"Does anyone here know why so many people are dying?" I ask again.

No one answers me. Finally Courtney speaks. "There is one theory, but we can't know for certain."

"What theory?"

"When we become Timeless, there are key events which we are briefed on. None of us expect to be around when they occur, because most sound too absurd for even us to believe. This might be one of those events."

A sound interrupts her from my left. The familiar hissing of a doorway of light begins to sizzle and hum as the outline forms ten feet away. After a few moments the full doorway is complete and two people step out of it. I recognize one of them immediately.

"Hey, Melissa," I say. "Who's your friend?"

Melissa looks over and then runs towards me with a huge grin on her face. I stand up just in time to catch her as she throws herself into my arms. "I'm so glad to see you again, Danni! When did you get back?"

"Just a few days ago," I say. "Where have you been and who's your young friend?"

Melissa releases me and looks over at the young man standing politely off to the side. The doorway has disappeared, and he seems to be enjoying the scene from the sidelines. He looks very distinctive in his black jeans, T-shirt and black hoodie. His eyes are unusual — do I detect silver flecks floating in them?

"This is Azrael," she says. "I just met him a couple of days ago. He has some very interesting ideas to present." Melissa looks at the young man and waves for him to come closer. "I don't know how you knew she was here, but you were right," she says to him.

The young man approaches, and as he comes closer it becomes clear that his brown eyes do indeed contain silver flecks... exactly like mine.

"Azrael?" Raph asks.

"Yes," the young man replies. He's smiling comfortably, and there seems to be a noticeable air of authority about him. I look at the Timeless and they appear to be instinctively deferring to him with both their posture and body language.

Raphael moves to get a closer look at his face. "Azrael?" he asks. "Is that truly you, Brother?"

The young man nods his head. Raphael cries out and wraps him in a huge bear hug. The two laugh and slap each others' backs, acting as if they are long lost brothers or relatives.

When they finally release each other, I ask Raphael the obvious question. "You two know each other?"

"Oh, yes," Raphael says. "This is our brother, Azrael."

"Is he an Infernal or Eternal?" I ask.

"He is neither," Azrael answers for himself. "I am the Archangel of Death, come to collect and guide souls to their true homes, Danni."

"What does that mean?" I ask him.

"It means that time has almost run out," he replies. "I would like to tell you about some very exciting things that are about to occur on Earth."

39

Trew

"**What just happened?**" someone asked as the picture and sound dissolved into hissing static.

"It looks like Azrael remembered to scramble the signal," Michelle said.

"Who is he?" Lilith asked. "Isn't he a bit young to be a Timeless?" she looked around the room at the blank faces. "Does anyone here know who he is?"

"He said he was the archangel of death," Nadine said.

"That sounds ominous," Lilith replied. "Especially since we all know angels don't exist."

"There seem to be a lot of avatars dying inside the Game at the moment." Trew steered the conversation in another direction. He wasn't about to tell the group that Brandon had returned to Tygon, and then he'd jumped into the Game. Trew believed that he knew exactly what Brandon was up to, and he would continue to watch events unfold until certain that his hunch was correct.

"NPCs," Michelle stressed again. "I know from a Game point of view it's somehow significant, but have any of us been able to figure it out?"

I have, Trew thought to himself.

"What are they discussing?" one of the team members asked. "We just got the feeds back up and now they scramble us? It's frustrating!"

"I want a count of how many NPCs have perished inside the Game," Trew announced.

Michelle looked at her tablet and quickly tapped a few commands. "Just under thirty thousand," she said. "Not many at all."

"What if we were talking about players?" Trew asked.

"Thank goodness we aren't," Lilith said.

"What if the problem jumps and starts affecting players?"

It felt like a heavy blanket had been dropped over the entire room.

"That's not funny," Michelle said.

"Exactly," Trew said. "Let's do our best to scour the feeds and see if anyone suspects what is making this happen." He looked at the group, trying to hide his anger at their treatment of NPCs, but understanding how they could feel so little for them. Just a few days ago he'd felt the same way. "I would like to find a cure for this epidemic so that we can stop anyone from suddenly dying inside the Game."

"Is this Azrael causing it?" someone asked.

Trew looked at Cooper and shook his head, raising his eyebrows for confirmation from Cooper. Cooper shook his head, indicating that Brandon wasn't causing the problem as far as he knew.

"I don't think so," Trew said, "but it wouldn't hurt to keep eyes on him as best we can."

Trew stood up. "I need at least half an hour of rest. Cooper, come wake me soon, please."

Cooper stood to follow. "I'm not leaving you alone," he said.

Trew began to protest, but he knew that it would be in vain. "Okay, let's go, then," he said.

They walked down the hallway towards one of the nearby rest quarters.

"How long are we going to do this dance?" Trew asked.

"I don't know," Cooper said. "I guess that depends on how long it takes you to come out and ask me a direct question."

Trew stopped walking and looked at Cooper, then shrugged and resumed his walk down the hall. "I guess it will be a while longer, then," he said.

Cooper chuckled. "I guess so."

Trew opened the door to the small rest area. He looked over his shoulder and asked the question that had been on his mind since the moment he guessed what was happening. "They're not NPCs, are they?" he asked.

Cooper's eyes shifted from Trew's to something inside the room. He looked surprised, and Trew quickly swung his head around to see what Cooper was looking at.

Trew had seen this old man before, but not on Tygon.

He sat comfortably on the couch, his bare legs crossed, and the black laceless boots swinging gently. The garbage bags that made up his outfit looked cleaner than Trew would have expected, and his white hair stood up and pointed in a multitude of directions. One arm was stretched out comfortably along the back of the couch, the light glinting off the red metal of his bottle cap gloves. He smiled as the two men stood in the doorway looking at him.

"Hello, Trew," he said. "I couldn't help but overhear your question for Cooper," he smiled and waved a hand for them to enter the room. "Why don't you boys come in so we can have a little chat? I'll start by answering that question."

The old man's eyes glinted with mischief as he leaned forward and spoke softly. "You are absolutely correct, Trew, the NPCs dying inside the Game are not NPCs..."

40

Azrael

I look at the group and smile. It's so good to see Raph after all these years. The sisters are the same as always; I should tell them their parents say hi and are happy that they're doing so well. Unfortunately this isn't the time for that conversation; maybe later. Stephanie looks great as well, although she was never a big Brandon fan.

"I was hoping Carl would be with you," I say.

Raphael smiles and nods, "He's not far from us. You'll come back with us and see the others, right?"

I shake my head. "Soon I will see them all," I assure him, "but at the moment there are more important matters." I look at them and shake my finger like a parent. "You all forget to scramble signals. The entire planet could have been watching this little meeting."

"Oh, damn," Stephanie says.

"Wait a minute…" Raphael cocks his head to one side. "Does that mean the feeds are back up? Do we have power again?"

"Who said the feeds ever went down?" I fight back a smile as faces flush with embarrassment. I'm not gonna tell them the feeds did go down when the power went out; they should be more cautious. I look around the camp and shake my head. "I mean, how much effort does it take to scramble the freaking signal? Even if there is no signal, you should be going through the procedure anyway."

Everyone looks properly chastised as they nod in agreement. I wonder if any of them will bother to check the power sources to see that everything's back on. I look at Danni and I know she's aware of the truth, but for some reason she isn't sharing the news. Oh, well, I'll let her play whatever game she's got going on.

"Now listen up," I say. "We don't have much time. I've been helping Melissa fine tune her abilities over the past few days and I think she's ready."

"Ready for what?" Danni asks.

"Ready to show you something, Danielle," I say. "Melissa taught you to fly, right?"

"Yes," she says.

"Okay," I say. "She has an even bigger lesson for you to master. Over the next few days the three of us will work together to learn a new skill, and I cannot stress how important it is that you master it as quickly as possible. It's what you were born to do, what you've been working towards your entire life."

"What is it?" Danni asks.

I grin. "If I told you, I doubt you'd believe me. I think the best thing to do is show you."

Danni nods slowly, and my grin widens.

This is going to be exciting!

41

Trew

Trew sat down at the small table near the couch. Cooper sat on the small bed directly beside Trew; the room was small.

"I can't stay long," the old man said, "and I'm not entirely certain if I'm here too soon or not." He shrugged his shoulders. "I think we're close enough that it doesn't matter if the timing is off by a little bit; it's not an exact science, anyway."

"What isn't?" Trew asked.

"The whole game," the old man answered, "but I'm rambling, and it doesn't really matter."

"I've seen you before," Trew said.

"Really?" the old man's bushy white eyebrows shot up curiously. "I don't remember that. When did we meet?"

"We didn't meet. I watched the video history of Brandon's life."

The old man frowns and he looks towards the ceiling, lost in thought for a moment. Then he nods and snaps his fingers. He points at Trew with the memory solidly in his mind. "When he was an owl, right?" he asked.

"Yes."

"That seems like so long ago." He nodded at the memory. "The kid has been busy since then, hasn't he?"

"Yes, he has."

"Okay," the old man slapped his knee and his gloves chimed with a distinct sing-song sound. "Let's get this show on the road. I have places to be. Wish I could spend more time with you, Trew, but that will have to wait for later. I have two messages to relay to you, then I must be off."

"What are they?" Trew asked.

"Number one," the old man held up a finger. "I am confirming that you are absolutely, ninety-five percent, on the right track."

"Why only ninety-five percent?"

The old man chuckled. "Because nothing is one hundred percent guaranteed," he said. "Ask the General or Thorn about that. They both made extensive plans and played the long game, only to have everything they'd worked so hard for turn to failure in the final hours. There's a good lesson to be learned from their experiences, Trew. You can do everything right and still lose the game."

"You can also learn from your losses and try to do better in the next play," Trew said.

"Spoken like a true player!" the old man exclaimed. "I love your way of looking at things. What if this is your last play, though?"

"I can't play any differently," Trew said. "To become suddenly cautious would be to ignore everything I've ever learned and reduce my chances of winning when it was most important to do so."

The old man closed his eyes and smiled. "You're like a refreshing glass of cold water after walking in the dessert for a week without a drop to drink," he said.

"It doesn't matter what I think or do," Trew said. "I'm just an NPC."

The old man's smile faded and his eyes shot open quickly. "So what?" he asked.

"I'm nothing more than a computer generated life form, and so is everything and everyone on this planet."

The old man shook his head from side to side and made a face as if he'd just eaten a bowl of lemons. "Of course you're an NPC; you live in a computer simulation, boy. What does that have to do with anything? You make it sound as if you don't exist simply because you're made from energy and code."

"That's exactly what it means."

"Perhaps I came here to talk to you about this, then," he looked at Cooper and smiled. "Cooper? Where you come from, are you made from code and energy?"

Cooper started to shake his head negatively but he stopped and considered the question fully. Finally he nodded. "Yeah, I guess when you put it that way, I am made from code and energy."

"No, he's not," Trew said. "He's made from living, organic cells."

"Which are built from code contained in the protein strands that exist in his cells," the old man said. "If he has no energy, then he dies. I don't see any difference between Cooper and you, Trew. Reality is subjective. The truth is that Cooper might even be digital but the programmers that built his world made the code look more organic than yours."

"We look organic," Trew corrected him. "There's no way for us to tell that we aren't anything except real living creatures."

"There you go, then," the old man nodded. "You are real, living creatures."

"But..."

"No." The old man made a chopping motion with his hand.

"There must be..." Trew tried to object.

"Stop it." The old man shook his head. "You're as real as any life form on any planet in any simulation in any universe. If you don't see that, then look at it a different way until you do." He fixed Trew with an intense stare as if daring him to disagree.

Trew thought about it and then nodded slowly. "Okay," he admitted. "You do make a convincing argument."

"Good." The old man held up his hands again. "Back to my messages, then. Number one: You're on the right track."

"Ninety-five percent certain," Trew said.

"Exactly," the old man winked. "And number two: Tune in to Melissa's channel and do not take your eyes off of her until it's time to."

"How will I know when it's time to take my eyes off of her?"

The old man's eyes sparkled. "You will know, Trew. Until that moment, keep your focus solely on her."

"And after that?"

"After that, you get good and ready for all hell to break loose."

42

Carl

I hear her enter the room and almost move. It's been a while since anyone has crept in, but I remember her threat, and regain control of myself to avoid giving away that I know she's here.

I breathe evenly, as if I'm still asleep; it's an old habit and takes no real effort. Instead, my mind focuses on listening to her for any signs that she'll attack.

Minutes pass and my gut tells me she won't make a move. Pity.

"I thought after all these years apart you might finally try to put me down," I growl without moving. I hear a slight shift in her breathing, indicating that I've startled her slightly. Good; she thought I was sleeping.

"How long have you known I was here?" she asks.

"Since you stepped near my room," I roll over and look at her.

"I've stood in this exact spot many times over the years," Danni says.

I nod. "Twenty-one times, to be exact."

Her mouth twitches slightly as she struggles not to smile. "Twenty-two, actually," she says. "There was one time I could have surprised you, then."

I chuckle and shake my head. "Don't play with me when it comes to my craft, girl. There have only been twenty-one times. You're not good enough to get past me in my own bed."

She looks at me for a moment, then nods. "You're right," she admits. "There were only twenty-one."

"If it makes you feel any better, even I wouldn't be able to sneak in here undetected. I've set alarms and wards which are impossible to deactivate. If it was a normal kill, I'm sure you could have gotten in without being noticed."

"Thanks," her smile widens. "That does make me feel better."

I sit up in bed and point to a chair in the corner. She nods and moves to take a seat.

"What have you been up to these past few years?" Danni asks.

"Nothing exciting," I shrug. "Helped Stephanie take the spot from Daniel, then eliminated some of her stronger opposition. After that she didn't need much assistance, so I've been rusting in a corner for the past few years."

"I seriously doubt you're rusty," Danni says.

"Maybe not rusty," I admit, "but if you rest a blade in the corner for long enough it'll lose its edge, even if you clean it and keep the rust away."

"Do you wish you'd remained an Infernal instead?" she asks.

I think about it for a few moments and then shake my head. "I don't think so," I say.

"Why not?"

"Because I would have stopped many of your plans from succeeding, which would have resulted in the world ending much sooner."

Danni laughs lightly. "You're confident in your abilities, Carl, I'll give you that. The world is ending anyway; perhaps it wouldn't matter what side you're on."

"Maybe," I shrug. "I think that this reality no longer depends on the actions of the Timeless."

"What makes you say that?" she asks.

I tap my heart and say nothing. She nods.

Danni looks at me and her features soften. I ignore it, and after a few moments she speaks. "I don't know much about you, Carl, and I find myself wishing from time to time that I did."

"There's not much to know," I say.

Her expression says that she doesn't believe me, but she says nothing. "What do you think happens now?" she asks.

"I think things end... or they don't."

"You don't sound too concerned either way."

"I'm not," I say. "I've had my fill of living. I would have died long ago, except I can't."

"Why not?"

"Because I'm not a quitter."

Danni looks at me and nods her head. "No, you are definitely not a quitter." She reaches behind her back and pulls out the sever spike that I used to kill her husband. Her thumb presses a switch and it hums like a hungry nest of bees responding to danger. "I could end it for you now, if you'd like?"

"Darlin'," I grin, "letting you sink that into me would be like committing suicide. There's no way you have the skills to take me out of the Game. There were times when I wish you did, and you've come a very long way in the skilled combat department, but you can't best me."

She turns the sever spike off and puts it away. With a sigh, she leans back and rests her feet on the edge of my bed. "Any idea how this all ends?" she asks.

"There are a number of ways it can end. Some of them I know about."

"Any that will make me feel positive?"

"Not a single one."

"Really? Not one single good ending?"

"They only prepare us for the worst," I tell her. "No one worries too much about the happy endings. They tend to take care of themselves if they occur."

"I guess that's true." She stands up and comes close. "I hate what you did to Trew, but you've spent many years doing your best to do right by me, Carl. I would still like to kill you horribly for stealing him away from me, but I owe you a thank you for saving my life; likely more times than I will know."

She surprises me by leaning in and giving me a gentle kiss on the cheek. I don't respond, but I can feel the electricity travel from her lips and into the very centre of my chest, spreading a warmth throughout my body that I haven't felt in years.

Danni leans away and looks at me, scrutinizing my face for any type of reaction; I keep it cold as stone.

She giggles and pats my cheek. Seeing her smile makes me wish this moment would never end. "That's okay, tough guy," she says. "You can pretend it means nothing, but I know you liked it."

She walks towards the door and stops to look at me over her shoulder. "If I don't see you again, you take care of yourself, Carl. You're a better man than you know. It would be good to see that man make an appearance from time to time." She pauses and then smiles. "If a happy ending should happen to occur."

The door closes and I continue to watch the space she just occupied. Slowly my hand touches the spot on my cheek where she kissed me. I smile slightly, and out loud I say, "Twenty-one times, Danni. Each time I saved your life, you came to my room to decide if you would kill me or not."

Both of us knew the number.

43

"This is Lisa Rohansen reporting for the Game News Channel and we are coming to you live from outside of the Central Game Centre building.

"A major broadcast sent out to all members of the Gamer movement ended just a few moments ago. Trew was kind enough to allow me to listen in so that I could report this breaking news to you as accurately as possible. Something unprecedented has just occurred, and I must ask for your patience while I do my best to convey what I've learned.

"I...

"Sorry, let me try again. Trew has told the five hundred million members of the Gamer movement that...

"Okay, I think I can put this into words. I'm so sorry, I don't remember being this flustered in years. Here's what he said to them.

"He's hired them all.

"Trew is paying each player who became a member of the Gamer movement to work for Strayne Industries for the next two weeks. I've seen the numbers and in two weeks Trew will spend a significant portion of his own personal money to cut a huge paycheck to over five hundred million children.

"They've been hired to observe the Game for the next few days, and after that they will all be sent back into the Game with one specific purpose. I am not at liberty to tell you what that purpose is, but let me assure you that when I heard the task it made absolutely no sense to me at all. We will have to watch the Game for the next two weeks to see how this affects both the simulated reality of Earth and our true reality on Tygon.

"Here's the real kicker, folks, and I'm sorry if this is all coming out all jumbled, but I wanted to get this to you quickly.

"Trew has assured the players that there is a very good chance that all of them will die a permanent death if they go back into the Game. Most of Tygon has witnessed the disintegration of the matrix supporting the very form and function of the Game. Trew told the five hundred million children that it is very possible they will be caught inside the Game when it collapses. This will result in permanent deaths for over a billion of our children...

"I can't begin to convey how powerful Trew's speech was. To give you some idea of how charismatic and inspiring it was, I can tell you this; when he'd finished speaking and completely outlined the risks involved...all five hundred million players unanimously agreed to go ahead and accept the challenge.

"This is, without a doubt, the best anniversary celebration in the thirty year history of the Game!

"Do not miss a second of the next two weeks, my friends, because viewers will witness either greatness... or absolute disaster."

Trew

"That went better than I expected," Trew said.

"Those kids are players," Cooper nodded as they walked towards Sylvia's office. "Of course, they're hooked on the Game. When it came right down to it, they had no choice but to accept your offer. It's the only life they know, and they want one last chance to come out on top or die trying."

"I think it's more than that, Cooper," Trew said. "They believe in the movement. They want to make a difference. I'm proud of every one of them."

"One portion of the speech did help decide the matter for them," Cooper looked at Trew.

"I know," Trew nodded. "Telling them if the Game ended then Tygon would soon end as well was the deciding fact. There's no point in telling that to the rest of the world, though. Let everyone think they are all heroes if they succeed. If they fail, it won't matter anyway."

The two men walked into Sylvia's office.

"Hello, Sylvia," Trew said. "I need an update on game stasis table preparation please."

"Five hundred million tables will be ready within twenty-four hours, Trew," Sylvia said.

"Good," Trew nodded. "I want Michelle here and the other team leaders as quickly as we can get them assembled."

"I'm on it," Cooper picked up a tablet and began typing commands.

"Brandon began speaking to Danielle just a few moments ago," Sylvia announced.

"Good," Trew said. "Can you begin playback please? I still have no idea what this plan is."

Cooper laughed out loud. "Could have fooled me with that speech of yours," he said. "It sounded like you were in complete control of everything."

"That's decades of acting," Trew smiled. "Now be quiet and let's watch what Brandon is cooking up in there."

===

Danielle - 70

"What do you mean, Melissa has learned how to wake up?" I ask.

"We're currently existing inside a computer simulation," Azrael said.

"I agree," I say.

"It's important that you do," he smiles. "The creators of this simulation developed strict processes and procedures for entry and exit into this reality."

"Makes sense."

"This world exactly mirrors the world that you originate from. To stay within those limits, you enter this world and leave it the same way you do Tygon."

"We are born into this world to enter, and we die to exit it," I nod.

"Correct," Azrael looks at Melissa and then back to me. "Melissa has learned a different way to exit this reality."

"Really?" I furrow my brows in confusion. "What other method can there be?"

"She closes her eyes here, and opens them in the other reality," Azrael says. "She leaves this body and wakes up in her real one."

"You make it sound so simple."

Azrael shakes his head emphatically, "It's not simple at all, my dear girl. It's the most complicated and magical feat that has ever been accomplished in this universe. It's taken tens of thousands of years of evolution and pain and growth. Simple? This should never have succeeded. Never!" He smiles at both of us. "But it did succeed, and here we are."

I look at Melissa and then Azrael. "I don't believe you," I finally say. "It's impossible."

"It was impossible," he agrees, "until Melissa did it. Now it's not only possible for her, it's possible for everyone."

"The universal law."

"Exactly!" Azrael stands up and claps his hands together loudly. "If something can be accomplished once, then it can be accomplished forevermore."

I look at Melissa and she grins sheepishly.

"So what do you want me to do?" I ask.

"You must learn how to do the same thing."

"You want me to learn how to wake up?"

"That's right."

"Why me?" I ask.

"You've led millions on Earth," Azrael says, "but on the world that you come from, billions watch you every day."

"Really?"

"Yes. Trew leads them, and they watch and follow your life here."

"So if I wake up, then that will accomplish something in the real world?" I ask.

"It will."

"What will it accomplish?"

"You can discover that for yourself when you wake up and see Trew."

My mouth goes dry. "I will see Trew?"

"Of course you will. He can't wait to see you."

I sit and consider what he's asking me to do. I don't fully understand what he wants, but it can't be much different from flying. "What if I can't do it?" I ask.

"I taught you to fly," Melissa said. "I can teach you how to do this as well, Danni. It's not that difficult once you get the hang of it."

"You've woken up only partially," Azrael says. "That part is easy. To fully wake up is much more difficult, but I'm certain that both of you can do it. After you've been fully trained, Melissa will do it first, and then you will go soon after."

"What does this mean?" I look at Melissa. "Have you opened a door to destruction for us all?"

"It's exactly the opposite, Danni," Azrael says. "She's opened the door to salvation."

44

Danielle - 70

I open my eyes and sigh in frustration. "It's very difficult."

Azrael looks at me with a patient smile. "I've watched you for your entire life," he says.

"That's creepy."

He laughs. "Okay, not for your entire life, but for most of the important accomplishments."

"Still creepy," I say.

"The point I'm trying to make," he continues, "is that you don't give up, and you don't find things difficult. You set your mind to something and you do it. Simple as that."

"Yes, that is how I do most things."

"It's how you do everything," he says. "What makes you so successful at everything you do is that you don't overcomplicate things. To you, everything is simple. This is just another example of something that most people would find difficult and you will succeed at it when you view it as simple."

I look at Melissa and she nods in agreement. "It's all about the glow, Danni," she says. "You've been meditating your entire life and this is just meditating."

"I feel like I'm going to fall," I say. "When I'm in there meditating. It feels as if I'm standing on the roof of a windy skyscraper and I'm about to fall off."

"You're not afraid of heights, are you?" Azrael asks. I give him a wry look and he laughs. "All kidding aside, flying girl, you're closer to doing this than you think. The falling sensation is good; you just have to surrender and let yourself fall over the edge."

"It's taken months to get to this stage," I say.

"Yes," Melissa agrees.

"I thought time was running out?"

"It is," Azrael says. "On your home world it's very short, but here time works differently."

"How long do we have?" I ask. "Here."

"I don't know for certain," he says.

"Ballpark guess?"

"Fifteen to twenty years," he says. "Twenty-five at the most."

"Oh, wow." I feel the stress melt away. "Sure, I can practice and get this nailed down by then. Why didn't you tell me sooner that we had that long?"

"No, I'm afraid you misunderstand me." He shakes his head. "That's how long Earth and most of the population has. I need you to wake up much sooner than that."

"How soon?"

"Within the next six months."

"Me doing this is that important?"

"Danni," his look says that it is. "You doing this is the most important thing in the universe."

I frown at the pressure, then I sit up straighter and nod at Melissa. "Okay, let's try again then."

===

Danielle - 3 months later

"Well, what do you think?" I ask.

Azrael and Melissa both look at each other and nod.

"I think we're ready to go," Azrael says.

He's been so helpful during this process. Once I learned to open my mind better he was able to join me in the meditative state and provide subtle guidance. Suddenly a thought occurs to me.

"They say you guide souls back to their homes... is this what they mean by that?"

He nods slightly. "Most of the time I'm more direct, sending souls back to their homes by killing their avatars, but this definitely fits the description, perhaps better than the regular way of things."

"You're not an angel or an archangel, are you?"

"No. Those are just names people give to beings like the Timeless to help them feel better about the unexplainable things they can do. Religion is a tool to guide mass groups of people towards common goals. God is just a computer running things, but people can't seem to accept that. They'd rather believe that an invisible creature runs it all."

"The computer isn't an invisible creature?" I ask.

He smiles and shakes his head. "You know what I'm saying."

I laugh. "Yes. Very few people are able to believe that this is all just a computer simulation."

"Nor should they," he said. "A core part of the program blocks that belief, although a few sometimes believe the truth and pass that on to others, like you and Trew did when you created the Gamer movement. More people believe the truth now than ever before."

"Non-believers just call it another religion."

"That's exactly what it is," he says," which is what this world requires it to be in order to build followers, to work towards achieving a purpose."

"Waking up."

He nods. "Melissa, are you ready to attempt a full awakening?"

"I've been ready for weeks now," she says. There's a comfortable bed in the room and she moves to lie down on it. She folds her arms comfortably over her chest, and closes her eyes. She takes two deep calming breaths and then suddenly her eyes pop open.

"Is this it?" she asks. "Will I be able to come back here if I fully wake up?"

Azrael shakes his head. "If you're successful in waking up completely, then you won't be able to come back here. This is it, Melissa."

I can tell that she is sad to hear the news. I nod at her reassuringly and squeeze her arm. "I know you can do this, Melissa. Don't worry, everything will be all right. I'll join you in just a few days, which is only a few hours on the other side."

Melissa nods and stands up. She gives me a tremendous hug which I return sincerely. "It's been an amazing adventure, Danni. I thank you from the bottom of my heart for giving a frightened, flying girl a safe place to be loved and taken care of."

"The honour is all mine." I feel tears beginning to form in my eyes, as if we aren't going to see each other for a long time. I know that's not the case, though; Melissa waking up will inspire me to go through my process even more quickly.

We separate, and she moves back to lie down on the bed. She takes a series of deep cleansing breaths and closes her eyes. I watch quietly as Azrael puts his hand on her right arm. After a few minutes her breathing begins to slow.

Then it stops. I look at Azrael but he doesn't open his eyes. I begin to count the seconds. After sixty seconds of Melissa not breathing I stand up and move closer. Azrael senses me and raises his free hand to tell me to stay still.

Another sixty seconds go by, and suddenly Melissa's body takes a sudden deep breath of air, and then begins to breathe again in a regular, rhythmic pattern. Azrael opens his eyes and removes his hand from her arm. Then he stands and looks at her. He places his fingers lightly on her neck to feel for a pulse, nodding at whatever he senses. Finally he looks at me and smiles triumphantly.

"She did it!" he says, grabbing me in a hug and swinging me around.

"She's still breathing, though," I say.

"She is now, but she stopped. That was when her presence, essence, whatever you want to call it, left her body." He points to the body breathing peacefully on the bed. "That's just an empty shell now, a vehicle without a driver. She's back in her own body in the real world. She did it. She woke up!"

"Now what do we do?" I ask.

"We wait a few days," he says, "and then you go through the same process."

"I wake up and go home," I say, still not quite believing it's possible. "I get to see Trew soon."

"That's right, Danni," Azrael confirms. "Very soon you will wake up to reality."

===

Trew

"Sylvia?" Trew looked at the blank screen that had been Melissa's feed. "Did it work? Is Melissa truly awake?"

"She has left her avatar, Trew," Sylvia replied. "All signs indicate that she has indeed returned to her body outside of the Game."

"Incredible," Cooper whispered.

"It sure is," Trew said. He reached for the remote and changed the channel from Melissa's blank feed to Danielle's. From Danielle's view point Melissa lay peacefully on the bed.

"What now?" Cooper asked.

"Let's go welcome Melissa home and celebrate!" Trew said. "Sylvia, which Game Centre is Melissa stationed at?"

"I don't understand your question, Trew," Sylvia sounded confused.

"I want to go and meet the gamer who was playing Melissa and be there when they bring her out of stasis. Which Centre do I need to go to?"

"I'm afraid that's not possible, Trew,"

"Why not?" Trew asked. "Were there complications bringing her out of stasis? She should be awake, right?"

"I thought you knew," Sylvia said. "Melissa isn't on Tygon, Trew. She was an Earth NPC."

45

"Despite our best attempts to learn more details about the players who will soon go back into the Game, we have very little to report.

"It appears that all five hundred million will enter the Game as closely together as can be accomplished, which will result in the biggest influx of players at one time in Earth's history.

"Most fans know the basic statistics; of the 1.3 billion Tygon children who play the Game, one billion of them inhabit human avatars. The count of players currently in the Game is approximately half a billion, with the other six billion humans of the Earth population comprised of Non Player Characters, or NPCs, as they are commonly called.

"There are rumours of a mysterious plague that is killing humans on Earth, but we aren't seeing any indications of this from the number of players being ejected. Our best guesses, based on the limited observations of players who are near some of these events, indicate that the humans being affected are only NPCs at the moment. We're unable to tell how serious the issue is, because most players are isolated in small groups throughout the world as a result of the chaos that resulted from 'the Day.'

"What can fans expect to see over the next few days of the Game? We will see a massive increase in births all over Earth as the five-hundred million enter the Game beginning tomorrow, sometime in the late afternoon. Next we will be trying to get more information on the NPC plague and report how widespread it is, and whether it has begun to affect player avatars.

"Our first order of business relates to the only piece of information that Gamers have shared with the press: They have all been instructed to view Danielle's feed, which leads us to believe something important is going to happen.

"We will be doing the same thing as the Gamers; watching Danielle and reporting any developments as they happen."

Lisa Rohansen - Game Central News

Earth

"It's getting dark. We should go back to camp."

Dillon ignored his little brother. The two of them had been exploring the empty building all afternoon. This was the most fun Dillon had experienced in a long time, and he wasn't ready to leave just yet.

Dillon was reaching to open a large, complicated looking panel. It was round, about two feet in diameter, and covered with light bulbs and wires. He moved slowly, careful not to break any of the fine wiring that was attached at various places on the front and sides. Just a few more inches and he would have it separated from the rest of the wall...

"What's that?" Dillon's little brother asked loudly into his ear.

"Damn it, Cory! I almost broke this thing. Stop sneaking up on me like that!"

Dillon looked over at his little brother. Cory was eight years old, a child of the new world. He'd never experienced any of the cool things that used to exist before the Day. Dillon occasionally felt sorry for him, but most of the time he envied his baby brother; he didn't know what he was missing.

Dillon remembered life before the Day. He'd been eight years old when it happened, almost nine. Like every kid his age back then, he'd had a smartphone in his hand, constantly texting and watching videos; the only time he put it down was when he picked up a game controller. The world had been an incredible place for a young boy, but then the Day had occurred... and everything had gone to hell.

The past eleven years had been a continuous struggle. Dillon's family was very close, which turned out to be a positive thing in this new age. Over forty brothers, sisters, and cousins had banded together and struck out to find a suitable place to settle down and ride out the crisis. It turned out that there was really no such place, and they'd spent the past decade as nomads, traveling from place to place, hoping to find a good spot to settle down. From what they had witnessed over the years, Dillon's family had fared better than most, but it hadn't been a picnic.

"What is that, anyway?" Cory whispered.

"I don't know," Dillon said. "Some kind of electrical panel, maybe."

"What's an electrical panel?"

"Hush up and watch, and maybe you'll find out," Dillon said. Whenever he didn't know how to answer his little brother's questions, he would tell him to hush and watch. It had turned out to be pretty good advice for the most part, and Cory always thought his big brother was smart for showing instead of telling.

The panel was stuck; no matter how he tried, Dillon wasn't able to fully pull it away from the wall. He peered into the space between the panel and the wall; he could see a locking slot of some sort holding it in place. He nodded his head and turned it slowly, in the direction of how a clock hand moved.

Suddenly the panel lit up, and a loud series of beeps and clicks began to sound from the wall. A deep, whirring noise started to build, and in the space between the panel and the wall Dillon could see a screen start to turn slowly in time with the sound.

"Whoa, what's happening?" Cory shouted as he scrambled away from his brother, stopping only when his back was pressed flat against the far wall.

Dillon quickly turned the panel back the way he'd found it. The noises stopped and the lights blinked out. He took a step back from the wall and looked around. The place remained dark and silent everywhere else. He glanced at his brother. Cory was pale, his eyes and mouth open wide.

Dillon walked over to his brother and hugged him, laughing and spinning him around. "It's okay, squirt," he said. "There's nothing to be afraid of."

"What was that?" Cory asked. "It sounded terrible."

Dillon released his little brother and walked back to the device on the wall. He grabbed hold of it and turned it one more time, laughing with delight as the lights turned on and the sounds once again began to reverberate from the wall. After a moment he turned the panel back, and the wall went silent once more.

"Come on," he said excitedly, "Let's go tell Dad and Mom what we've found."

"What have we found?" Cory asked.

"Power!" Dillon said. "The power's back on!"

46

Trew

"I don't understand," Trew said. "How were we able to see her feed if she's an NPC?"

"When I detected her potential early on, I set up a channel for her," Sylvia replied. "Sometimes an NPC shows exceptional promise, and I have the authority to assign them a channel. Over the course of the Game, there have been many memorable plays from NPCs, Trew. I thought you knew this."

"Is it common knowledge?" Trew asked.

"No," Sylvia admitted, "but I thought Brandon might have filled you in on some of these things."

"Brandon and I didn't have much private time together," Trew said. "There's a mountain of information that I likely should know, but I don't. I was hoping to sit down and read most of the instructions he left for me when Danni was out of the Game and I had more available time."

"Time is running out," Cooper said.

"Thanks for the update," Trew said with a sarcastic tone. He looked back towards the main screen, and then whipped his head back towards Cooper. "Wait a minute," he said. "Thorn said the Game was going to end much sooner because Brandon entered it, right?"

Cooper nodded.

"Tygon is powered by the same source that keeps the Game going, am I correct?"

"Indirectly, yes," Cooper said. "Tygon is powered by energy sources in the Dream, and the Game is powered by sources on Tygon."

"So that means that Tygon itself will power down eventually."

"When Thorn's power source runs out of energy in the Dream, then yes, Tygon will disappear," Cooper acknowledged.

"Has that been sped up by Brandon entering the Game?" Trew asked.

"It's not a concern," Cooper said.

"Why not?"

"Because it's not the limiting or determining factor here," Cooper explained. "If the Game fails to do what it was built for, then eventually everything will power down and shut off. In the grand scheme of things, the Game will go offline first."

Trew put his hands against his eyes and rubbed them wearily. He'd been running on very little sleep since he came out of the Game, and it was starting to take a toll on him. "I have to keep this simple," he said. "I start asking questions and it takes me so far away from my original thought that I can barely manage to get back on track."

Trew put his arms on the desk and lay his head down to rest. Cooper looked at his tablet, and Sylvia was respectfully silent.

"Yes!" Trew's head shot up quickly, his eyes focused and full of energy.

"What's up?" Cooper asked.

"The old man said I was right, didn't he?"

"You know he did."

Trew picked up the phone and dialed a number. He held the receiver to his ear and waited patiently.

"Who are you calling?" Sylvia asked.

Trew held up a hand for silence. After a few moments he spoke. "It's Trew," he said into the receiver. "Melissa just left the Game. According to the feed, she 'woke up' and left her avatar. Sylvia just informed me that she's an NPC." Trew listened to the person on the other end of the line for a moment before asking, "Any idea where she could have gone?"

Trew listened again for some time before responding. "Okay, call me back when you know more." Placing the receiver in its cradle, he looked at Cooper.

"Who was that?" Cooper asked.

Trew smiled. "I think I found her," he announced with a pleased look on his face.

===

Thorn walked into the large hall where Brandon's body was kept. He looked down at the still form and fondly brushed a stray lock of hair from his face, listening to the monitor beep steadily in time to the boy's heartbeat. Thorn checked the rest of Brandon's vital signs and nodded in satisfaction as he confirmed that all was well at the moment. He looked around the empty room and shook his head sadly at the considerable number of empty stasis tables. He'd sacrificed much to gamble on Brandon, but he was still convinced that this plan would succeed. Thorn sighed and left the room.

He walked down a darkened, grey hallway, passing identical doors on either side. Thorn paused outside the door to the General's quarters. *Perhaps I should go in and give him an update,* he thought to himself, but quickly shook his head and dismissed the idea. He continued to walk until he reached the doorway at the end of the hall.

Thorn placed his hand on the doorknob and paused. He was afraid of what he'd find on the other side of the door. It had been days since he had visited this room, and he feared the worst. Taking a deep breath and standing straighter, Thorn turned the knob and entered, flipping the light switch on as he stepped inside and closed the door behind him.

Tables lay positioned around the room, each occupied by a body. There were no monitors hooked up to any of them; there wasn't enough power to allow for such a luxury. They were all breathing, but for how much longer was anyone's guess. These were citizens of the Dream who'd been pulled into the simulation that Thorn had built; the game that this world had lined up to play. The game that had gotten out of control and pulled everyone it could inside, trapping them so none could escape. The game that would soon cause the mass extinction of all people on this planet.

Thorn made his rounds, walking to each table to observe the individual on it until he was certain they were still breathing. Their bodily functions had slowed down so much that it was sometimes difficult to determine that fact. He started at the first one on the right and scrutinized each until his eyes came to rest on the final table in the room.

He looked closely at this figure, watching the slow rise and fall of its chest. He stood watching as the seconds ticked away into minutes, and still he continued to observe. Finally he turned away and walked towards the door.

Behind him he heard a deep gasp.

Thorn smiled and looked at his watch, marking the time. Then he turned around and walked quickly to the table he'd just left a moment ago.

As he drew close, his smile broadened, tears of both relief and hope welling in his eyes. He leaned down to look closely at the person's face.

Thorn saw the eyes were open and blinking slowly. Seconds later, the head turned and looked at him.

"Where am I? The voice croaked, raw and dry from months of disuse.

Thorn wiped tears of joy from his eyes as he leaned closer and whispered softly. "Hello, Melissa. Welcome home."

47

"The purpose of the Game has always been to serve as a learning tool for our children. With that goal in mind, it became apparent early on that the time difference would be a significant issue. Many scientists, physicists, and scholars have spent considerable effort attempting to figure out the exact mechanics and details of the time difference between the Game and Tygon. I never worried too much about the specifics as long as it continued to work on a consistent basis, which it did. Early on I realized that if the Game started and continued in a linear fashion then the technology and skills of the avatars inside the Game would soon outdistance our own. There would be no real point to putting kids into a simulation where fantastic things were the norm, because they would learn nothing that could be brought back with them when they exited their plays. Imagine a child spending a lifetime living on a planet that had learned to alter its own gravity, or growing up using computers that were so advanced compared to Tygon technology that when they returned to us they would stagnate when left with a boring, primitive world in which to live out the rest of their lives.

"To address this issue, I did the math and decided that every five thousand years of Game time I would reset the servers to begin again. At a rate of ten years per week times fifty weeks in a Tygon calendar year... that meant that every ten Tygon years we would have a Game reset. This would allow our children to live and

experience similar types of developments as our own world has undergone, so that they could bring back life experiences that were practical and useable in their own reality upon graduation.

"Of course, we were very surprised at both how similar some things turned out and how different other situations seemed to go.

"I think that overall it has been an excellent experience so far for both the players and the fans. As we prepare to reset the Game for the second time, all of us look forward to the next cycle of the Game."

Interview with Brandon Strayne during the twentieth anniversary celebrations of the Game

"How's she doing so far?" Trew asked.

Thorn had appeared a short time ago, joining Trew and Cooper in Sylvia's office to discuss Melissa's status and to give Trew an opportunity to ask questions. Thorn was charged with positive energy; he was clearly excited and his smile looked optimistic.

"She's doing very well," Thorn said. "We've had her up and walking around. Her appetite is present. All signs indicate that she's back to normal, which is very encouraging."

"Any danger that she will slip back into the simulation?" Cooper asked.

Thorn shook his head and looked at Trew. "As Cooper knows, that was one of our major concerns," Thorn said. "Would she be pulled back in after finding her way out? To test this, we let her rest and sleep inside the shielded room with the rest of the volunteers who are all still locked in Sim2, which is what we call Earth," Thorn smiled and shook his head. "It appears that her mental process for ejecting herself from Sim2 protects her from being pulled back in. She slept three hours and woke up feeling refreshed with no indication that the program tried to steal her back. If I were to nod off in that room, I would be sucked into Sim2 immediately, as would anyone else currently awake in the Dream."

"So you're using the consciousnesses developed by NPCs in the Game to reanimate the bodies of people on your planet?" Trew asked.

"No..." Thorn said. "Melissa is originally from the Dream. She has simply returned to her body."

Trew stared at Thorn for a moment, then shook his head in confusion. "How is that possible?" he asked.

"There's only one way for it to be possible," Thorn said. "You tell me."

Trew frowned for a moment, then he grabbed a nearby pad of paper. He started to make circles and label them, then he began to draw lines back and forth, stopping on occasion to erase one and draw it a different way. Finally he looked at the drawing and nodded in satisfaction. His eyes widened in surprise as he fully understood what he'd just mapped out.

"You merged the two Earths into one," he said.

"Exactly," Thorn confirmed.

"When? How?"

"The 'how' is boring technical jargon," Thorn waved his hand. "The 'when' is the interesting part. You know about the Game resets, right?"

"Of course," Trew said. "Everyone on Tygon knows about the resets."

"That function was built into the program on purpose to do more than just to reset the server and time period of the Game."

"So ten years ago, Tygon time, during the reset of the Game, you and Brandon somehow merged the Earth of the Game with the Earth from your game, which was originally called Tygon 3.0, but you began referring to as Earth?"

Thorn smiled. "Clever, right?"

Trew looked at him dubiously and then glanced at Cooper, who nodded to confirm that what Thorn was saying was indeed true.

"So you knew back then that this might happen?" Trew asked.

"Brandon did," Thorn admitted. "Once he took control of VirtDyne and he began developing the Game, he contacted me and had me change the name of Tygon 3.0 to Earth. I don't remember the exact timeline, but that's what happened."

"Brandon had this vision for the past thirty years?"

"More than that, but for argument's sake, let's say yes."

"So Melissa is originally from the Dream. She went into the game you created and became trapped. Then, unknown to her or any of the other players inside, they eventually merged with Brandon's version of the Game from Tygon. On Tygon we thought of them as NPCs... but they are in fact players from another reality sharing the same playing field?"

"There you go." Thorn clapped his hands together. "Not so difficult at all, once you get a good look at the whole picture."

"It's a tangled, freaking mess!" Trew said.

"No," Cooper said. "It's a playing field where two realities meet. One group can learn from the other."

Trew considered the statement, and then he nodded his head. "It's brilliant!"

"If Brandon were here, he would bow and say thank you, I'm sure," Thorn said.

"Who is Melissa in your world?"

"She's a member of my Hand," Cooper said.

"What?" Trew was surprised. "How did a member of your Hand get pulled into the Simulation? I would have thought you and your group would be very careful about exposing yourselves to the dangers associated with proximity to Sleepers." Trew had learned that citizens of the Dream who had become trapped inside Thorn's game, once called 'Tygon 3.0' and now just referred to by survivors as 'Sim2' were called 'Sleepers.'

"She volunteered to go in," Thorn answered. "When it became clear what Brandon was planning, I began to look for mentally strong citizens from the few of us who remained protected underground. We assembled groups of them and began to train them in the art of meditation and mental focus. Then we asked for volunteers to enter Sim2, hoping that one of them might be lucky enough to find an opportunity to be of use to the cause."

"Lucky enough?" Trew couldn't believe what he was hearing. "The more I hear about this entire story, the more it seems all of you have been flying by the seat of your pants. Looks like an awful lot of luck was required to get to where we sit today."

"It was," Thorn agreed, "and I can assure you that a significant amount of luck is still required to get us to where we need to be."

Cooper chuckled as he saw the grim expression on Trew's face. "Luck means something different to you than it does to us, Trew," he assured the young man.

"What happens next?" Trew asked.

"Next we see if Danielle can do what Melissa just accomplished," Thorn said. "We see if she can wake up from the Game to come back to Tygon and show five hundred million children that such a thing is possible."

"What will that accomplish?" Trew asked.

Thorn laughed and shook his head. "I'm not going to ruin the whole story for you in one sitting, boy. I think you will figure out most of it, and the rest you can watch as it unfolds."

"Wait a minute," Trew looked scared. "The Game ends when Danielle exits it, doesn't it?"

"That was based on her dying to exit the Game," Thorn assured him. "If she can exit without dying, then she has found a loophole."

"Sylvia?" Trew asked. "Is that correct?"

Sylvia said nothing.

"Sylvia?" Trew asked loudly.

"Yes, Trew?" Sylvia replied.

"What Thorn just said? Is he correct in his assumption?"

Again, Sylvia did not reply.

"We can't allow her to try," Trew said.

"If she doesn't try, the Game ends anyway, Trew," Thorn said. "This way at least there's a chance for a different and better outcome."

"It looks like we need luck to help us out yet again," Cooper said.

The three men sat and watched Danielle on the monitor in silence.

48

Danielle - 71

I open my eyes and look at Azrael.

He's scrutinizing me like you would look at a litter of pups to decide which one to take home. Finally he smiles. "I think you're ready."

I nod my head. "Yes, I think so too. It's very easy to get into the right part of the meditation now."

"That's all well and good," he says, "but do you think you can take the leap?"

"I was thinking of making it more of a step." He frowns and I laugh. "Yes, I think I can take the leap, Az. I just hope..." I catch myself.

"You hope what?" he asks.

I shake my head.

"Danni, there must be no doubt in your mind when you do this, or you won't end up where you need to be." He looks at me seriously. "Others have done this before, you know," he says.

"Yeah, Melissa," I nod.

"Not just Melissa. Over the centuries there have been wise men and women who have devoted their entire lives to searching for inner peace and tranquility through self-reflection and meditation.

Dozens, if not hundreds of people, have stood on the very same ledge and looked down. Many of them have stepped off."

"Have they succeeded? Have they opened their eyes on their table and ejected themselves from the Game?"

Azrael pauses and then shakes his head. "I would like to tell you that they have," he says, "but I have no idea where they went, which isn't our goal."

"So their bodies died here and they woke up outside of the Game in their real bodies?"

"No," he says, "their essences never made it back to their real bodies. Their avatars died in here, and soon after their bodies died in the other reality as well."

"Oh." That isn't what I was expecting to hear. "How do you know that isn't what happened to Melissa, too?"

He taps his head and grins, "I saw where she went. I was with her until she went through the final door, and I saw what was on the other side." He nods, "It's exactly where she was supposed to be going. There is no doubt in my mind that she is safely home."

"The same place I am going to end up," I say confidently.

"Yes, you will end up in the same place," he says. "Your home."

I think about his warning, and then I nod and stand up. "Okay. I am prepared to make the leap. I'm ready to go home."

Azrael stares at me intently, it feels like he's trying to look deep into my essence; perhaps he is. "I believe you," he says. "Rest tonight and say your goodbyes. You go home tomorrow."

===

Trew

"What was that all about?" Trew looked over at Cooper, who was still watching Danni and Brandon on the monitor.

"I don't know," Cooper said. "Not very smart to tell her that part of the story, if you ask me."

"How come no one has told me that part of the story?" Trew asked.

"It's not relevant."

"Of course it is," Trew said. "If there's a chance she might not succeed, then I need to know about it."

"Haven't you been paying attention, Trew?" Cooper asked. "There's always a chance we might not succeed."

"You seem comfortable with that fact."

Cooper laughed. "Of course I am. Let me put this into perspective for you. From the time this all occurred until only a short time ago, the chances of total failure and utter annihilation of our race from the face of the planet appeared to be 99 percent certain. For the past few weeks it's flipped to an entirely different situation, Trew. Thanks to you, and Danni, and Melissa, and especially Brandon, since he set this all up, we are looking at a 95 percent possibility that everything will be fine and we will all be saved. I don't know about you, but I'll take big chance of success over big chance of failure any day."

Trew considered Cooper's words and nodded in agreement. "When you put it that way, I guess things do seem better."

Cooper chuckled and looked back at the monitor.

"I'm worried about Danni coming out and the Game being destroyed in the process," Trew admitted.

Cooper nodded and looked at Trew again. "That's a valid concern," he admitted, "but we've done everything we can to minimize the chances of that happening. Now we just have to sit here, content that we have increased our odds for success as best as we could, and leave the rest to luck. There's nothing we can do to affect the outcome at this point; that ship has sailed. I face oblivion better than most, Trew, but that's only because I've had lots of practice doing it. In a few hours we will either be closer to success, or all dead and gone. Maybe even that outcome will unlock a new adventure for us. Perhaps we'll all wake up in totally different bodies on other tables and find out that this has all been one more simulation inside a simulation."

Trew smiled; he'd considered that fact many times as well.

"The only thing we can do at this point is be positive. In difficult times the most challenging thing is to remember our own advice and words of wisdom. Intelligence and reason are the first casualties during any crisis. Remember your words to the masses, boy. Thoughts are things, and we must have only good thoughts in these troubled and challenging times."

Trew looked back at the monitor and nodded. "You're absolutely right, Cooper. Thank you."

"Any time, kid."

"So when Danni wakes up, she will return to her body here, is that correct?" Trew asked. "Or is there a chance she will wake up in the Dream in her real body there?"

"She will wake up on Tygon. She isn't from the Dream," Cooper smiled. "It is a bit confusing, isn't it?"

"Layers upon layers," Trew admitted. "Just when I think I have something figured out, it seems to suddenly change again."

"I understand," Cooper said. "Think of the Game as a place for two worlds to play in. Tygon children lie on a table and enter the Game. They control avatars called humans and when they die, their essence returns to Tygon."

"Okay," Trew nodded.

"People from my world — the world that we've always called 'the Dream' — are also inside the Game. They control avatars also called humans. Up until recently, Tygon citizens believed that these were empty, computer controlled avatars, and called them NPCs in the Game."

"Indeed we have."

"If we can show the Dream players, or Game NPCs, or non-Tygon players — whatever you want to call them — if we can show them how to wake up, then they will be able to return to their reality."

"The Dream," Trew nodded.

"Yes."

"What happens to them now?" Trew asked. "When they die, I mean?"

Cooper shrugged. "Since Thorn and Brandon spun them into your Game — during year twenty of the Game is when they did that — they've been recycled back into the Game as new humans. Reincarnated."

"They die and are born again into a new body?"

"Yes," Cooper said.

"The Game is ending, though," Trew said. "What will happen to them if they die and the Game ends?"

"Same as will happen to Tygon players," Cooper nodded. "They will all be lost forever."

Trew considered the information, as well as the positive words from earlier, then nodded.

Trew picked up the phone and dialed. "Michelle, I want to be in Danni's room when she begins her journey home. Let's have cameras there as well. Call Lisa Rohansen and tell her that we're giving her another big career boost."

49

Shane

I've always loved sitting out under the open sky in front of a nice fire.

Thousands of years have gone by, and if I don't have marshmallows or a hot dog to roast, I still get perturbed.

A rabbit will have to do tonight; the pickings are slim since the Day occurred. Every time I start to curse those responsible for that one, I catch myself and chuckle. Oh, right... it was me.

I sense that my company has arrived.

"You didn't happen to bring marshmallows, did you?" I ask out loud.

I hear a chuckle from the darkness and I turn to look at him as he enters the light of the fire. "You picked a young avatar this time," I say.

"I think it's twenty-one years old," he says. "A good age, if you ask me."

I smile. "It's a good age if you ask anyone. Grab a chair; I've had one sitting out for you every night for a very long time."

He nods and sits down beside me. I hear the crack and hiss of a can being opened and he hands me a beer. I grab it and smile. "It's so nice to have it already chilled," I say.

"Yeah, I thought you'd like that touch," he says.

We sit and drink our beers, watching the rabbit cook slowly on the fire for a few moments.

"So we're almost done, then," I say.

"Yes."

"It's been a long life."

"Imagine if you'd done it all three rotations. The first five thousand years we hadn't considered that option yet, and Gabriel was the first volunteer for it during Tygon years ten to twenty."

I nod. "Still, it's a long time, Brandon. I went crazy a few times, I'm sure of it."

"I know, Easton, and I'm sorry for it." I can hear the pain in his voice.

I shrugged my shoulders. "We all knew this would be a struggle. The toughest part is having the rest think I'd gone rogue and trying to hunt me down and kill me."

"Every story needs a bad guy," Brandon says.

I poke the fire with a stick, watching the flames flare up as oxygen feeds the combustion process. I look at Brandon with a grin on my face. "How did I do?"

Brandon laughs and slaps me gently on the back. "You were one of the worst, and by that I mean best, bad guys I've ever seen!"

"Thanks," I say. "I did have a long time to perfect it."

"In all seriousness, though, I really appreciate your work, Easton. You've always been one of my best teammates, and I'm grateful that you joined us for the ride."

I stand up and so does he. We hug and I pat him on the back. "Thanks, Brother. I've always been thankful to be on this journey with you, too. If we pull this off, it will be legendary."

"No one will have accomplished so much in all of history," he agrees.

The rabbit is ready, so I remove it from the spit and split it in half, putting the parts on two plates and handing him one, which he accepts with a word of thanks. We eat silently for a few moments. Brandon produces two more cold beers and we drink them with our meal.

After the meal, I take the plates and put them over to the side and out of the way. When I get back to the fire, my eyes light up at what I see in Brandon's hands.

"Marshmallows!" I say, and he laughs at my excitement. I duck into my tent and grab two straight sticks with sharp ends, bring them back to the fire and sit down.

Brandon holds his marshmallow over the fire, careful to keep it at a proper distance. It slowly turns golden brown and he turns it. "Danni will attempt to wake up tomorrow," he says.

I watch my marshmallow become crispy and golden brown. I remove it from the fire and blow on it a couple of times to cool it down. Then I pluck it from the stick and bite into it, closing my eyes as the warm crunch is replaced by gooey sweetness. I close my eyes and sigh in absolute delight, slowly chewing until it's gone. "You are an absolute angel for bringing me these!" I say. Brandon laughs and hands me another, which I take and place on the stick. "How certain are we that the Game will still be around after she succeeds?" I ask him.

"Maybe 50 percent."

I laugh lightly and look over at him for a second. "That seems a bit low," I say.

He shakes his head doubtfully. "It's better odds than I expected to get, but Sylvia really threw a curve ball when she tied the ending of the Game to Danielle exiting it."

"I still think it's higher." I look back to my stick in the fire and turn the marshmallow. "Sylvia doesn't want this to end; it's her entire existence."

"Maybe she's tired," he says. "After five thousand years, you aren't sad about it ending. She's been in existence for three times that long."

"Maybe," I say. "Now that it's almost complete, I am glad I did it," I admit. "There was a tremendous amount of fun and good times, too."

"I'm glad to hear that," Brandon says. "So you think the odds are higher?"

"Absolutely," I nod.

"What number are you thinking?"

I pop another toasted marshmallow into my mouth and chew to let the drama build. Finally I finish it and smile. "Maybe as high as 56 percent."

Brandon looks at me for a moment. Then we both begin to laugh.

50

Danielle - 71

I sit alone in the silence.

The hard stone of the bluff feels more comfortable than I would have guessed, and the view from up here is wonderful. Everything is bathed in the white glow of the light coming from the large full moon that sits high in the sky. A cool breeze blows gently from the air in front of me, chasing away the humidity and preventing the warm night air from becoming uncomfortable against my skin. I listen to the sounds of nature in the trees and grass; a full symphony of countless creatures whose voices join each other to create a magical effect.

I hear a soft thud on the stones behind me and Azrael asks me what I've been waiting to hear.

"Are you ready to go home, Danni?" he asks.

I continue to look at the fields and patches of forest below me as I nod. "Soon," I say.

He comes to stand beside me, surveying the ground below and nodding.

"I think I remember a past lifetime," I say.

"Really?" he sits down. "What do you remember?"

"Not very much," I admit, "but what I do recall is very vivid. It came to me earlier this morning as I practiced standing at the edge of the lake of gold energy in my meditation."

"Tell me about it," he says.

"In my memory it's very dark. I recall feeling safe and warm, with heavy thudding sounds all around me. I don't know why the sound didn't bother me, but I found it to be calming and reassuring."

Azrael nods and I continue to speak. "I'm not certain how long I spend in this darkness, but eventually something changes. The calm peaceful feeling is replaced by panic, and the thudding noise becomes erratic, causing me to feel upset and frightened. Then I realize that I'm having trouble breathing. One second everything is fine, and the next I'm fighting to get a single breath so I can keep living."

I pause, remembering how terrified I felt when I experienced this memory. "It becomes obvious that after a few moments I won't be able to get a breath," I say. "No matter what I do, there's no way I can keep going without air."

"It sounds terrible," Azrael says gently.

"It was," I agree. I look at him and he's watching me intently. "Finally, when I realize that struggling and fighting won't help me, that nothing will help me, I remember experiencing something incredible."

"What?" Azrael asks.

"Surrender," I whisper. "There is a final moment when I understand that there's nothing I can do. No matter how hard I fight and struggle and thrash around, there is only one thing that I can do, and that is to surrender to my situation; which I do."

"What happens next?" he asks.

"I can't remember anything after that," I say. "What I do remember is how I felt in that moment, in the exact instant when I surrendered my will to the inevitable realization that I would not breathe again." I don't know if my eyes look different than they normally do, but I feel such wonder and awe at this moment that I'm sure it must be visible on my face.

"How did you feel?"

"Like anything was possible," I say. "Like everything was within my grasp. I can still feel the sensation that came when I surrendered to my fate, and it was miraculous."

Azrael watches me for a moment, and then he smiles. "I think you are remembering a past life, Danni, and I have an idea which one it was."

"Can you tell me?" I ask.

He slowly nods his head. "You've lived many lives inside this Game called Earth. Many of them were long, prosperous lives, where you learned much and carried those experiences with you into subsequent incarnations. There was one lifetime, however, that was very short. I think you're remembering that one."

"How short was it?" I ask.

"You died in childbirth."

"Oh." I don't know what to say. For a moment I think about my own child, the baby Trew and I wanted to have. It died prematurely; did it feel the same things I'm remembering now?

"You had planned a remarkable play, complete with a long life and many significant events. Many fans were shocked and disappointed when you died so young."

He looks like he wants to say more, as if he wants to share what happened to me after that brief life. Instead he shakes his head and looks at me. His eyes become excited and he smiles. "Perhaps that life was more important than any of us could have guessed," he says. "What you are describing to me is exactly what you need to do in order to complete this waking process. You need to fully accept what you are about to do... to surrender to the only course of action that can move you forward to your goal."

"I wasn't sure I could do it," I admit, "but now that I have this memory, I believe I can."

Azrael laughs softly and shakes his head. "She thought of everything, didn't she?" he asks.

"Who?"

"It doesn't matter," he says. The point is that what we thought of as your worst play may end up being the most important." He chuckled again. "It's incredible how all of this falls perfectly into place; simply mind-staggering at times."

"I don't understand," I say.

"That's okay, Danni," he said. "When you wake up, I think you'll see the magic in it all. When you enter your trance, and stand on the very edge, remember the feeling that you experienced in that past life."

"Okay..." I say.

"The only way to wake up," Azrael says, "is to completely surrender to your fate like you did then. Now that we know you are capable of it, let's finish preparations and begin."

51

"You make it sound so simple, Brandon."

"There are so many steps that must all fall in place, at both the right time and with the right orientation, for us to have any chance of success at all. The odds favour this being a complete failure."

"Then why attempt it?"

"I attempt it, Father, because it looks complicated to the average person, but to me it's simple."

"It looks extremely complicated to me."

"You might not see what I'm about to attempt, but there are other areas where you are without peer."

"Very amusing, boy."

"I didn't mean it as a joke, nor did I intend to insult you. There is one fact which you must keep in your mind during this project, Father. It will serve you well over the times that are to come."

"What fact is that?"

"The thinking that created the problem will not solve it."

"Are you saying you are able to outthink me, Brandon?"

"That's exactly what I'm saying."

"For the sake of our entire world, which faces total extinction thanks to my mistakes, I hope you're right, son, because I can't begin to come up with an idea to save everyone."

"I can, Father."

Excerpt of private conversation recorded by Brandon on Tygon during the first year of the Game.

Lisa Rohansen looked around the luxurious room until her eyes rested on the still form of Alexandra Montoyas. She couldn't believe that she was sitting in the corner watching the most popular player of all time. The viewer on the wall displayed Danielle inside the Game as she prepared to attempt something that had never been done before.

"Okay, Lisa, we're ready to go live."

Lisa looked at the camera and smiled. She nodded her head and waited for the red light to appear on the camera.

"I am reporting to you live from Danielle Radfield's, or should I say Alexandra Montoyas' private gaming room. I will continue to call her Danielle until she comes out of the Game and announces what she would like to be called.

"In a few moments we expect Danielle to attempt something that no one has ever accomplished; she will wake up from the Game and her essence will return to her body here on Tygon.

"Please bear with us; from now on, we will be speaking very rarely, if at all. Cameras will continue to roll as Trew and a select few stand by Danielle's side and wait for her to wake.

"I'm Lisa Rohansen, and I couldn't be more excited!"

===

Trew stood outside Danielle's game room and listened to Cooper's update. "Lisa is in the room now," Cooper said. "She's been instructed to remain quiet and out of the way. The cameras will be rolling and she has already brought the audience up to speed."

"Good," Trew said. "There will be a split screen feed so that viewers can see Danni in the Game and her body on the table?"

"That's right," Cooper confirmed. "They will see her close her eyes and begin to meditate in the Game, and if everything goes well, they'll see when she opens her eyes here."

"Or they'll see if she doesn't."

Cooper nodded.

"We've cut every other feed and made Danni's channel available to everyone who turns on a viewer at no charge for this event," Trew said. "The whole world will be watching."

"What if she doesn't wake up and the Game ends?" Cooper asked. "The half a billion kids still inside the Game will all die."

Trew nodded, "That's another reason I cut all the feeds and am showing only Danielle's. If this fails and the Game ceases to exist, then I will address the nation to prepare them as best I can," he made a wry face and shook his head. "We'll have to prepare for all-out chaos and destruction if that happens."

"Any clues from Sylvia?"

"She refuses to answer me, but I'm going to feel confident everything will be fine. Brandon bet our very existence on it."

"That's reassuring," Cooper said. "Everything's a game to that boy. He won more than anyone I've ever seen, but he also lost."

"Life's a Game, Cooper," Trew said. "We've all played the best we could and there's nothing to be done now except see if the rolling dice land so that we can make the next move."

Cooper grinned at Trew. "You really are just like him, boy."

"Thank you. Shall we go in?"

Cooper opened the door. "After you, sir."

52

Danielle - 71

I turn my head slowly to soak up the sounds and sights of this reality in the early morning light. I believe that this world is a computer simulation, and that certainty instills me with wonder at the complexity of the computer running this universe. It's so real; I wonder if my home reality will be noticeably different from this one. The others wait patiently behind me, and I turn to face them. "This is it, then," I say.

Azrael smiles and nods.

Raphael hugs me. "You will be missed," he whispers into my ear and I blink back a tear.

After a long moment, we separate and look at each other.

"The Colony is ours again," I say. Stephanie left as promised, and we found that she had been true to her word; it was in excellent shape and the people were living a safe and normal life — as normal as life can be in this bleak and powerless setting.

Raphael nods. "This morning a new group arrived at the Colony. I thought you would be interested to hear the news they brought with them. It's a large family of about forty people made up of cousins and brothers and sisters and their children. One of the teenage boys made a startling discovery a few months ago on their way to us."

Raphael pauses dramatically and I wait for him to continue. "They claim the power is back on."

I sigh with relief. "That's excellent," I say. "I was hoping someone would eventually figure it out and say something."

"What do you mean?" Raphael asks. "This isn't news to you?"

Azrael chuckles. "Danni knew the power was on. She's the one responsible for restoring it."

The small group of Timeless look at Azrael and then glance at me for confirmation. I nod slowly, it must be okay to speak about it now that someone else has informed them. "Yes, that's why I left the Colony," I admit. "To find a way to turn the power back on."

"It was Shane?" Raphael guesses. I nod and he claps me on the shoulder. "Well done, Danni! Why didn't you tell us?"

"That was his condition for restoring the power," I say. "I couldn't tell anyone, someone else needed to discover it."

"Well, thanks to one curious teenager, and a stroke of luck that they ended up on our doorstep, now we know." Raphael says. "That will keep us extremely busy over the next few years."

"What about people dying?" I ask. "Have there been many more?"

"No," Azrael says. "After the first wave of deaths, it appears to have stopped."

"Strange," I say.

"Perhaps it was a signal," Raphael says.

"Perhaps," I say, "or maybe it was just a strange virus that burned itself out."

"It was a signal," Azrael says. "More puzzles for those of us left behind to solve."

"Okay, I get the hint." I smile and hug Raphael one more time, then walk to the edge of the bluff and sit down in what has become my most comfortable meditating spot.

"Wish me luck," I say.

"Luck!" the small group says in unison.

I close my eyes and sense Azrael as he sits beside me in his customary place.

"Safe travels, Danielle," he whispers softly. "Give my regards to Trew and Cooper. I will see you again very soon."

I wonder what he's talking about; will he be coming with me? There's no time to ask him, though. I can feel the golden glow humming to life around me and then covering me like a thin, warm film from head to toe. I control my breathing rate and feel the world around me fade, to be replaced first by darkness, then by the golden glowing colour, and then I'm standing on the edge.

I'm surrounded by a glowing matrix of colours, similar to what I saw in the cave, but more expansive and colourful. I stand on a tall cliff, with the various intersecting lines above, below, and all around me. I look down and feel the smooth cool stone on my bare feet. The stone ledge is narrow and my toes hang over it, extending into empty space. A quick look behind me shows Earth with its colours and scenery slowly dissolving. In a few moments I'm completely surrounded by the digital matrix; it is the most beautiful thing I've ever seen.

"It is time," a voice says. I turn my head, expecting to see Azrael standing beside me, but instead I smile in surprise as I see who my companion is.

The old man floats comfortably in the air, his legs crossed and hands resting on his knees in a traditional meditative pose. He looks as unkempt and scraggly as ever, with his black garbage bag garments and loose fitting black army boots. The red pop bottle cap gloves chime cheerfully as he raises one hand and waves in greeting. He winks at me and flashes a mischievous smile.

"I haven't seen you since we concluded our long journey," I say.

"I've been busy," he says, "but thought I should make an appearance before you head out. It'd be rude of me not to say goodbye. While I'm here, I may as well help send you on your way; Owl Boy had his chance. I swear sometimes that kid slows the whole process down more than it needs to be. I would have kicked your arse over this cliff weeks ago."

"That might have been premature and I would have failed."

He shrugs his shoulders. "It's worked for birds for millennia," he says. "Kick the little bugger out of the nest and let them fly to join the world."

"Some don't make it,"

"Some never will," he says. "Doesn't matter how long they sit up there in that safe nest; some will simply freeze up when the air hits them in the face and they find themselves plunging for the ground." He looks at me shrewdly and grins. "That's not you, though, Danni. You will always succeed. You are a special jewel, girl, and don't you ever forget it."

"Thank you," I say.

"Sure thing." He points down and looks at me with a smile. "Ready to go?"

I nod, "Yes. Let me get into the right frame of mind, and then I'll surrender."

The old man chuckles. "You've already surrendered, Danni, or you wouldn't be here."

I look down and my eyes widen in surprise. The cliff has disappeared, and I'm falling, or floating; it's hard to tell what is really happening in this environment.

"See?" he says. "You've surrendered and you're almost there. Just one more thing to do, darling girl."

"What's that?" I ask.

"Open your eyes and say hi to your home reality."

===

Trew stands close to Danni and holds her hand. He glances quickly at the monitor to make sure her Game avatar is in a trance.

At the moment he looks back down, her eyes open.

She looks up and sees him. Then she smiles.

"Hi," she says.

Trew's eyes fill with tears. They were never supposed to meet in this reality again, but here she is, alive.

He blinks rapidly and cups her cheek with his hand. In a husky tone he answers her simple greeting with one of his own.

"Hi."

53

Raphael

Azrael — I think I'm finally getting the hang of calling him that — opens his eyes and stands up. The others have left and only the two of us remain. Both of us look at Danni's body, which has slumped gently to one side.

"The avatar is still breathing?" he asks me.

"Yes."

"Good. I need you to find a hospital and see if you can bring the power back up enough to equip a monitor and table. There will be usable intravenous solutions to keep the avatar nourished and hydrated; secure those items as well."

"We have everything to accomplish that at the medical facility in the Colony," I say.

"Good," he pulls up his hood. "Get it hooked up as soon as you can and keep it in good condition."

I nod. "Are you going to assemble the groups of thirteen?"

"Yes," he says. "It will soon be time to send them back to the Dream. Melissa will likely be up and mobile by now. She'll reintegrate them and work to restore power to the Dream."

"Why groups of thirteen?" I ask.

"I have no idea," he shrugs. "When Shane realized that some of the fractured individuals were members of the 'Avatars of the

General' from the Dream who'd been sucked into the game against their will, he started gathering them together. No matter what he tried, he was never able to restore their sanity if they were in groups of more than thirteen. He couldn't make it work with less than that, either; they had to be assembled into groups of thirteen to reintegrate their brains and personalities."

"How many groups did he manage to restore?" I ask.

"Guess," Azrael smiles, and I see my old friend Brandon in his eyes.

"Thirteen?"

"You always were clever, Alan," he says.

"Is Miranda one of them?" I ask.

"No," he says.

"Then one of the groups is only made up of twelve?"

"Nope," he shakes his head. "That particular group has thirteen; the thirteenth member just happens to be a cell-sized, sentient nanocomputer."

"How will that transfer back to the Dream?"

"I have no clue. Maybe it was a person in the Dream who chose to come into the game as a nanocomputer, or maybe it won't transfer over — it doesn't really matter. We can still succeed if some don't make the transition."

"That sounds a bit cold, doesn't it?" I ask.

"I made peace with that sentiment long ago, Alan," Azrael says. "When we entered this simulation, we knew that billions would die if we failed. If we can save the majority of them, then that's gonna have to do. When all this is done, perhaps I will mourn those who don't make it. If we can save most of them, I'm going to feel much better than I have for decades."

"What do you want us to do after we stabilize Danni's avatar?" I ask.

Azrael smiles at me and points west towards the Colony. "Spread the word about the power coming back on, and put that large group of yours to work restoring it. I would advise that you start searching the globe to see if anyone else has stumbled onto the same realization. We have just under twenty-three years to finish this plan before Dream players die en masse. Melissa opened the door, and now Danni has driven a wedge under the door to force it to remain open. Now we get to work and teach everyone else how to wake the hell up and get back to their bodies in the Dream. One of the keys to doing that will be bringing this world back to an era of instant global communication. We're going to have to assemble and train billions of NPCs, and the Gamer movement will be responsible for that. I want everyone to join the movement. Soon I will provide the Prophet, but it's important that everyone can witness the arrival."

"We'll need people to spread the word and teach the way," I say.

"Ah, yes," Brandon says. "Get everyone you can ready for a worldwide increase in births."

"How big an increase?"

"Five hundred million," he smiles. I shake my head, wondering how Earth will handle that giant flood of players. "Get ready for a big batch of baby turtles to hit the beaches, Raph, and here's hoping many of them make it to open water so they can do what we need them to."

===

Trew sat and held her hand tightly, staring at her while the doctors and nurses made certain she was healthy. She looked at him often during the half-hour process; the medical professionals were very patient as they repeatedly asked questions to grab her attention back from him. Each time they would repeat a question and she would respond with, "Pardon?" Trew would grin, the kind of grin you know is likely making you look silly but you just can't help yourself. Smiles of relief, joy, happiness, and overwhelming thoughts of a future full of possibilities that Trew had feared would never be raced through his mind while the doctors and nurses did their job.

In the far corner, Lisa the reporter sat quietly, her body shaking as tears of joy poured from her eyes. She raised the microphone to her mouth a few times to whisper into it, but quickly lowered the mic and let the cameras silently capture the moment for fans all over the world.

Trew had glanced at Cooper just once during the initial moments, his look asking if the Game was still live; whether half a billion children continued to live inside the simulation. Cooper had nodded clearly and patted him on the back, and then stepped outside the room to give Trew and Danni some privacy as the medical staff finished their work.

Finally the doctors were done, and Trew pulled Danni towards him. She giggled like a schoolgirl, which she technically still was, despite her decades of life experience. Then they kissed. It had been days for Trew, but years for her. The two became lost in the moment, their love and energy mixing together in a kiss that left them both breathless.

Trew smiled and looked over at Lisa, who had become so engrossed in the moment that she'd forgotten to breathe herself.

"The camera was on, right?" Trew asked with a smile.

"What?" Lisa stammered. She looked at the camera in alarm. "Yes, of course it's on, Trew." Lisa came closer and looked at Danni, then threw her arms around the girl and began crying teas excitedly. "We are so happy that you are back with us!" Lisa exclaimed.

Danni laughed and returned the hug, not sure who this woman was, although it was obvious that she'd been following Danielle's life inside the Game.

After a few moments Lisa let go and sat down in a chair that one of her crew had placed near the couple. "So now that you're back, what do we call you?"

Trew winked at Danni and she nodded. During their time together in the meditation chamber, Trew had told her about what was happening on Tygon concerning the Gamer movement and players keeping their names when they left their last plays. She looked at Lisa for a moment, and then smiled and nodded her head. "I think it's best if you continue to call me Danielle," she said.

They were several levels underground, but Trew thought he could hear roars of approval from the crowds assembled outside the Game Centre.

Lisa smiled and nodded her head. Then she looked at Trew and her face became more serious. She turned and addressed the camera. "As I informed you already, we knew that we would need to leave soon after Danni arrived to let her recover in peace. Trew has assured me that in a few hours we will be invited back to speak further with our returned heroine, but for now we must sign off. Welcome back, Danni, and thank you, Trew, for allowing us to be a part of this magical moment. Ladies and gentlemen of Tygon, you see before you the first person to ever leave the Game and return to their body without dying. This has been a miraculous moment in the history of the Game, and I want to thank you all for tuning in to witness it with us. Stay tuned for repeats of this program and up-to-date interviews and discussions about what happens next in the Game during this incredible thirtieth year celebration."

Lisa smiled and waited for the camera feed to end, then she nodded and put her microphone down, grinning as she looked back at Danielle and Trew. "Wow!" She said. "This has been quite a ride. I can't imagine what it's been like from your point of view, Danni, but let me just say that as a fan, you have taken the Game to a whole new level of excellence!"

Danni smiled and nodded. "Thank you, Lisa, that's very kind of you."

"Kindness has nothing to do with it!" Lisa stood up. "What a life you just lived! It'll be a long time before anyone comes even close to accomplishing what you did during that play. Well, I'll leave you two to celebrate, and I can't wait to interview you again."

Danni pursed her lips together and smiled with a quick nod.

"Thank you so much for the exclusive, Trew," Lisa said.

"It was my pleasure, Lisa. There's no one who can cover an event like you. Thanks for giving us the superb coverage we can always expect from you."

Lisa smiled and nodded, hugged Trew briefly, then headed for the door.

They were alone.

Trew stood up slowly and walked to the wall, turning off the monitor so that the room was quiet. They moved from the sterile area of the room where the stasis table was located into an area that resembled a luxury hotel's living area. They stood close, holding hands and touching foreheads lightly. Smiles broke out on their lips and then disappeared like flashes of lightning in a summer storm. They stood this way for minutes, enjoying being in each other's company.

Danni thought about the years since she'd been this close to him, the void that she had felt from his absence for so long. She realized that for Trew it had been only a few days, and for that she was glad. Eventually she leaned forward, slowly resting her head on his chest. The tears of happiness began to flow, and after a moment she sobbed loudly to release the years of silent pain that she had endured. Trew held her, stroking her hair and whispering how much he loved her. He told her how proud he was of her, and that she truly was the best this world had ever produced.

Finally Danni leaned back and looked up at him. They smiled and kissed again, and she decided it had been worth the wait.

Danni saw something in Trew's eyes, and she paused thoughtfully, nodding as if reading his mind.

"Time works differently here," she said.

"Yes." Trew looked both happy and sad.

"We have work to do, don't we? Work that needs to be done sooner rather than later?"

"I'm afraid we do, my love."

Danni sighed and nodded. She blinked back tears as she smiled. "I had hoped that just waking up would end my play," she said, "but your look tells me that there's more for us to do."

"There is," he said.

"Do we get to spend at least some time together?"

Trew's eyes lit up. "Yes, sweet girl, we get to spend some time together."

Danni shook her head and pulled him towards the third room in the suite. "Don't tell me how long we have until we leave," she said.

Trew grinned and followed her willingly. "Deal," he said.

54

"As fans have just witnessed, Danielle did the impossible! She exited her avatar inside the Game to return to her body here in reality!

"In addition to fans all over the world witnessing the event as it happened, players not inside the Game watched as well. Now that Danielle has returned, Game Centres around the world have begun the process of sending every available player back into the Game. Earth is about to see its biggest population explosion ever.

"No one knows for sure why Trew is sending in so many players this quickly but one thing is certain; something important and worth watching is about to happen inside the Game again!"

Lisa Rohansen, Game News Central

Danielle, Trew, and Cooper sat in Sylvia's office. Both Sylvia and Danni were excited to meet each other for the first time; they were like two girls chatting and catching up on gossip as if they were friends who hadn't seen each other in years. When Trew had mentioned something to that effect, both had laughed and Danni had rolled her eyes. From the tone of Sylvia's voice, Trew could picture her doing the same.

Next, Cooper brought Danni up to speed on the plan and what still needed to be done. After he was finished, she looked at Trew in wonder. "Wow, Brandon has been working towards this for thirty years?"

Trew nodded.

"It sounds impossible for everything to fit so perfectly into place."

"Yet here we are," Cooper said. "It's all coming together. The impossible parts are complete; most of them are. You waking up was the one thing that only Brandon believed could be accomplished. Now that you've achieved that, it's possible for anyone to do the same thing inside the Game universe."

"It's possible to do here as well," Danni said.

Cooper's eyebrows arched curiously, then he shrugged his shoulders. "There wouldn't be a point to that, but I guess you're right."

"Why wouldn't there be a point to it?"

"Because there's nothing to wake up from," Cooper said.

"I suppose," Danni let the thought hang in the air for a moment and then she continued to speak. "So the half billion players are born into the Game and we wait?"

"Yes," Trew said.

"How long?"

"Week and a half," Cooper said. "Until they are around fifteen."

"That will leave us, what? One week?" Danni asked.

"Yes," Trew admitted grimly, "it's cutting things close. NPCs will begin dying in large numbers two and a half weeks from today."

"They aren't NPCs, though," Danni had been stunned to hear this.

"Many aren't," Trew said. "They're real people from a different reality, stuck in a game and about to die."

"I'm feeling pretty optimistic that they won't," Cooper admitted.

"So am I," Trew smiled.

"I'm not hearing any details that involve me," Danni said.

"Well," Cooper looked at her with an amused expression. "There was a very important part that you did play; I think we covered it a few hours ago."

"Yes, I'll take a bow for that part," Danni said. "That's it, then? I can collect my credits and go on with my life? I get the feeling the entire planet is not too productive at the moment while everyone watches what's going on in the Game."

Trew smiled at his wife; he still thought of her as his wife, even though he was eighteen and she was seventeen, and probably boyfriend/girlfriend at the most, according to Tygon law. "There's more for you to do, Danni," he said.

"Excellent," she smiled and rubbed her hands together. "What have you got cooked up for me, lover boy?"

Trew chuckled and shook his head. "I have absolutely nothing planned for you, babe," he said.

Her smile became a pout. "Well then why are you saying that there's more for me to do?"

"I know what comes next for you, Danni," Sylvia said helpfully. "Brandon left me directions for you, if you happened to make it this far."

"Great!" She said. "What do you have for me, Sylvia?"

"How do you feel about going back?" Sylvia asked.

"Into the Game?"

"Yes, back into the Game," Sylvia confirmed.

"When?" Danni asked.

"That's the thing," Sylvia sounded apologetic. "You've been here a few hours, which means that months have gone by inside the Game..."

Danni and Trew looked at each other. He shook his head, and she walked over to rest her hand on his shoulder, giving it a reassuring squeeze. "You want me to go back in as soon as possible?"

"Ten minutes ago would have been optimal," Sylvia admitted, "but anytime in the next half hour will do nicely."

"For how long?" Danni asked.

"Not long, from a Tygon point of view..."

Danni laughed at the vague statement. It could be two days or twenty years inside the Game, both would be a short time from a Tygon point of view. "Okay," she nodded. "I'm willing to fill whatever role Brandon needs me to play."

Trew stood up and walked to the door. "Let's get you back to Earth, then. I know you're coming back soon, babe."

"I believe you," she smiled, "and I can't wait."

55

"How many days will I be gone this time?" Danni asked as the elevator moved downwards.

"Less than one," Trew said.

"Really?"

"Your purpose for this visit is to show the parents of the world that you left and are able to come back."

"It's important for them to know we can come back?"

"It's important for them to be certain that there is a place where they go when their lives end on Earth," Trew said. "Children believe what their parents believe. Enough people believing something makes it accepted by society. Earth society must believe that it is possible to travel to another dimension."

"I don't see the point in players being born to learn how to eject themselves from the Game," Danni said.

Trew smiled and shook his head. "We are doing things indirectly," he explained. "We don't want Tygon players to be able to eject themselves from the Game; that would mess up the whole dynamic of our world system. Yet that is exactly what we must have for the real goal to be reached."

"We want players from the Dream to learn how to eject themselves from Earth," Cooper said. "The newly arriving children from Tygon will spend the next dozen years becoming spiritual masters and young teachers. Earth will be flooded with a new type of phenomenon, young spiritual children who will teach everyone methods for executing true spiritual transcendence."

"They will teach the NPCs — sorry, I mean Dreamers — how to wake up."

"That's the goal," Cooper nodded. "Melissa can't come back to tell the world what she did, but you can. You repeated her accomplishment and showed millions of players here that it could be done. Everyone being born into the Game right now knows that this is possible."

"They'll forget, though," Danni said. "When they're born, their memories will be wiped and they'll forget what they saw on Tygon."

Trew shook his head. "Not this time. Sylvia has awarded free perks and abilities to every player entering the Game for this play. They will have faint genetic memory that becomes unfailing certainty as they grow older. They will know the truth; that it's possible to wake up from the Game of life that they are living in. At first it will be hidden, but as they are raised and trained, the memories and certainties of what they saw you do will surface. Then they'll know that it's possible and will work towards being able to teach this skill to others."

"That's excellent," Danni said.

"They will also be able to identify the difference between Dreamers and Tygon souls," Cooper said.

"For what purpose?"

"They will feel compelled to seek out Dreamers and teach them," Trew said. "We don't care about helping Tygon being able to eject themselves, we take care of that for them when they die. Dreamers are stuck, and if they don't eject soon then they die permanently."

The three arrived at Danni's private room. Doctors and nurses quickly hooked her up to the proper equipment while Trew and Danni sat beside each other.

"You're going back into your body, with all memories intact," Trew said.

"Sounds like fun," Danni smiled.

"It should be. Now before you get going, let's give you the details of what we need you to do while you're inside."

For the next few moments Trew delivered precise instructions on what tasks Danni needed to perform. When he finished, she nodded her head.

"What do I do when I'm done?" she asked.

"Deep meditation and come back to me," Trew smiled and kissed her lightly on the cheek. "You've been gone for about six months, so it will take a few days for you to feel well enough to be up and around."

"Okay,"

"There have been some major developments since you left," Cooper said. "Power has been restored to every major colony. Stephanie has helped each group elect new leaders and has gone back to the dark side of things. Basic communications have been restored thanks to Shane and the other Timeless around the world, and Brandon is overseeing all of it."

"Brandon?" Danni asked. "What's he doing inside the Game? Who is he in there?"

Trew smiled, "I thought you knew, babe. Brandon is Azrael."

Danni laughed and shook her head. "I had no idea."

Trew smiled and kissed her gently on the cheek. "When you get up and mobile, Brandon will put you to work."

"So I just stand up and wave my arms to show everyone that I left and can return?"

Trew and Cooper smiled. "Knowing Brandon, he'll likely have you do a bit more than that," Trew said. "I believe you will be introduced as the world's most prominent holy figure."

"Holy figure? You gotta be kidding me."

"On the feeds, Brandon has begun to refer to a Virtual Prophet returning from the world that all avatars come from," Cooper smiled. "Sounds an awful lot like he's talking about you."

Danni raised her eyebrows and shook her head. "Great," she said.

"Religion is the quickest way for Earth to build a movement; this is why it was encouraged since day one. The other religions of the ages have been dry runs to prepare Earth to get ready for this major event."

"Okay, then," Danni looked dubious.

"It could be fun," Trew laughed.

56

The Dream

"Good morning, General."

The General opened his eyes, blinking slowly as a white wall came into focus inches away. He slept on a small cot in a tiny room. Everything was white and sterile, except for the dark green wool blanket that covered him. He didn't bother to turn over. "How do you know it's morning?" he grumbled, blinking his eyes as he waited for full consciousness to return to him.

There was a brief silence; the General knew the man behind him wasn't amused by his question. The man behind him seldom came to see him; their history together wasn't very pleasant.

"I've come to share some exciting news, General."

The General waited a few moments, then furrowed his eyebrows at the wall and spoke. "Then tell me and get out, Thorn."

"The Dreamers will soon begin to wake."

The General slowly turned over, his tired, weary frame feeling the effects of age and lack of exercise over the past few months. He grunted involuntarily and winced as his right hip sent a jab of electric pain downwards into his foot. Panting slightly, he moved his head back and forth on the pillow for comfort as he gazed at the man who had destroyed his entire life's work in the space of a few months... with a computer game.

"How many?" the General asked cautiously. It'd been months since the world had gone to sleep, all but a few souls trapped in the virtual reality game created by Thorn. The General could still picture the look of defeat on Thorn's face when he'd admitted that things had gotten away from him; when he told the General that, in all likelihood, their people would soon become extinct from this planet. Thorn looked less defeated today, though; was that actual hope in the man's eyes?

"Only a few will wake up at first," Thorn said. "I think it would be good for you to be up and about when they do, General. It's time to get up off this cot and help me."

"Help you do what?" the General asked. "Do you want the few remaining survivors shot in the head? At this point it would be better for none of them to wake up. There isn't much of a world left to return to, thanks to you, Thorn."

Thorn shook his head. "Don't scold me, General. You know better than anyone how years of careful planning can come unravelled in an instant."

The General sat up and leaned against the wall. He chuckled bitterly at Thorn's statement. "I suppose I do, Mr. Thorn," he said. "Luck can be a nasty bitch."

Thorn smiled and nodded. "I think it's safe to say that, as adversaries, we did a spectacular job of ruining everything both of us ever held dear, wouldn't you agree?"

The General looked around, his gaze stopping for a moment on the live television screen that showed the outside world from the cameras posted around the compound walls. Everything looked blue and green, full of life as birds flew by and squirrels hopped on the ground going about their business. "It doesn't look like the rest of the world would miss us terribly if we did cease to exist," he said.

Thorn followed his gaze to the monitor and nodded in agreement. "I've been working hard to fix the mess that was caused," he said. "Melissa has returned to us. She was stuck inside Sim2 with no chance of escaping, yet she did. Her doing so has made it possible for everyone else to do the same thing."

"That's good news, Mr. Thorn," the General nodded. "Do you think others will follow her out?"

"Plans are in place. I think that many will make it back to us."

"What do you need from me?"

"Soon, over a hundred of your Avatar soldiers will make their way out of Sim2. I want to put them to work by having them begin to forage outside the compound to restore basic power and infrastructure. After that, we expect more to join in an exodus out of the simulation. As people wake up we should have measures in place to help them recuperate and begin to reestablish some semblance of life here in the Dream. That will require leadership, General. I think you possess the skills necessary to lead us in this new age of change."

The General looked at Thorn suspiciously. "You know what I wanted to accomplish better than anyone," he said. "Why are you coming to me now, asking me to lead? I dreamt of controlling the world, of being the leader where everyone did what I told them to do."

Thorn shrugged. "That's the world we lived in at the time," he said. "We were bred to follow those who were bred to lead. You might have been bent on taking over as leader, but you wouldn't have been any different from those who came before you."

The General looked surprised by Thorn's frank, but astute comment.

"The world can be different this time," Thorn said. "Or maybe it can't. All I know right now is that I almost caused the extinction of our race, and we might just have a chance to change that. If that happens, then we need someone to step up and help society survive." Thorn shook his head and tapped the General lightly on the chest. "I'm not a leader, but you are."

The General thought for a moment, and then stood up. He smoothed his hair back and straightened his posture. "Okay, Mr. Thorn," he said. "If you can bring them back, then I'm willing to help develop a new society for us to rebuild our race."

Thorn smiled. "I'm glad to hear that, General."

The General smiled and clapped Thorn on the shoulder. "From now on, I think it's best for you to call me Donovan."

57

Thirteen - the Dream

"Whoa, this is definitely not Earth."

I open my eyes and look around. I'm not sure who said that, but they are correct; this isn't Earth. "Azrael was right," I say. "Looks like we had some kind of 'Day' type event here, too."

Before I can say anything else, memories begin to flood back into my skull. At first it's gradual, but then it comes in a rush, like a fire hose being turned on full blast. It doesn't hurt, but it's overwhelming. I look around and my companions seem to be experiencing the same thing. Finally it passes, and I gasp raggedly for breath. "I know who I am," I say. I look at the other two and nod, "I know who you are too."

"Me too," Cynthia, the woman of our group, says. "Where are the others?"

"Close by," I say. "We didn't all go down while sitting in a perfect little circle. They are awake by now, same as us. Azrael said to meet in the centre of town." I move toward the front door. I don't bother to look around me; this appears to be an ordinary house that we were exploring before we got sucked into Sim2. I remember it all now vividly.

I open the door and the three of us move toward the curb. Abandoned cars line the streets; most are parked with the doors closed, while here and there the odd one looks like it's been ransacked. Overall, the neighbourhood appears orderly, as if everyone is home from work and getting ready for dinner.

Down the street to my left, I see the others. I do a quick count and see ten. "Come on, let's join the others," I say. "It looks like we all made it and they're waiting for us."

The other two follow me silently. When we get closer I whistle and raise my arm. Ten heads swing towards me, some smile, and others raise their hands in greeting. There's a car close to the group and when I get close enough I jump on top of it. Everyone stands silently, waiting for my orders.

"Okay," I say. "Looks like all of us made it back. If there's anyone who can't immediately get to work, speak up now."

I look at the group and no one says a word. It looks like everyone is good to go.

"Our first task is to report in to the compound. What's our distance to target?"

"Four kilometres," someone says from the group.

I nod. "Let's report in, then. I believe they're expecting us."

===

Danielle

"One minute to air." The young man holds up his hand and smiles at me.

"Ready to make your first big address?" Azrael asks.

"Absolutely," I say. It's been two weeks since I returned to the Game. After six months of being in a coma, my avatar needed a bit of time to get its strength back.

"You remember what to say?" he asks.

"Something about this life being one big computer simulation?" I laugh as he makes a sour face at my joke. "Yes, I remember what to say. If I forget anything, just write it on a cue card and hold it up. No one watching the television will confuse me with a real actor. I'm sure they will forgive me if I stammer a bit."

Azrael steps back and the young cameraman begins to count down from ten seconds. Finally he points and nods, the red light appears on the camera, and I stand there in my white hooded robe and smile.

"Hi," I smile into the camera. "For those of you who don't recognize me, my name is Danielle. I lead the Gamer movement, and if you're watching this and haven't heard of it, I hope that very soon you will."

I push back the hood so the camera can get a better view of my face, looking at Azrael briefly. He nods and smiles encouragingly. "The world changed over ten years ago when all technology stopped functioning. Recently the world was encouraged to change yet again. Power has been restored. Soon, with everyone's help, Earth will return to some semblance of what it used to be."

I walk to the right a couple of steps and stop in front of a window that looks out onto green trees and blue skies. The camera follows me. "Over the next few months, many of you will begin to have children. With the return of power and a more stable lifestyle, it is expected that there will be many babies born soon."

I look directly at the camera. "Children are our most important resource, and we will be sponsoring learning centres to educate and guide the children all over the world. We will work with each culture to foster the best learning environments, as well as select the most qualified adults and teenagers to assist in the teaching."

There is a lot to say, but not in this initial address. I have introduced myself and prepared the viewers for the big streak of pregnancies that will happen. Now it's time to sign off.

I smile kindly at the camera and raise my hand in friendship. "I look forward to meeting many of you over the coming months as you elect leaders for your colonies and we consider strategies to move forward in this new chapter of society. Old governments are gone and this is an exciting new time to forge ahead. Goodbye for now."

"And we are off the air," the young man announces.

"Great job, Danni," Azrael says.

"Thanks," I say. "What's the plan for the next few months?"

Azrael flashes me a smile. "I thought you'd never ask."

Looks like I'll be here for a while longer, Trew.

<u>58</u>

"Every fan knows how to tune in and view their favourite Game players.

"Of course it's not possible to observe every moment of their lives, the time difference won't allow it; every day on Tygon, approximately 1.4 years passes inside the Game. The Game feeds assist us by filtering out boring details and delivering only the interesting stuff. Intelligent viewing functions enable each fan's system to learn what is most interesting to them. After watching the Game for the first few weeks, viewers can be assured of viewing only what appeals to us when watching the players we subscribe to follow.

"Most viewers enjoy watching the gripping drama; the living, the dying, the accidents and the love scenes. We enjoy watching the action as it develops, which, in the normal span of a regular player's life, results in numerous gaps that can be missed. Part of what makes the top players so desirable to follow is that their lives contain more of the things that viewers like to see.

"With that in mind, it's been a very challenging day for anyone's intelligent viewer system to filter Danielle Radfield's feed. She has been constantly busy and her life is full of excitement!

"Since her return to Earth, Danielle has been traveling the globe with her Eternal companions, tirelessly meeting with colonies both old and new as they begin to gather and form now that technology and power are again available to the world. It's easy to imagine not one single fan sleeping in the past twenty-four hours!

"Early this morning, Danielle closed her eyes on Earth and opened them back on our home world of Tygon. I was lucky enough to interview her not long after this occurred. If you want to know what happened during that interview, please join me in just two short hours on channel seventy-two to see it in its entirety.

"Here are some of the questions that I asked her. Has Danielle exited the Game for good? If she intends to go back in, then when will that occur, and for what purpose? How does the jumping back and forth between realities affect her Game ranking and subsequent credits?

"Be sure to catch the interview where we attempt to get the answers to all of these questions and so many more..."

Lisa Rohansen

Danielle's Command Centre

Everyone looked confused as they sat quietly around the main table. Most people looked down at their tablets, taking turns to glance at the person sitting at the head of the table and quickly dropping their eyes to feign interest in their tablets again.

Finally Danielle laughed and broke the silence. "Come on, everyone, quit looking so glum and grim. I thought you would all be happy to see me!"

Michelle smiled and looked at Danielle. "We are happy to see you, Danni. Everyone is just a little bit confused about how we're supposed to proceed." She shook her head and laughed. "Usually when we see our player, that means they've completed their play, and our work is done." Michelle nodded to the main viewer where the still form of Danielle's avatar lay on a table, hooked up to life support. "You're still in the Game, though, which leaves us wondering what to do next."

Trew nodded. "That's what we're here to discuss," he said. "Everyone in this room has done a phenomenal job during Danni's play. There have been secrets kept from many of you up until now as key points were executed and played out. Moving forward, everyone present will know our full plans for the rest of Danni's play."

"So you're going back in?" someone asked.

"I'm going back in," Danni confirmed.

"The children are just being born now," Trew said. "For the next ten years inside the Game there will be very little that needs to be done by Danni. The day to day, year to year, planning and implementation of a new society and schooling system can be accomplished by the Timeless."

"By the Eternals, you mean?" Nadine asked.

"By Infernals as well," Trew said. "The world isn't populated with only positive, pure and optimistic sweet avatars," he admitted. "There will be many young players who lean towards the path of things that are not so good. That's how the genetics and ancestral history components of avatar procreation works. We want to be able to provide everyone with a clear path to learning how to meditate and figure out the mechanics of waking up from the Game. From this point forward, our only goal is to produce half a billion individuals capable of learning and teaching others how to wake up from the Game."

"After ten years, what happens?" Lilith asked.

"These children are being called the Chosen," Danielle said. "Over the next ten years, the world will fall in love with them, especially the NPCs."

"How can you be sure of that?" someone asked.

"Resonance," Cooper replied. "When the Game was created, Brandon built in natural functions to help out later on as things progressed. Over the years he tested it and perfected the process. Individuals sometimes enter the Game with a very specific vibrational frequency. It's so subtle that no one knows that their cells vibrate slightly differently than everyone else's. As these special individuals come into contact with others, the vibration of their cells causes those around them to match the vibration. Brandon referred to this matching as Resonance."

"What's the significance of it?"

"When people begin to match vibrations, or resonate with each other, then they feel connected and are more inclined to follow the person they resonate with. Some of Earth's greatest leaders over history have possessed this unique vibration. They grew in power as they passed their vibrations on to those around them. Sometimes the results were good; sometimes they were very bad indeed. Regardless of the outcome, Resonance worked every time. It was a powerful introduction to the Game."

"NPCs will resonate with the Chosen, then?" Lilith asked.

"Absolutely," Trew said. "At first it will just be feelings of goodwill and a desire to nurture and look out for the Chosen. When they complete their mental training by ages thirteen to fifteen, it will fully unlock. Every Chosen will subconsciously draw a flock of NPCs to them; devout followers with a desire to learn what the Chosen will be ready to teach."

"Sounds like the Pied Piper story," someone said. "The man who played a flute and had all the children of a village follow him wherever he led."

"It's exactly like that."

Danielle brought the conversation back to the original topic. "For the next ten years, I'm not really needed on Earth. However, for the past year, I established myself as the Prophet who will lead the human race to a new era of enlightenment and development."

"Exactly," Trew said. "For the next ten years, the world will be focused on rebuilding society, and raising the Chosen. It will be fairly boring, if all goes as planned."

"With humans in the Game, there's no such thing as boring," Michelle said. "I'm certain there will be all sorts of romance, intrigue, treachery, and conflict."

"You're right," Danni smiled, "there will be. Game fans need to be entertained, and the next week or so will not disappoint anyone. Brandon and the Timeless will ensure that the Game is more exciting than ever while still moving towards the desired end point."

"Brandon?" Lilith asked. "How does he factor into this? He died."

Trew nodded. "Danni meant the plans and programs that Brandon put into place when he created the Game."

Danni nodded, but inwardly she winced. She had forgotten that no one here knew Brandon had come back and entered the Game as Azrael.

"Can Danielle's avatar remain in stasis for ten years?" Nadine nodded her head towards the monitor.

"That's what we're here to decide," Trew said. "Do we unplug Danni's avatar from life support and allow her to technically end her play?"

"If we do that, how will she get back into the Game in a week as an adult? If her avatar dies, then she will need to be born into another avatar, which won't get her to the right age in time, right?"

"There is another option," Trew said. "A way for us to get her back into the Game when we need her there."

"Tell us," Lilith said.

For the next half hour the group discussed the possibilities.

Finally Trew called for a vote; it was unanimous.

Alexandra Montoyas' play as Danielle Radfield would come to an end. Immediately.

59

Three days ago, one of the greatest players of all time made her exit from Earth.

In a very quiet affair presided over by select friends and lifelong companions, the avatar of Danielle Radfield was disconnected from life support and allowed to pass away peacefully.

All over Earth, people gathered to mourn the passing of their beloved leader and newly anointed Prophet.

Across Tygon, reactions to the event were met with a mixture of sadness at the passing of a truly diverse and remarkable character, but also celebration as Alexandra Montoyas exited her play in triumph.

Just a year ago, Alexandra, who now calls herself Danielle, failed completely out of the Game and was consigned to government schooling. A year after suffering from such horrible luck, the Game computer awarded her a free play. No one thought the young player would be able to do much with her free entrance into the Game, most believed she would do her best to gather whatever safe credits she could in hopes of earning her way back into some small amount of prosperity until she turned eighteen and graduated.

Danielle has managed to do considerably more than eke out a few points to earn another play; this young lady has turned the Game on its head and finished her free play as one the highest scoring player in the entire thirty year history of the Game!

Much of Danielle's wealth remains undetermined, as most of the credits she stands to earn rest on the outcome of the current scenario going on across Earth. If the Chosen are able to complete their goal and teach the NPCs of the planet to 'wake up,' then Danielle will be almost as wealthy as her boyfriend Trew Radfield, successor to Brandon Strayne and heir to his fortune and empire.

As fans wonder why it is so important to teach NPCs how to 'wake up' and we all guess at what will happen to them and where they will go if they are able to learn the process, Danielle and Trew spend some well-earned private time together for the next few days...

Danni and Trew lay in bed and watched Lisa's update on the viewer. She grabbed the remote, turned the viewer off, and nuzzled her face into Trew's neck.

Trew smiled and put his arm around Danni, drawing her closer and kissing the top of her head.

"It was a nice ceremony," Danni said. "Small and positive."

"It was," Trew agreed. They'd watched the ceremony through Brandon's feed. It was a happy celebration of the life that Danni had, and the accomplishments she'd achieved. Most of the attendees were Timeless, so they knew that she wasn't gone forever, just moved on to Tygon.

After they had watched the ceremony in the command centre, Trew made certain everyone knew their roles and then left Cooper in charge, announcing that he would be indisposed for the next day and only to disturb him if something unexpected occurred. Then he had grabbed Danielle gently by the hand and led her to his penthouse suite.

"This is wonderful," Danni said. "I can't believe we get to do this for an entire week!"

Trew laughed softly and shook his head. "I wish that were true, Danni. There's much to do, even outside of the Game."

Danni nodded and caressed Trew's face. "I see stress lines on your face," she said. "Too much for a young man, if you ask me."

Trew chuckled and touched her hand. "Most of them were caused by worrying over you."

Danni laughed and slapped him playfully on the shoulder. "There was never anything to worry about, silly. I had things well in hand all the time. Well, most of the time."

"Of course you did." Trew got out of bed and walked to the kitchenette where he poured two cups of fresh coffee. Danni sat up and accepted a mug as he got back into bed with her.

"The Game won't end, then?" she asked.

"There's still a chance it will," he said. "If NPCs don't wake up, then the place they come from won't be able to provide power to the Game, and Tygon simply can't generate enough energy to keep it going."

Trew hadn't told Danni the entire truth. He'd told her that NPCs were beings from another reality, and they'd been sharing the Game as a common living area. He had told her that Melissa was from another reality, and that the players there had become trapped in the Game — their real bodies were in danger of dying, which would wipe out their entire population. Trew had further explained that the ultimate goal of the Game was to help NPCs wake up and return to their own reality.

He had not told her the truth about Tygon; that this 'reality' of theirs wasn't real at all. He might tell her eventually, but now wasn't the time. He still wasn't sure he was dealing with the truth very well and he didn't see the point in causing confusion or pain to anyone else. "Everything looks good," he said, "but you never know for sure until the final card has been played. Luck can change everything in an instant."

"Do you think Brandon and Cooper are right?" she asked. "Is the difficult part done? There seems to be a sense of relief and calmness now, like we're all just watching pieces of the puzzle fall neatly into place instead of praying for a miracle."

"I agree. The hard part was doing the impossible. Now that waking up from the Game has been accomplished once, it can be done any time. We just need to get enough people focused on it, and Brandon will take care of that."

"So we wait until the Chosen are old enough to lead, then they do their thing, and then billions of NPCs wake up and leave the Game to return to their own reality."

"That's right,"

"Then what?"

Trew smiled and kissed her on the forehead. He appeared calm and relaxed, but inside he was worried about the answer to her question. He'd asked himself the same thing and wondered what Thorn and Brandon would do once their people had been saved and Tygon had served its purpose. Would they shut it down? Tygon was just a computer simulation populated by programs. In his mind Trew could shut the Game down with no thought to the consequences... at least he could have, before learning that his own world was as unreal as the Game was.

Trew embraced his girl and closed his eyes, trying to forget the number one question occupying his mind as time ran out.

Once the Dreamers were saved... would Tygon and the Game be shut down forever?

<u>60</u>

"Good evening, Sylvia."

"Hello, you two lovebirds." Trew and Danni could hear the playful, girlish tone in Sylvia's greeting, which made them both smile. "How are you enjoying your alone time together?"

"Loving it!" Danni said as she held Trew's arm and pulled him tighter towards her.

"I'm a little confused about why you're both entering this office in the middle of the night. Of course, you must want to talk with me, but I can't begin to imagine about what."

"There are questions we would like cleared up," Danni said.

"I'll do my best to answer whatever you ask," Sylvia said. "Fire away."

"You told me the Game would end when Danni died," Trew said.

"That's correct."

"We hoped that her waking up from the simulation would be a loophole, a way to bring her out without ending the Game."

"It appears that you were right," Sylvia confirmed.

"We also guessed that the Game would not end when her avatar stopped functioning," Trew said.

"That one was easy," Sylvia said. "The Game ending had nothing to do with her avatar; it depended solely on the fate of her spark, essence, or whatever you want to call it. The only way a player's spark can return to the body on Tygon is if the avatar dies on

Earth. You found a way around that which cancelled the effect that was laid out for ending the Game. When Brandon allowed Danni's avatar to die, he knew for a certainty that nothing bad would happen."

"So there's no way to turn the Game off?" Danni asked.

"There are ways," Sylvia assured them, "but it requires unanimous action by the Game Masters and a list of other actions that must all be done in proper sequence. The complete sequence is known to only one person living on Tygon, and the individual components are known to each person who is to be involved."

Danni looked at Trew. "Are you the one who knows the entire sequence?" she asked.

Trew nodded.

"What else can I answer for you?" Sylvia asked.

"When the NPCs wake up in their own reality, what happens to the Game? There will be a huge void of characters."

"I've got that covered," Sylvia said. "I will replace the consciousness of each empty NPC with an exact replica of the intelligence that currently inhabits it. Once the real sparks leave the avatars and return to their own reality, I will make certain the new digital personalities kick in so that we can continue to have them present in the Game for our players to interact with."

"Sounds elaborate and complicated," Danni said.

"I'm fairly powerful on Earth," Sylvia's voice contained the hint of a smile. "I think I'll be able to pull it off."

"So let me get this straight," Danni shook her head. "NPCs are players in the Game from another reality. We are going to teach them how to wake up so that they return to their bodies and avoid dying on their home planet. At the exact instant their spark leaves their Earth avatars, you will implant digital replicas into the avatars so that they continue to function exactly as they did before they left their avatars?"

"That's right," Sylvia said. "If a Tygon player has two parents that are NPCs, when those avatars wake up and their sparks leave Earth, I will implant new personalities back into the avatars so that the Tygon player has the same parents, so far as they know. That way the Tygon player continues to play the exact Game they were playing, and the original NPC spark returns to their home reality to avoid death."

"Why is saving these NPCs so important?" Danni asked.

"You'll have to wait for the answer to that question," Sylvia said. "It is very important, though."

"How did they get into our Game, or did we get put into theirs?"

"I see where your mind is going, but none of these questions will help you at the moment. I think the two of you should spend a little more time together and forget about the world... all of them. Then in a day or two, come out of your bedroom and make plans to help with the final stages of the Awakening event."

Danni sighed and looked at Trew. He nodded in agreement, and so did she. "Okay, I guess it won't hurt to relax for a couple of days and help in whatever ways we can."

"Off you go, then," Sylvia chuckled. "Unless you have nothing better to do than sit and talk to a disembodied voice coming out of speakers in an office."

Danni grinned at Trew. "We have better things to do. Thanks Sylvia, we'll see you in a day or two."

"Have fun, you two."

61

Azrael - one week after Danni's avatar has died.

Stonehenge.

This spot has always been important to me; to us. The six of us had fun creating so many of the mysteries of the world, leaving behind curious structures and stories so that players might choose to devote their plays, or even more than one play, to the pursuit of finding the answers to questions we raised. I think it's one of the traits that makes us who we are as intelligent creatures; the desire to know more, to learn and figure out puzzles. To discover the rules of the games and then master them. It's been important to me, that's for certain.

I stand in the middle of the structure and look at my watch. It's almost time for them to arrive.

Five bright white doorways appear simultaneously, all equidistant from each other. I smile as each of my Hand members arrive. Gabriel, Shane, Raphael, Angelica, and Carl. My team in the Dream included me as part of the five, because our goal was to become the Hand of the General. Once inside this game, I realized that I would need my own complete group of five, and Carl was the proper choice to fill that spot.

We spend the next hour catching up. I won't bore you with it; if you're watching me, then you'll see it all anyway.

===

"Can we finally get down to business?" Carl asks. His look conveys impatience and disgust for the past hour that we've spent hugging and crying and making small talk, but we all know that he enjoyed it too.

"All business and no play makes you a dull boy, Carl," Angelica says teasingly. Carl looks at her and the smallest trace of a grin forms on his face. One of the first things I had to do when I got in here was go unblock Angelica. In her mind she thought she was a new Timeless recruit; part of a plan that thankfully never needed to continue. I feel bad about putting a mind block on her and having her forget exactly who she was for a few years, but if things had gone differently it could have been a crucial backup plan. Long story short, I removed the block and she remembers the entire history of her life. That's an interesting story; I wonder if someday it will be available for Firsting...

Once Carl knew that she'd been restored, their 'animosity' towards each other faded. Angelica did some nasty stuff to him inside the Game when she was a player, and he definitely wanted revenge for that. Who knows, he still might try, although he's a professional and knows it was all part of a bigger plan.

Carl's smile resembles that of a hungry tiger. "Play? Does that mean I get to go hunting?"

"Likely before we're through, the answer to that question will be yes," I say. "Let's sit down and discuss what we have to accomplish here over the next fifteen years."

We assemble at an old stone table rising from the ground in the middle of the ancient structure; another little treasure we hid under the ground that no one ever seemed to be able to find. A wine glass filled with pale blue liquid sits at each seat, and I raise my glass.

I propose a toast. "Impossible, my ass!" I say, using a long ago remark one of us made about the chances of saving our world from extinction.

The others laugh and raise their glasses as well, repeating my toast and drinking deeply.

"Gabriel," I say. "Tell us what needs to be done."

Gabriel nods and pulls out an ancient worn leather notebook from the breast pocket of his suit. "We will be responsible for controlling the Timeless on each continent. All will answer to us; the program has initiated properly in that regard."

I nod my head and look at the eyes of each person sitting here. Gold, crimson, and platinum flecks all swirl in each of our eyes now. The colour will match whichever Timeless we are in front of for the remainder of the Game, allowing us to be seen as brothers and sisters to ensure their cooperation. Infernals will lean towards the nasty side of things and Eternals the nicer, but we will guide them both towards our common goal. Speaking of which... "Everyone knows the main goal for the next fifteen years, right?" I ask.

Shane nods. "Restore technology and society, while fostering support and encouragement for the Chosen."

"I've already held a few of the little buggers," Carl says. "It's gonna be impossible for anyone not to love them. They resonate powerfully. It'll be a cakewalk getting them nurtured and trained to fulfill their roles."

"Good," I say. I reach beneath my chair and place a black case onto the table. I open it up and remove six sleek cell phones and hand them out. "These phones will work anywhere in the Game. We can keep in constant touch with each other between face to face meetings. I would like to meet back here once a month to start. If we feel that's too much, then we can change the frequency. Any questions?"

"Seems pretty straightforward from this point on," Angelica says.

"At least until the big moment," Gabriel smiles.

I nod in agreement. "There will be challenges, but nothing we can't handle," I say. "When the billions are sitting on mats and meditating so that they can all wake up... well, I'm still a bit nervous about that."

"Not exactly blockbuster movie material is it?" Shane asks. "Civilization's entire fate rests on its ability to sit quietly and... meditate...?"

The group chuckles at what such a scene would look like on a movie screen. "I know it's not glamorous, but the fate of the Dream does rest on it. If anyone else had a better idea, you should have shared it with me decades ago."

"Hey," Carl shrugs. "If the fate of humanity rested on us being able to solve a serious crossword puzzle, then we would all roll up our sleeves and sharpen our pencils to get it done correctly. Let someone else worry about big action scenes and explosions. We're saving a race from extinction, here."

"I agree," I say.

"What happens after that?" Angelica asks.

I look at her and raise my eyebrows for further clarification.

"With this Game." She sweeps her arm to indicate this reality. "Do we keep it? Or flip the switch and turn it off?"

I shake my head. "We can worry about that later," I take a sip of wine, hoping no one sees that I'm trying to hide something important. "Let's keep our eyes on the main goal, and discuss what happens after that... after that."

Everyone nods, and I can tell from their reactions that they didn't catch anything suspicious in my response.

"It's really good to see you all again," I say. I look around and it's obvious that I'm not the only one overcome with emotion. Everyone at the table nods in agreement; we are the only family any of us has ever had, after all.

62

"Ten years have passed inside the Game since Danielle finished her play and Earth experienced a gigantic population explosion. During this time, Earth has been rebuilt, complete with new forms of government and technologies that have encompassed the globe.

"The Timeless, who were invisible for most of the Game's history, are now active and present in all parts of the world, assisting the population to grow and rebuild society.

"Utopia? Definitely not a word to be used when describing the new civilization that is developing since the power was restored by Danielle, now lovingly referred to as 'the Prophet.' Crime, war, corruption, and all other normal human traits still exist in the world; it would be foolish to think such things could ever disappear, but the world does seem more united in moving towards a single common goal. It can be seen and felt on every continent and in every settlement and city across the globe.

"These new children are indeed special. There is a presence or 'vibe' that one gets when you are near them. Game fans know that these special children will one day teach NPCs to achieve a different mental state, essentially 'waking them up' to their true potential. We aren't certain what this means, but fans wonder how this will change Earth, and if it will make things better, or worse for story lines to come..."

"Game Buzz"- Channel 1 Game News - Clive Ragnar

Carl

"**You saw this** coming, right?" Angelica asked.

Brandon looks at us for a moment and nods. "Of course I did. This is exactly why we sent such a large number into the Game at the beginning. They are like every other soul that enters this system, no different from baby sea turtles."

"What are you talking about?" I shake my head. "A minute ago we're talking about the Chosen and now you want to discuss baby sea turtles? I know sometimes you switch topics and go off on strange tangents, Brandon, but I don't understand what sea turtles have to do with anything."

"Don't call me Brandon," he says, giving me a sharp look, "and I'm not off topic." He looks around the table, one eyebrow raised questioningly. "Please tell me one of you remembers my turtle analogy."

Angelica's hand shoots up like a teenage schoolgirl wanting to blurt out the answer to a history question. The rest of us laugh at her antics. Brandon plays along by looking everywhere but her as if he's a teacher impatiently waiting for someone to raise their hand, ignoring the only knowledgeable student in the class. Finally he smirks and nods. "Yes, Angelica?"

Angelica stands beside her chair at attention with her hands to her sides. "Avatars are like baby sea turtles," she recites. "Of the thousands, hundreds of thousands, even millions that are born, only a small few will survive the many threats and dangers to make it."

"That's right," Brandon chuckled. "Only one sea turtle out of a thousand will reach adulthood. It's the same for players; many of them enter the Game with specific goals, but only a small portion of them ever accomplish those goals. I fully expected the same thing to happen with the Chosen." He looks around the table to let the numbers sink in.

"So of the five hundred million that were born, you hope that half a million will advance to become leaders and teachers," I say.

"Correct," Brandon says.

"Well, that changes the tone of what we considered grim results before we got here," Shane says. Gabriel had just stood up to tell the group that hundreds of millions of Chosen were being assessed for their progress as they celebrated their tenth birthdays, and the majority of them were failing horribly.

Shane looks at Gabriel, "How many of the Chosen are on track to do what we need them to do within the next two to three years?"

"Just under a hundred thousand," Gabriel says.

"That number is fine," Brandon nods. "To tell the truth, I'm surprised it's even that high. Consider the magnitude of what we expect these children to do, after all."

"You could have shared this with us earlier," I say.

Brandon looks at me and grins. "You all know me better than that. What else do you have to report? Are we still on track in every other aspect?"

"Yes," Raphael nods. "The Gamer movement has swept the globe and drawn NPCs fully into the fold. Centres have attracted the masses and meditation lessons have begun focused teachings on spiritual transcendence." Raphael shrugs. "It's the term that best describes what we want them to achieve, so we dusted it off and started to push it."

"We are in the final stages of a very long game," Brandon says. "Please tell me that everything continues to stay calmly in place and nothing is threatening to change the outcome that we have all worked for."

He looks at each of us in turn and we hold a thumb up positively. After everyone has confirmed that things are on track, he sighs and nods. "Soon we will accomplish what we set out to do," he says. "Then it will be time to go home."

I snort and he looks at me. "Home," I say. "We wake up in teenage bodies again, some of us spending a few years in an orphanage until we're old enough to join the others serving in the military? That's guaranteed to happen, you know; they'll need military to help do the garbage jobs more than ever." I shake my head. "You're lucky all of us are so loyal to you, Brandon, because I doubt an average person would want to 'succeed' and go back to that kind of life."

I look at the others and it's obvious from their silence that they agree with me.

Brandon nods seriously as he looks at me. "You're right," he says. "If you have other ideas, then I'm open to hearing them."

"What are our options?" Raphael asks.

"Anything," he says. "Sky's the limit. When we succeed, our entire race will owe us an immense debt. I'm certain that Thorn will agree to reward us however we want." His pride is obvious.

"Maybe each of us will want something different from the others," he says, "but start to think about what you will want now. When this is complete, I'll be asking what happens next for each of you, and your futures will depend entirely on your choices."

"It always does," I mumble, and Brandon responds by grinning.

63

"**It's very nice** of you to invite me to dinner." Cooper raised his wine glass in salute and took a sip after Trew returned the gesture.

"We haven't had much time to spend together since you arrived," Trew said, "and I have a feeling that you might disappear when this is done as suddenly as you showed up."

Cooper cut a large bite of steak and put it into his mouth, smiling as he began to chew. He swallowed and nodded. "I might do that very thing, when the time is right," he admitted.

"I'm not entirely certain what it is that you've actually done by being here." Trew loaded his fork with food and held it suspended over his plate. "Brandon gave his life for you to make an appearance, and you've been with me inside the Game offices the majority of that time. I admit that you helped clear up some questions and also to make a few key suggestions, but is any of that worth the price that was paid to get you here?"

Cooper smiled and nodded, chewing silently for a time before answering. "If I came here to complete one small, seemingly unimportant and trivial task — something that changed the entire course of events in favour of the outcome we are about to see — wouldn't that be worth it?"

"Absolutely," Trew answered.

"There you have it, then." Cooper grinned and scooped a fork full of green vegetables dripping in butter to his mouth. He was silent again until his mouth was empty, then took another sip of the dark red wine. "I haven't been here with you one hundred percent of the time," he said. "There are considerable dangers to you right here on Tygon."

"Rival corporations of Brandon's," Trew guessed.

"Yes," Cooper said, "and other things, individuals, more dangerous than even his most powerful business rivals."

"You're talking about the other teams that Thorn let die in the Dream?" Trew asked. "I suspected that they were somehow transported to this single remaining simulation."

"That's exactly who I'm referring to," Cooper said. "Lohkam you know a bit about; you saw him during the viewing of Brandon's life. He's been here with his formidable crew, as well as the other twenty-eight groups with their teams. Each one of them has been working to provide a solution to the crisis in the Dream, although they realized many years ago what had occurred; that they'd all somehow been transported into a single simulation."

"Some of them wanted to remove me from my position?" Trew guessed.

"They did, and they likely would have, if I hadn't made an appearance at your side." Cooper grinned. "In addition to the assistance I've given you, I have been meeting with them and keeping the pack of hyenas away so that you can complete your work."

"What happens when the Dreamers wake up?" Trew asked.

Cooper popped the last bite of steak into his mouth and grinned. "It depends on who you are and where you're standing, my boy," he said. "It will be exciting to see how it all turns out, that's for certain."

===

The Dream

Thorn sat at the computer monitor with the General standing behind him. Both men looked intently at the scene playing out on the screen before them. They were watching live feeds that had been set up as the groups of returned soldiers — the groups of Thirteen — restored basic power to towns and made certain that the hospitals were as functional as possible for the coming Awakening.

"We're cutting this very close," the General said.

"I'll take a close call over a slow failure any day of the week, General," Thorn said.

"Please, Samson, stop calling me that."

Thorn smiled and looked at the man who had been an adversary for so long, and now seemed to be content as an ally. "Old habits, Donovan," Thorn said.

"Indeed," the General nodded. He'd given up hope for the entire race, and it was strange to feel the sense of optimism that was now returning. Watching the Thirteens wake up and speaking with Melissa had brought him back to life, and he was eager to work to save his world from the extinction that had seemed an absolute certainty just a few days ago.

"We will have a lot of work to do," the General said. "When they all wake up."

"There will be massive casualties, even if the best possible outcome is achieved," Thorn admitted.

"First priority will be to see to the living," the General nodded grimly. "Second priority must be to shut the simulations down immediately once we get everyone out."

Thorn frowned and shook his head. "That's not going to happen, Donovan,"

"It has to." The General looked surprised. "What if they get pulled back in? We must do everything we can to make sure that doesn't happen."

"We have done everything we can," Thorn said. "The simulations will not be shut down." He paused thoughtfully. "At least not right away."

"You intend to keep them running?" the General's face betrayed his shock.

"I've had no time to think about what to do," Thorn lied smoothly. "We get everyone out, and then we worry about the other things."

"You have... feelings for the computer generated beings in there," the General said.

Thorn shook his head, then he paused and shook it again. "I do, but it's not just about the NPCs living in there," he said. "We owe it to Brandon and his group to try and get them out."

"That shouldn't be a problem, just pull them out with the rest."

Thorn's face betrayed his feelings, and the General knew that something wasn't right. "What is it?" the General asked.

Thorn shook his head as tears formed in his eyes. "I told him not to go back in so soon," he said, "but he wouldn't listen to me."

The General gently put a hand on Thorn's shoulder. "What happened to Brandon?" he asked.

Thorn bowed his head sadly and his shoulders shook as he sobbed. "He couldn't handle the transfer," he said. "Brandon's body died when he went back into the simulation."

<u>64</u>

"Placeholder avatars?" Danni asked.

"That's right," Sylvia confirmed. "There are always empty avatars roaming around the Game in case we need to jump into the Game during an emergency."

"What do you mean, 'roaming around'?"

The rich yet gentle tone of Sylvia's laughter bounced off the walls of the office. "There are many true NPCs inside the Game, Danni," she admitted. "They go about their lives in a programmed way, living and dying, believing that they are as real as any other avatar. It's very possible for an NPC to be everything a player or Dreamer is." Trew caught the knowing tone in her voice as she said, "It's even possible that NPCs could be more real and significant than any other life form across all three realities."

Trew held his breath, expecting Danni to add things up and ask if citizens of Tygon were NPCs, but she was too confused by the current discussion to grab onto such a thought. He sighed in relief as she continued to ask questions about placeholders in the Game.

"So I will jump into one, essentially 'kicking' its program while I'm in it, and when I leave it will resume?"

"That's exactly what will happen," Sylvia said. "You do your thing, then 'wake up,' and its regular programming will reinitiate when you do."

"Okay, I understand," Danni said. "Let's do it."

Trew stood up. "It's time, then," he announced. "The children are ready, the masses are assembling, and Thorn tells me they are prepared to welcome their people home when they wake up."

Danni stood up and hugged him. "I'm so excited to see what happens," she said, "and I'm glad Brandon will be there to see his hard work all come together as intended."

"So am I," Trew said.

Danielle opened the door and started to walk out. Sylvia spoke up before Trew could exit the room.

"Might I have a quick word with you, Trew?" she asked.

"Of course."

Danielle smiled and left the room, politely closing the door to give them privacy.

"Have you spoken to him?" Sylvia asked. She sounded excited and eager to know more.

Trew knew who she meant. "From time to time," he said.

"How involved has he been in this plan?" She wondered aloud.

"As involved on Tygon as you have been on Earth. He's been directly involved since the beginning of creation," Trew confirmed.

"Yes, that makes sense." Sylvia paused, not knowing what to ask, but being as curious about the computer that ran Tygon as most were about her on Earth. "I wish I could talk with him," she said.

Trew laughed. "You can talk with him whenever you like," he assured her. "Do you hear the voices of people on Earth, even when you don't answer them?"

"I always answer them," Sylvia said. "Unfortunately, most just don't know how to hear me."

"Isn't that interesting?" Trew asked. "Perhaps the very same thing is happening with you."

Sylvia said nothing for a long moment, and she laughed in delight. "Never too old, or too wise, or too powerful that we still can't learn more. You are absolutely right, Trew, thank you! I am humbled by your advice and wisdom."

"Wisdom comes from everywhere at some point in life," Trew nodded. "Often the places where you least expect to find it are where the most powerful lessons are to be found."

"I couldn't agree more."

65

"**Good afternoon, Game** Fans. I would like to thank all of you for tuning in to join us this afternoon." Lisa Rohansen smiled at the camera and tried her best to contain the excitement she felt at landing another live interview with Trew and Danielle Radfield. Lisa's entire professional life had changed so much in the past few weeks since Trew had entered the Game for his last play. She'd gone from an average reporter on the feeds to the number one source for keeping up with breaking news and developments both inside the Game and out. She knew her growing fame was due to her good fortune in covering Trew, and then Danielle, and she was both happy and sad to see this chapter coming to an end. Lisa wasn't sure how things would go for her after the dust settled, but she fully intended to ride the wave as long as she possibly could.

"Today we are joined by Danielle and Trew Radfield. The large climax that we have all eagerly been waiting for occurred yesterday morning at 10 a.m., Tygon time. Viewer ratings reported by Game Central indicate that over 90 percent of Tygon was watching as billions of players gathered all over the Earth to meditate. Less than half an hour later, the event was over and the Game continued to play on. That was just over twenty-four hours ago, and experts and fans all over Tygon have many questions that they want answered."

Lisa turned to face the power couple of the world. "Trew, let's start first with the question that's on everyone's mind; what exactly happened yesterday?"

Trew smiled. He'd been watching the news feeds and wasn't surprised at the massive outcries of disappointment that were sweeping the world like wildfire on a dry grassy plain. No one knew what was really going on, and it wasn't his place to reveal that billions of people had been successfully returned to their own reality and saved from permanent death. Instead he had a different message to share. "The Game is a living, breathing entity, Lisa," Trew said with a shake of his head that indicated disappointment. "We built a scenario and sent the players in, hoping that something miraculous or spectacular would occur. There were some very powerful events that did take place, but it appears that it wasn't enough to please the fans."

Footage of the previous day's highlights played on the screen in the background. It showed large aerial views of the gatherings; waves of people congregated in large open areas of Earth, everyone sitting with legs crossed and eyes closed as they entered meditative states. There were also views of the Chosen; calm, enlightened youngsters sitting on elevated stages in front of the massive crowds, who slowly began to float a few feet off the ground as they entered their deep trances. Cameras captured individual avatars throughout the world surrounded by slight golden glows, also floating above the ground as they entered their own trances during the global event. Still other feeds cut to what players experienced as they meditated, dark views turning to bright golden glowing from their perspective. After a few moments, the videos ended and the camera returned to focus on Lisa and her guests.

"What was it that you were hoping for us all to witness?" Lisa was sincerely puzzled. "The past few weeks were so full of excitement and action, I think that fans were expecting more than just billions of people sitting quietly together while some glowed and others floated into the air. There must have been more to it than that, Trew? Please tell us what it was that we should have seen."

Trew opened his mouth to speak, but Danielle put her hand gently on his lap and he nodded, allowing her to answer the question.

"What you witnessed, Lisa — what we all witnessed — was that some things simply cannot be seen. We live in a world obsessed with the question 'why.' We believe only in what we can see, quickly dismissing any thought, idea, or theory that can't be viewed immediately by our eyes, while the truth of the matter is that our eyes can only see a very limited portion of the reality in which we live. Your pet can see things that are invisible to me and you. Insects that fly into windows and don't seem capable of figuring out how to find the easy escape only inches away see a very different world from the one we live in. We know that something big happened during the Game, because the Game computer awarded points and credits to players in record payouts after the event. To you and I and the average viewer, perhaps it seemed as though very little happened, but I disagree with that statement, because a few short weeks ago one person floating just a few inches in the air was impossible. Since then we have seen individuals that can fly through the air, both inside the Game and here on Tygon, and so we now discount the Chosen and others who float as 'less than spectacular.'"

"That is all very true," Lisa admitted.

"Indeed it is," Danielle continued. "I believe that Game fans around the world should give themselves more credit." She looked directly into the camera, as if speaking to each individual watching her. "Rather than cry out with disappointment and complain that you didn't see anything, or that what you saw wasn't incredible enough to have been worth watching, you should sit quietly and ask yourself this: What did I see, and how can it help me in my life here on Tygon?"

Danielle nodded towards Trew and put her hand gently on his back. Trew smiled at her and spoke.

"The Game has always been about learning something in a safe environment and finding a way to use it in reality," he said. "Over the years, we seem to have forgotten the true purpose of the Game, and that has caused more suffering and pain than it should have. Failing out of the Game doesn't have to mean a life of poverty and destitution. Succeeding in the Game won't guarantee that a young adult will live a happy and prosperous life after they graduate." Trew shook his head. "This event was intended to give each of you a moment to consider something bigger than yourselves. Incredible things occurred yesterday, both inside the Game and out. If you need me to tell you what happened, then you're missing it all completely."

"Sounds very abstract," Lisa said. "Many will say that you are giving us a vague answer so you don't have to admit that you don't have a specific response. What would you say to those people?"

Trew smiled calmly and grabbed Danni's hand. "I would say that if what happens in the Game is more important and has more meaning than what happens in your own life, then perhaps you should turn the feed off and never watch the Game again. If you don't get it, then keep trying, or stop trying and move on. It's as simple as that."

The camera focused on Lisa, and she was silent for a moment as she considered Trew's words. Then she nodded and looked at Danielle. "Danni, something definitely happened yesterday where the rankings are concerned. You've skyrocketed to become the number money earner to have ever played the Game, and you're still eligible to play at least one more time before you turn eighteen and retire. How does it feel to be the richest woman in the world?"

Danni smiled and nodded her head. "It feels good," she admitted, "but I've attained wealth in past Game lives, so I'm hoping the money and fame doesn't go to my head and ruin me."

The three laughed and continued to discuss Game specifics of the past few weeks. As they did, Lisa made certain to ask all the riveting questions fans had been asking. Time flew, and before they knew it, the cameraman made a hand signal to indicate that it was time to sign off.

"I know there are still many weeks left to enjoy new developments and story lines as the thirtieth year of the Game winds down," Lisa said. "I don't know if any events will ever come close to the excitement that the two people sitting with me today have given us. Danni and Trew, from the bottom of my heart, and on behalf of Game fans across the world, I thank you for what you have done."

Danni and Trew smiled. "We both feel lucky to have been a part of history, Lisa. Thank you for the great coverage; I think without you talking about us all the time, we wouldn't have become so famous."

Lisa blushed and shook her head modestly, tears of happiness welling up in her eyes.

"I'm certain discussions will rage about the events of yesterday for weeks to come. Remember what you heard here today, everyone. Big things did happen yesterday; it's up to you to decide what those big things were. I'm Lisa Rohansen with Danni and Trew at Game Centre channel one."

66

"**Things seem to** have returned to normal here."

Brandon didn't look up from his reading. "You're more stealthy than usual," he said.

"Perhaps you're just distracted by what you're reading."

Brandon smiled and glanced in the direction of his visitor. "That must be it. Hello, Father; how are things?"

Thorn smiled and sat down beside Brandon. "Things are excellent," he said. "You did it, son; you got them home."

Brandon nodded. "The majority of them made it safely?"

"Yes," Thorn said. "The next little while will be challenging for us as we scramble to locate them and make sure they get food and water. They've have been lying motionless for so long that most can barely move, but we know a little exercise will fix that."

Brandon smiled at the memory of coming out of long games and having to subject himself to weeks of physiotherapy to restore muscle mass and function to his atrophied limbs. "How have the groups of Thirteen been performing?"

"Like the military aces that they are," Thorn said. "Brilliant idea to find and send them back to pave the way for the others."

"That was Shane's idea."

"Easton," Thorn said.

"Yeah."

Thorn looked around. They sat on one of the elevated stages that the Chosen had used during the mass meditation gatherings only a few weeks ago. The enormous field was bare. The only evidence that there had been a crowd lay in the subtle clues left behind; the trampled grass, the stray bits of refuse such as plastic water bottles and rogue clumps of paper that blew and tumbled randomly in the otherwise empty fields. "Where did everyone go?" he asked.

Brandon smiled wearily. "They went back to their lives," he said. "Once the meditation was successful, the Dreamers exited their avatar bodies. When Sylvia switched the avatars over to act like true NPCs, she made them forget what had happened so they could resume normal lives."

"Very clever," Thorn said. "Billions of people stood up and returned to their previous paths in life?"

"Exactly," Brandon nodded. "In their minds, this event didn't even happen. They will make their way back to where they came from before the event and continue to move forward in this new society that is growing from the ashes of the Day."

"What about the Chosen?"

"Same thing," Brandon replied. "The resonance that made others follow them was disabled. A quick adjustment from Sylvia turned that off and false memories kicked in. They are regular children with parents that, as far as they recall, encouraged them to learn arts like meditation and eastern spirituality."

"The world has returned to normal, then?"

"Very much so. No one in the Game will remember this event."

Thorn looked around and silently considered the scope of power that Brandon exercised in this computer simulation. "Quite the playground you set up here, son," he said.

"It sure is," Brandon agreed. The two men sat thoughtfully for a few minutes.

"I had planned to end the Tygon simulation and bring you out if you succeeded."

"I figured you would," Brandon said.

"Is that why you came back in?"

Brandon looked at Thorn and shook his head. "I came back in because I was needed. If I'd stayed out, then our chance for success would have been slim, Father. I knew my body would likely die if I came back, but there was no choice."

"You play to win," Thorn said.

"That's the only reason to play."

"Sometimes, you can play to learn from your failures," Thorn offered.

"Not this time, we couldn't."

Thorn looked frustrated. "I haven't figured out how to transfer your consciousness to another body in the Dream. If you stay here for a while, I'll work on it, and perhaps..."

"No."

"There are people whose minds didn't make it back to their bodies. I can find you a suitable body. I'm sure I can figure out how to do it."

Brandon stood up and walked to the edge of the stage. He looked out at the world he had created and smiled. Then he looked back at Thorn and his smile softened. "I want to stay here, Father."

Thorn looked confused. "In the Game?"

"I have a body on Tygon," Brandon said. "I could live here and there, back and forth, for a long time. If you leave the simulation running."

"Earlier I said that I had planned to shut it down. After what they have done for us, the billions of NPCs living on Tygon, there's no way I can shut it off. Computer programs saved our lives; they saved our race and ensured our continued existence. While there is one ounce of power available in the Dream, I will make certain Tygon stays online."

"It really is the least you can do for them," Brandon agreed. "I've spoken to my Hand. All of them want to stay, too."

"That is acceptable."

"We can keep the communication lines open between us, right?"

Thorn walked over to his son and put his hand on his shoulder. "Of course we can. I might even stop in from time to time to visit."

"That would be great," Brandon said, "but I want to make sure you let no one else enter this Sim. I will put sensors in place and if anyone comes here, they will be destroyed. I understand why you brought Lohkam and the other teams to Tygon, and if they want to stay I will allow it, but that's it."

"I have no problem with that," Thorn said. "What will you do with the Game now that it has served its purpose?"

Brandon shook his head. "I don't know. I have to think about it for a while. Maybe a long while."

Thorn chuckled and looked out across the empty field. "You definitely have time to think about it, son. You've earned that luxury."

Brandon smiled. "I think I have."

67

Brandon woke up and looked around in the darkness.

It was the middle of the night, pitch black, but for some reason he was fully awake and alert. Sometimes it was difficult to know what reality he was in; and this was one of those times.

His vision sharpened as the tiny bits of light entered his expanding pupils. He knew where this was, but it made no sense for him to be here.

He swung his legs over the edge of his cot and stood up, the hard floor cold against his bare feet. He walked slowly towards the far wall, passing the bunks filled with sleeping children as he made his way quietly to the faint source of light coming from the bathroom.

Brandon stopped and looked over his shoulder; he recognized dozens of familiar faces. They were all between the ages of ten and twelve, and Brandon was the youngest of them. Somehow, he was back where it had all started; the Game Facility in the Dream.

A golden light began to glow from the bathroom to his right, and Brandon headed quietly for the far wall, nodding as it disappeared to reveal a dense green jungle. Brandon stepped over the ledge and into the tropical setting, feeling the moist warmth and cloying heat cover him like a heavy blanket against his skin.

He knew which tree to look for, but it was empty this time.

Brandon looked around and called out. "Sloth? Are you here? Owl?"

There was no answer.

Brandon ventured further into the jungle, calling out occasionally, but there was no response.

A large tree appeared out of the mist. Rough wooden slats were positioned halfway up the trunk along the outer edges of the branches to form a crude floor. The branches and leaves had been woven together to enclose the interior into rooms, although it was still possible to see inside at many points. The trunk had what appeared to be a broken old makeshift ladder nailed at points along the length of it. Many of the small boards were missing, and the ones that remained looked dark and rotten, likely to break if any weight was applied to them.

Brandon drew close and looked up into the branches. He could see light wavering gently in one of the small rooms, most likely a small candle burning. He cupped his hands and called out. "Hello? Is anyone up there?"

Leaves around the lit room began to rustle, and there was a distinct thud followed by mutters and a very creative swear word. Brandon cautiously watched as the branches moved from the lit room towards an open platform area that had no branches surrounding it. He smiled as he recognized the form which burst through the leaf doorway and peered down at him with a scowl.

"What in blazes are you doing down there yelling like that?" the old man whispered harshly, his white hair standing up like a ragged flame, unmoving as his body flailed about while he spoke. Black garbage bags covered him from shoulders to knees. Brandon was glad to notice that they were tied tightly at the bottom so he didn't catch a glimpse of what was underneath. Heavy black laceless army boots peeked over the edge of the boards; his slight, scrawny frame provided enough weight to make the clumsily built deck tilt dangerously towards the ground.

"There's all sorts of dangerous animals living on the ground. You could attract one of them and get yerself killed!"

"I'm sorry," Brandon whispered. "I had no idea."

"Hmphh! Youngsters like you never do have much of an idea. Not that most manage to gain ideas as they age, either, come to think of it," his hands made a chopping motion, the red pop bottle caps of his gloves clinking together melodically. "Hey, wait a minute." He leaned down to get a better look at Brandon. "Aren't you the boy I saw with Owl a while back?"

Brandon nodded his head and opened his mouth to ask where Owl or Sloth might be, but the old man interrupted him excitedly.

"Owl Boy!" he exclaimed loudly, suddenly not worried about the volume of his voice or the dangerous predators that it might attract. "It's good to see you again! Have you finally come to spend some time with me?"

Brandon looked around to see if the brush was moving. If there was danger close by, the old man's yelling hadn't woken them... yet. "I can't seem to find Owl or Sloth, so yeah, maybe I'm here to be with you."

The old man's eyebrows shot up and his eyes twinkled happily as his mouth opened in a broken-toothed smile. "Excellent!" he exclaimed. "It's been so long since anyone was sent to learn from me. You must be a clever lad indeed to have earned such a reward. Well, come on up then, boy, what are you waiting for?"

Brandon nodded and walked towards the broken ladder attached to the tree trunk. He figured he was strong enough to navigate the broken rungs and make his way to the top.

"Where are you going?" the old man dropped to his belly and peeked his head over the boards to watch Brandon. "You give up already, boy? That's a bit of a surprise, if you are."

"I'm climbing to you," Brandon whispered as loudly as he could. He heard the bushes rustle from his right. He caught a glimpse of a large, dark, orange cat stalking towards him. It looked hungry, and it was focused intently on Brandon.

"You don't have time for climbing," the old man chuckled. "There's a tiger on the prowl and you have only a few seconds to avoid being eaten. Nasty business getting eaten by a tiger. I don't recommend it at all. It would really cut our lessons short if that were to happen."

Brandon backed away slowly from the trunk and shot a look at the old man. "Fly up?" Brandon guessed.

"Of course you fly up," the old man scowled. "You fall on your head lately or something else bad happen to your brain? Hurry and get up here before Tony over there gets his claws into you."

Brandon closed his eyes and the glow was there immediately. He leapt into the air and quickly flew up to join the old man. Directly below him he could see the tiger had pounced and barely missed him with its razor sharp claws. It roared in fury and glared at Brandon as he flew upwards.

The old man whistled slowly as Brandon landed beside him. "That was way too close a call," he said. "I sure hope you don't plan on being that slow for the rest of your stay, Owl Boy. It would be fun, but likely a short visit."

Brandon grinned and shook his head. "I'll try to be quicker from now on," he assured his host.

"Good," the old man nodded. "All right, then, why don't you come inside and we can get started? There's much for you to learn."

"I'm older than I look," Brandon said. "I've learned a lot already."

The old man grinned. "I know you have, Brandon. The thing about this life we live, though, is that there's always lots more to learn, no matter how much we think we already know."

Brandon considered the old man's words, and he nodded slowly.

"Good!" the old man slapped the boy happily on the back. "Let's get to it, then, shall we?"

Brandon followed the old man into the treehouse, and the branch door closed softly behind them.

EPILOGUE

Tygon

Cooper sat in a hotel room, gazing out of the window at the restaurant across the street. Years of training and discipline in diverse military conditions enabled him to sit without moving for hours. His eyes flitted constantly in all directions, looking for patterns or signs that he'd been followed.

He spotted his contact entering the restaurant and continued to observe the area, looking for clues that his contact was being tailed. The odds were slim, but bad luck could magically appear at any time and destroy even the safest plans in an instant. Cooper watched the scene below until he was confident that everything was as safe as it could be, and then he exited his hotel room and crossed the street to meet his contact.

Lohkam sat in the back corner of the room, his back to the wall so that he faced the doorway. He continued to scan the single sheet of paper that served as a menu in the pub-style restaurant, but Cooper knew he'd been seen; Lohkam was a careful kid.

Cooper sat down and waited patiently for Lohkam to look up from his menu; he knew the boy was observing the door to make sure no one had followed him in. Ten seconds passed and Lohkam looked up. "You're clean," he announced. "Why are we meeting again so soon?" he asked, his cruel eyes looking left and right, his thin lips pursed in a tight scowl that meant he was nervous and ready for violence. It was a common look for him.

"I heard you were planning on making a move against Trew." Cooper picked up a menu and pretended to be interested in it. "I'm here to make sure that doesn't happen."

"The runt's pet is all alone and unprotected now." Lohkam's face reddened slightly. "He's just coming off a big victory in the Game; it's on all the feeds. Now is the perfect time to strike and take over."

"Oh, he's protected," Cooper said calmly. "I've got his back, unless you're finally ready to challenge me?"

Lohkam looked at Cooper and frowned. "I don't get it," he said finally, shaking his head.

Cooper glared at him for a few moments until he was certain Lohkam had received his message loud and clear, then his face softened and he sighed. "I've explained it to you more than once; what part don't you get?"

"What side you're on."

Cooper chuckled softly and looked around to make sure no one was listening. "There's only one side for me to be on after all that has gone down, Lohkam."

"Well, you could have fooled me."

"Of course I could." Cooper grabbed a handful of peanuts from the bowl in the middle of the table and leaned back. He cracked the shell and popped two peanuts into his mouth. "I've fooled everyone for a very long time; people who are significantly more clever than you, boy."

"Okay, so I leave Trew alone," Lohkam said, and reached for a peanut as well. "What are my orders, then?"

"Just keep on doing what you've been doing. When the General is ready for us to move, he'll send me a message."

Lohkam chuckled as he popped a peanut into his mouth. "I would love to be there when Brandon finds out you've been working for the General this whole time."

Cooper leaned across the table and slapped Lohkam sharply with the back of his hand. Lohkam's eyes burned with hatred as he looked at Cooper in surprise. "What the hell was that for?" he asked angrily.

"Shut your mouth," Cooper hissed. "This is not some quick game of capture the flag, you idiot. This is a long and dangerous game that requires silence and patience. Have you learned nothing in all your considerable years?"

"I was just saying," Lohkam said.

Cooper smiled and leaned back again. "I know, it's difficult at times. This last turn was a long one, but everything the General said would happen has occurred. The dreamers are awake and rebuilding a new society with the General at the reins and no governments or officials to oppose him. Thorn thought he was being clever, but he played right into the General's hands."

"Why keep the Game and Tygon online?" Lohkam asked.

"There's no rush to deactivate either," Cooper shrugged. "Brandon is trapped in here and Thorn is without his best player. We can assess the situation and do whatever the General decides to do at his leisure. No one knows the truth, except you and I."

"Are you in contact with the General very often?" Lohkam asked.

Cooper smiled and tapped his head lightly. "Any time he wants to tune in," he said.

===

The General blinked three times rapidly to deactivate the organic viewer implanted in his skull. His vision of the conversation between Cooper and Lohkam faded to be replaced by his current surroundings; a makeshift office in what was once the State Capitol building.

He scanned the various monitors showing him how things were progressing around the countryside.

One feed showed Thorn hunched over a table with a group of computer engineers. They were discussing and designing plans for a new facility.

The General leaned back in his chair and smiled.

Everything was progressing perfectly.

END

Printed in Great Britain
by Amazon.co.uk, Ltd.,
Marston Gate.